I0838433

Promise of Danger

UNDERCOVER MAGIC BOOK FOUR

Cover Design by CReya-tive Book Design

Edited by Mo Sytsma of Comma Sutra Editorial

Proofread by Suzi of Royal Reads and Dominique Laura

To the maple trees that donated their blood and the coffee beans that gave their lives so that Second Cup could keep me stocked in lattes, this book exists because of your selfless sacrifice.

And for Sarah K, the best Robin who's ever lived, we've come a long way and lived through many iterations of this book. Thanks for sticking by my side through them all.

*"Someone who's willing to burn the world down
to protect the one person they care about . . .
that's a man I understand."*

\- Raymond Reddington, The Blacklist

Promise of Danger

CHAPTER 1
NORD

Nord held the Director's dagger out to Lina, feeling inexplicably anxious. The last time he'd been this twisted up by hope for a woman's consent and the simultaneous fear of her rejection, he'd been thirteen and on the brink of stealing his first kiss from his neighbor, Yngrid. Since she'd been five years his elder and vastly more experienced, his uncertainty had been more than justified. But this was Lina, which made things infinitely simpler and more complicated in the same breath.

She'd only just learned of her new nature. Perhaps she wasn't ready to fully embrace it yet. As for him, since leaving home, there hadn't been anyone he could share that part of himself with, let alone wanted to. This was uncharted territory . . . for both of them.

Nord couldn't help the slight tightening in his gut. He wasn't sure why a rejection of her berserker felt like a rejection of him, but there you had it. The true source of his unease.

After everything they'd been through, it should have been laughable. Hell, surviving the Transference alone proved that they both accepted and understood the darkest parts of each other. That they belonged together. The Ancient Ones wouldn't have blessed them with their gifts otherwise. But even knowing all of that didn't ease his uncertainty.

His mind continued to whirl with his jumbled thoughts until the wave of her emotions washed over him, calming him almost instantly. The only things he picked up from her were joy, surprise, and an abundance of love.

"I would love that," she said, her smile radiant as she moved closer.

Nord's chest expanded like a helium balloon as exuberant relief filled him. He wasn't sure which of them were more excited by the prospect of making her first ring, though he'd hazard a guess it was him. Something about sharing that piece of his history with her called to the man he'd once been, waking him from his centuries-long slumber.

He set the dagger down on top of the dresser and rubbed his hands together expectantly. "We just need to make ourselves a forge—"

The rest of his words were lost as time just . . . stopped. Nord had the sense of walking into a room, intent on completing a task, and then losing his way. Like he'd immediately forgotten what he was doing there as soon as he crossed the threshold.

It was a peculiar sensation. He seemed alert, though only in that half-asleep, last-moments-before-waking sense. The kind where your conscious mind floats between the dream world and reality, not fully able to discern the difference between the two.

His disorientation was such that he didn't immediately realize anything was wrong. Not until a sharp throb of outrage pierced through his mental fog and he could focus enough to gather himself. It was then he realized several things at once.

One: he couldn't move his body.

Two: it wasn't his anger that broke him out of his disorientated state.

And, perhaps most concerning of all, three: his berserker was nowhere to be found.

Alone, each of those clues was troubling but held a variety of plausible explanations. When taken together, however, those truths only equated to one infuriating possibility.

Crombie.

Not only was the fae scum the only chronomancer he knew, but he'd taken every opportunity to abuse his ability when he wanted to neutralize Nord and corner Lina. Lina, whose growing rage continued to flood his senses. Although, this time, the feel of his mate's fury wasn't quite enough to summon his own.

Whatever had kept his consciousness awake during Crombie's temporal pause hadn't done the same for his inner beast. Since Nord was only ever aware of Crombie's tampering after the fact, he could only assume the difference this time had something to do with his newly acquired powers.

Or, more specifically, his new bond with Lina.

Was it possible that because she wasn't trapped by Crombie's power, neither was he? At least, not entirely? It certainly seemed to be the case. Perhaps he could use that to his advantage and access his power to break the last of the way out.

Nord had no way of knowing whether his magic was a match for Crombie's, but if ever there was a time to find out, this was certainly it. Who knew if he'd ever get another opportunity to test the theory.

As if summoned by the thought, his magic stirred, and just that initial tingle of its presence was enough to erode more of Crombie's hold on him. Nord blinked. When his eyes reopened, he could actually see the room. He hadn't broken the hold enough to hear what was happening, but it wasn't hard to fill in the blanks as Crombie stalked out of the shadows toward Lina, his lips tilted in a mocking smile, his eyes hard. Lina's back was facing Nord, and while he could not see her expression, the rigid set of her spine and shoulders painted a clear enough picture. She was utterly livid.

A sentiment Nord shared.

He drew on more of his power, feeling it uncoil and stretch as it filled him. Once again, it burned away at Crombie's hold. Even though Nord didn't have a picture in mind of what he wanted to do with his power, he continued to draw more of it until he could not only see and hear, but had regained complete control of his body once more.

He waited only long enough to see Crombie reach for Lina. It was like someone had pulled the trigger. Nord exploded forward, the sheer momentum of the act—combined with Crombie's surprise— sending both men to the floor.

Lina gasped, but wisely stayed out of his way. This was a show- down that had long been coming.

Pity, Nord thought as he fisted one hand into the red silk of Crombie's shirt. The rest of the thought followed as he slammed his other fist straight into Crombie's nose. *I would have enjoyed seeing him painted in his own blood.*

There was a satisfying crunch as Nord's knuckles connected with the other man's face, and he couldn't quite control the savage smile that stretched across his face.

"Surprise."

He cocked his fist back, preparing to land another brutal punch when Crombie seemed to break free of his own stunned stupor. In a seemingly impossible move, his hand snaked out and caught Nord's fist before it could connect a second time.

"I think once was quite enough," he drawled.

"It wasn't nearly enough."

"Yes, well," Crombie said, not even breaking a sweat as he shoved Nord off of him with all the effort one might use to swat a fly, "I don't recall asking for your opinion."

Crombie's strength shouldn't have been a match to his own, and yet . . .

"Nord!" Lina shouted, her eyes wide with shock as he flew across the room and crashed into the small bedside table, sending both it and him toppling to the floor.

His forehead smacked the corner of the upended furniture, and he had to shake off stars as he pushed himself upright. Blood trickled into his eye from the resulting gash, but he didn't do more than blink it away as a very welcome fury began to take over. At least pain had managed to do what his magic had not.

Finally. It was high past time Crombie learned firsthand exactly what a berserker was capable of.

A low, predatory snarl escaped as Nord caught Crombie's eyes. His lip curled up in an anticipatory grin that would have sent a wiser man for the door.

Crombie merely lifted a brow as Nord took a menacing step forward. "Well, this is an unexpected turn of events . . ." He sighed as he smoothed down his wrinkled shirt. "And while I'm nothing if not adaptable, I'm here to collect what was promised"—his head snapped up, and he pinned Nord with a fierce glare of his own—"and I have no intention of leaving without it."

Then his hand shot out, catching Lina by her wrist. She let out a startled gasp as he yanked her closer. She fought against his hold in earnest, her panicked gaze finding Nord's furious one as he charged forward.

"Crombie, you don't have to do this," she said, nails scraping over the hand he had shackled around her wrist. "We can talk—"

Lina's pleas fell on deaf ears as Crombie smirked.

The sight of it filled Nord's veins with ice. "Don't you dare—"

"See you around."

"No," Nord roared. He jumped, going airborne in a desperate attempt to close the last few feet that separated him from the woman he loved. He barely registered the snap of Crombie's fingers over the rush of blood in his ears.

Less than a second later, Nord's body met with empty space. The very space Crombie and Lina had just occupied.

Nord spun in a circle, heart and mind both unwilling to accept what he could so clearly see.

Needing an outlet for his rage, Nord let out a cry of pure fury. The walls shook from the force of it, but it wasn't nearly enough. Spinning around, his gaze landed on the dresser. With another furious shout, he picked it up and hurled it across the room, not so much as flinching as shards of wood rained down upon him. It was still nowhere near enough. So he kept going, systematically destroying everything he could get his hands on.

Nothing helped.

If anything, the destruction of their room only fueled his rage. Not only was furniture a poor substitute for his actual target, but as the seconds ticked by, there was no escaping the truth.

Chest heaving, body covered in sweat, Nord was forced to finally admit defeat.

Crombie was gone, and he'd taken Lina with him.

CHAPTER 2
FINLEY

He hovered by the bedroom door, ready to duck out at the first sign of Quinn waking, knowing full well the Satori heir would hardly appreciate his bedside vigil. She'd been out for well over twelve hours now, and Finley had spent more of them by her side than he'd ever admit. Especially to her.

At first, he'd told himself he was just keeping his promise to Nord and Lina by checking in on her. But as the hours passed and she barely stirred, he recognized the lie for what it was. He wasn't watching over her out of any sense of duty. He was satisfying his own needs by ensuring she didn't stop breathing.

Ever since he'd met her, there'd been a sense of knowing. A familiarity that would have been more appropriate with someone he'd known for years instead of a handful of weeks. It bothered him, that feeling. Kept him awake at night trying to suss out just what it meant and where it stemmed from.

Both his waking and sleeping thoughts were devoted to trying to solve the riddle that was Quinn Satori. Not just who she was, but how she'd ensnared him so completely. It wasn't anything as simple as attraction—though she was quite possibly the most stunningly beautiful creature he'd ever seen. But gorgeous women were a dime a dozen, and he'd sampled more than his fair share. Beauty alone would never be enough to lure him. And while he appreciated her quick wit and clever tongue, he'd known plenty of sophisticated, intelligent women in his lifetime. Never once had he experienced anything quite like this.

It was safe to say Finley had never been this captivated by a woman.

Ever.

Each time he thought he had her figured out, some new layer revealed itself, sending everything he thought he knew about her spiraling into chaos. Perhaps that was par for the course when dealing with an Animagus with ties to a sphinx, but since Quinn was the only one he'd ever spent any time with, he couldn't say.

The lack of concrete answers meant he was constantly on edge. It was also why he felt the need to deliberately provoke her. He wanted to get under her skin the same way she'd so effortlessly wormed her way beneath his. At least when they were trading insults, his fascination didn't feel so one-sided.

Finley sighed and scrubbed a hand over his face. Quinn had him so tied up in knots, he didn't know if he was coming or going anymore. If she was any other woman, he'd just fuck her and be done with it, but he already knew it wouldn't get her out of his system. He was starting to think, fuck her or not, Quinn Satori would never be out of his system.

He stepped out of the doorway, taking a few quiet steps closer to the bed—and its occupant. Moonlight streamed in through the window, bathing her in its soft glow. Not for the first time, Finley was struck by how vulnerable she looked lying there with one hand curled beside her head on the pillow, her berry-colored lips parted, and the long sweep of her lashes casting shadows on her porcelain skin. Awake, Quinn was a force to be reckoned with. Asleep, she seemed delicate and in need of protecting.

Finley's lips twitched up in a small smile. Quinn would likely gut him if she ever heard him refer to her as delicate. Not only that, she was so stubborn, she'd probably purposefully put herself in danger and then try to rescue herself, just to prove that she absolutely did not require his protection.

But, want it or not, it was hers.

And so, he was coming to realize, was he.

Finley blew out a defeated breath and gave in to temptation. Reaching out, he trailed his knuckle down her temple and over her velvety cheek. As he moved his hand along her jaw, he ran the pad of his thumb across her plump bottom lip, his body relaxing as her warm breath washed over his fingers.

He lingered for a moment, sweeping his thumb over her lip a second time as he imagined the various ways he might taste her mouth the first time. Despite the gentleness of his touch, there was nothing sweet or soft about the scenarios playing out in his mind.

Of all the delicious possibilities, one in particular appealed to the darker part of his nature. The part that craved control and submission. He could so clearly imagine Quinn delivering one of her patented smart-ass remarks, thinking she'd just won whatever argument they were having. Only this time, instead of returning her barbed comments with one of his own, he'd grasp her just beneath her jaw so he could feel her pulse skyrocket beneath his fingers as he pushed her back into the wall and shut her up with his lips.

There was a change in Quinn's breathing, and Finley's eyes snapped back to her face in time to see her eyelids flutter. Knowing he'd pushed his luck too far, he snatched his hand away and made a hasty retreat.

He'd almost reached the door when Quinn's groggy voice called out, "Where do you think you're going, Batman?"

Finley closed his eyes and inwardly cursed. *So close.*

"Finally decided to rejoin the world of the living?" he asked, turning back around to face her.

Even rumpled with sleep, she took his breath away. *You are so fucked, mate.*

"I had the craziest dream."

"Oh?"

Quinn yawned and stretched. "Yeah, Lina was trapped in a night garden talking to snakes." She chuckled and then seemed to notice how dark the room was. "Wait, how long was I out?"

"All day."

She frowned. "Yikes. Did I miss anything?"

He tucked his hands into his pockets. "Besides Lina raging out? No, not really."

"What?" she asked with a disbelieving laugh. "You're joking."

"Afraid not. You were out when she went after the Director, and then you'd already left when she almost lost it on Nate. Nord took Lina off to work out the rage, by the way. Not sure when they'll be back."

If Quinn had any reaction to the news that they were alone, she didn't let on. She just asked, "Nate?"

"The head of the Brotherhood's cleanup crew."

"Ah . . ." She let out a low whistle. "Man, I wish I could have seen Lina in action."

"Me too."

"What do you mean? Weren't you there?" she asked, her brows dipping low.

"I was, I just ah . . . missed most of it," Finley said, rubbing the back of his head.

"Bastard knocked you out too, huh?"

Finley nodded sheepishly. He wasn't used to being taken out of the game so easily. It wasn't sitting well.

Quinn gave him a sympathetic smile that quickly turned impish. "At least we got the last laugh. He may never realize it, but Colin's lucky I let him remember his name. That piece of shit won't hurt anybody ever again."

"There is that," he agreed.

Finley's satisfaction at the part he played helping to dismantle the Director was eclipsed by the pride he felt at Quinn's. He had to give it to her. The woman was a pro when it came to exacting revenge. He wasn't sure what it said about him that the thought both terrified and aroused him.

He cleared his throat.

"So, Lina's a berserker," Quinn said, thankfully unaware of the turn his thoughts had taken. "That's going to be fun." Making a face, she added, "Shit, this is going to require a new nickname."

It was Finley's turn to give her a confused look. "Come again?"

She rolled her eyes. "Not that it's any of your business—"

"You're the one that brought it up."

"—but I only just settled on calling her 'Li.'"

"An inspired choice, to be sure."

Her eyes narrowed threateningly at his dig, and Finley couldn't help his answering grin. Every time one of his barbs landed, it felt like a minor victory.

"Well, I couldn't exactly keep calling her 'Queen E' when she doesn't go by Evalina anymore—it didn't make sense."

"Obviously not," Finley murmured, amused despite the inane topic. Only Quinn could make something so superficial sound so vital.

He listened as she prattled on about various possibilities until finally, she let out an exasperated huff and pinned him with her aubergine stare. "What do you call Nord? Maybe I can come up with something for Lina to match."

Finley raised a brow. "I call him Nord."

Quinn groaned. "I should have known. A man as uptight as you clearly lacks imagination."

You want imagination, princess? I'd be more than happy to show you just how creative I can be when properly inspired.

Then her attention sharpened once more, and she ran her eyes up his body. Finley felt her blatant examination like fingers raking across his skin. Shivers of anticipation raced over his body and seemed to coalesce directly in his cock.

"So this is what casual looks like on you. I have to admit I wondered."

It took a second for her words to register. Generally, he had no trouble following her rapid shift in topics, but she was on a roll and he was more than a little distracted. When they finally did, Finley glanced down at his gray slacks and white button-up. He hadn't paid much attention when grabbing clothes after his shower. He'd been more interested in getting back to her.

"How is this any different than what I usually wear?"

Quinn gestured with her hand. "For one thing, your sleeves are rolled up, and there's not a tie or jacket in sight. All I've ever seen you in is a suit. I was starting to think you slept in one."

His lips curled up at that. "Imagine me in bed often, Satori?"

Finley was ready for one of her customary shutdowns, but Quinn surprised him by swinging her bare legs out from under the blanket and over the side of the bed.

Hands planted on either side of her thighs, she leaned forward. The move shouldn't have been seductive, but even clad in a V-neck and sleep shorts, Quinn was temptation itself as she purred, "And if I do?"

Finley was ready to push her back onto the mattress and show her exactly what he wore to bed, but a distant roar sent all thoughts of sex and seduction scattering.

"Did you hear that?" he asked, craning his head as if it would help him locate the source of the sound.

Quinn's brows furrowed. "Hear what?"

Finley held a finger up to his lips as his ears caught the faint sound of a crash. "Something's going on outside," he whispered, moving to the window.

Back against the wall, face angled toward the window, Finley carefully pushed aside the heavy curtain.

"What do you see?" Quinn asked, creeping over and tucking her body behind his.

Finley let the curtain drop. "Nothing."

"And you're certain you heard something?"

Finley gave her a look.

She held up her hands. "Just asking, sheesh." When the next crash came seconds later, followed closely by others, even Quinn heard them. She paled. "Okay, but what are the odds whatever's causing the ruckus has anything to do with us?"

Finley didn't bother answering.

Quinn sighed, correctly interpreting his silence. "I was afraid of that."

"I think it's coming from next door," he said in a voice just barely above a whisper.

"I thought the house was abandoned?"

"It is." Which made the disturbance even more worrisome. "Stay here. I'll go check it out."

"You want me to stay here? By myself? What if this is all some elaborate scheme to separate us? It wouldn't be the first time someone used a trick like that to draw us out."

"Alistair's wards will protect you—"

Quinn crossed her arms and raised a brow. "Because wards are foolproof. Yeah, totally."

Finley bit back a groan. This must be how Nord felt every time Lina refused to stay put. "We don't know what we're going to find out there. It could be dangerous—"

"More dangerous than staying here with no means of defending myself?"

"We both know that's not true, Satori. You're perfectly capable of defending yourself."

"Um, have you already forgotten what happened to me back in that alley this morning? I think the Director proved easily enough just how useless my defenses actually are."

Finley frowned. The likelihood of anyone breaking through the wards was slim to none. But now that she'd pointed out the possibility, he couldn't ignore it. He knew of one creature in particular who didn't seem to have any trouble with wards. And if there was one, there could be others.

He let out a pained groan, squeezing the bridge of his nose between his fingers. If this was some ploy to get Quinn alone, he couldn't play into their enemy's hands.

"All right, fine," he snapped. "We'll go together." Finley tore the curtain from its rod, drawing on his power to convert the material into a more appropriate outfit for her to wear. Tossing it to her, he ordered, "Get dressed."

Quinn opened her mouth to say something. She must have realized she'd already pushed her luck far enough when she saw his expression because she wisely shut it and pulled on the pair of pants.

"So you can be obedient."

"Don't get used to it."

Finley shook his head and busied himself by checking his weapon while she finished changing her clothes. That done, they crept down the stairs and out the back door.

The crashes and bangs grew louder as they carefully made their way to the neighbor's back door.

"What the hell is going on up there?" Close as they were, Quinn practically breathed the question directly in his ear.

"Nothing good," Finley answered.

"It sounds like someone let a tornado loose inside."

Finley eyed the light spilling out from the upstairs window and spotted a massive shadow zooming past. "Let's hope it's only a tornado."

Making quick work of the lock, he slowly pushed open the door. With all the racket upstairs, he needn't have worried about being overheard, but it was second nature to take precaution. After a quick sweep of the first floor, they made their way to the second. It wasn't hard to find the source of the noise. Only one door was open, with light pouring out of it.

Standing just off to its side, Finley glanced over his shoulder at Quinn. For the first time, he accessed his Guardian magic to speak directly into her mind. It was something he rarely did with anyone outside of the Brotherhood, and definitely not without their permission. Not only because it was an intrusion, but because it required far more power to send even the simplest thoughts. Given their current situation, however, he felt justified in breaking his rule.

"Stay behind me, got it?"

Quinn nodded, her eyes wide.

Weapon in hand, Finley peered around the doorway and went still. "Nord?"

His friend stood in the center of the room, chest heaving, sweat dripping down his face and torso. The destruction surrounding him was absolute. Not a single piece of furniture remained untouched. From what Finley could tell, when Nord had run out of things to destroy, he'd started taking out his rage on the walls themselves. Blood was smeared across its white surface, disappearing into too many holes for Finley to count.

Quinn lightly touched Finley's back and peered around him into the room. He heard her startled gasp, and then the slight quaver in her voice as she asked, "Nord . . . where's Lina?"

Finley knew the answer to that as soon as he'd seen the state of the room. There was only one thing that would send his friend's rage spiraling like this. But Quinn, it seemed, needed to hear it.

Nord slowly lifted his head, his expression terrifyingly blank and his voice dead as he uttered one bone-chilling word. "Gone."

CHAPTER 3
NORD

"Gone? What do you mean 'gone'?" Quinn asked, her voice unsteady.

"What about that is unclear?" Nord snarled as he stalked forward. "She's gone. Vanished. Taken. Stolen. Not. Fucking. Here." A terrible crash accompanied the last word as he slammed his fist into the wall so hard the entire house quaked.

"Mate, you need to calm down before you send what's left of this place falling down on top of us," Finley said.

Nord's head whipped to his friend, his eyes flashing with uncontrollable rage. "Don't you dare tell me to calm down."

Something like understanding flashed in Finley's eyes, but he didn't back off. "You're no help to her like this."

The blow would have hurt less if Finley had used his fists. His words too closely echoed Nord's own thoughts.

He'd never felt more worthless in his life. He'd been there. Right. There. And it still hadn't been enough to protect her. That fucking pissant managed to steal her anyway. What good was the vow he'd made when he couldn't seem to keep it?

Shame swirled inside of him, colliding with his bottomless fury. It was damn near impossible to stand still when the need to destroy pulsed in his veins, but he managed through sheer force of will. Well, force of will and the knowledge that Finley was right. He needed a clear head if they were going to find Lina. Or as clear as he could get, anyway.

Tearing the room apart blunted the edge of his temper, but only just. Any reprieve would be short-lived until Lina was back in his arms and Crombie was in the ground. So long as he had a target—and a plan that would lead him to it—he could focus through the worst of his wrath.

Without either of those things, without Lina to anchor him, there'd be no stopping the ruthless monster he'd become in his quest to sate the bloodlust. He'd witnessed the bloody aftermath of a berserker who'd lost his mate. It was not the sort of thing one ever forgot. The body count the man had left in his wake had been staggering. The only reason his reign of terror even ended was that after the seventh day, he took his own life to escape the blinding madness.

Nord had been too young and stupid to realize what it meant at the time. That the collateral damage he'd been so impressed with resulted from a broken heart rather than prowess. It wasn't until many years later that he realized the man he'd so admired had been ripped open by his grief. But it wasn't until today that Nord understood what it would mean if someone found a way to permanently separate him from Lina.

His clansman had done all of that because of a broken heart. If Nord lost Lina, he'd be a man without a soul. So if he truly lost her, if there was no chance of ever getting her back, there would be no stopping him. He'd raze the entire fucking world to the ground before he would ever contemplate joining her.

Thankfully, for him and the rest of the world, that was not the scenario they were currently facing. Lina was alive, and he knew who she was with. Now he just needed to figure out how he was going to get her back. In order to come up with a plan, he'd need to rely on Quinn and Finley. They knew his quarry better than he did.

"Let's start at the beginning," Finley demanded, slipping into the role of competent Guardian as he holstered his weapon. "Who has her?"

"Crombie," Nord spat. Just uttering the name had his body vibrating with barely restrained fury.

Finley's face darkened, but Quinn visibly relaxed.

"Well, that's a relief," she said, sagging against the door frame. "For a second there, I was sure you were going to say Mikel."

A growl rattled in Nord's chest. The last thing he needed right now was a reminder that there were other, potentially far deadlier enemies after his woman.

"I don't think you're helping," Finley said under his breath.

"I'm just saying, it could be worse. With Crombie, we have an advantage. We know he's unlikely to hurt Lina because he needs her alive, so she can steal whatever it is he's after. Plus, he's always had a thing for her."

Another snarl slipped free.

"Quinn," Finley said in a low, warning tone.

"I'm just stating facts. Crombie *likes* Lina. I'm not saying any of us have to be happy about his crush or the demented lengths he's taken to be alone with her, but the truth is we should be thanking our lucky stars he's the one we're dealing with. That's a good thing for us because we know he isn't going to hurt her. It means we have time."

Nord forced himself to breathe, hating that another man's obsession with his woman might be the only thing keeping her safe.

"So where would Crombie take her?" Finley asked. "His club?"

Quinn bit her lip, her eyes growing unfocused as she considered it. "No," she said, drawing the word out as if she was thinking out loud. "Too public, even with its secret rooms. The District is filled with employees and surveillance; there's a high chance they'd be seen or overheard. He wouldn't risk it."

"His house then?" Nord asked.

She seemed to weigh the option, tilting her head side to side as she considered. "That's more likely," she finally answered. "Guaranteed privacy, at the very least. He'd definitely bring her to a location he had full control over. Somewhere we couldn't get to easily. He owns other property, but nothing as remote as his estate. At least not in town."

Assuming he's still in town.

Tension thrummed through Nord, knotting his muscles and sitting heavy in his chest. He couldn't allow himself to consider the possibility Crombie had taken Lina somewhere outside of his immediate reach. Nord's hands trembled, and he balled them into tight fists. The only thing keeping him on this side of sane was the knowledge that he was going to find her and bring her home. Sooner versus later. He didn't think he'd stay sane long if he had to deal with 'later.'

Quinn flinched as his gaze met hers, and Nord realized she could read everything he was feeling in the single look.

"We're going to get her back," she promised softly.

He nodded, unable to form anything resembling an actual response.

"If they're at his house," Finley mused, oblivious to the silent conversation passing between Nord and Quinn, "we're not going to be able to break in the same way we did last time. Even if we could, with Crombie there, it's not like we can just sneak around and search for Lina."

Quinn blew out a breath. "We need a distraction. Something Crombie can't ignore, so even if he's in the same place, he's looking the other way while we're there."

"What's important enough to make Crombie ditch Lina after going to such extreme lengths to take her?" Finley asked.

"Crombie's only ever cared about two things," Quinn muttered, coming into and out of Nord's field of vision as she paced up and down the hall, "himself and his hoard." She was out of sight when she let out a long groan. "Oh my God, of course."

By the time Nord could see her again, Quinn had her phone in her hand.

"What are you doing?" Finley asked.

"Ordering pizza," she replied dryly, glancing up only long enough to roll her eyes at him. "What's it look like I'm doing?"

"Calling someone," Finley answered, his voice dripping with as much sarcasm as hers. "What I haven't figured out is why."

"I know somebody who might help us create our distraction. Obviously."

"Obviously?" Finley parroted, quirking a brow. "Is it really a good idea to bring anyone else into this?"

"I don't see you coming up with any ideas, Batman," Quinn snapped as she lifted the phone to her ear and waited for whoever it was on the other end of the line to pick up. She didn't have to wait long. "Linc, hey—"

Her flood of words came to an immediate halt, causing Nord's chest to tighten, but then an exasperated smile lifted the corners of Quinn's mouth, and he relaxed.

"Sorry. *Zilla.* A mutual friend of ours is in trouble. She could use your help."

It took Nord half a second to place the name. When the bouncer's face swam up in his mind, he couldn't decide if Quinn was insane or a genius. With her, the two were not necessarily mutually exclusive, but could they really trust one of Crombie's lackeys? Even one who'd sworn allegiance to Lina after she drunkenly knighted him?

Quinn fell silent once more, and he and Finley exchanged an uneasy glance as the silence stretched. Sweat rolled down Nord's back, and his hand trembled once more as the leash he held on his fury began to slip.

"Put it on speaker," Finley whispered.

Quinn flipped him off and ignored the request. A second later, she broke out into a full-blown grin. "You were, were you? Well then, what would you say if I told you I have some information that could help you with that?" There was another beat of silence, and then she chuckled. "Serendipitous, huh? I suppose it is, because I just so happen to know about a break-in involving one of Crombie's prized items . . ."

There was a brief pause, and then Quinn lifted her eyes to Nord's. There was no missing her relief as she silently mouthed, "He's in."

CHAPTER 4
LINA

A sharp tug in the vicinity of her belly button was Lina's only warning before the bedroom vanished. For one endless moment, her body felt as if it was being shoved through a vacuum. The pressure was so great it seemed like her insides were attempting to swap places with her outsides. Just as her lungs began to seize with the need for air, it was over. Nord's bedroom was replaced by a glittering night sky and greenery as far as the eye could see.

Not that Lina was in any state to appreciate the unexpected beauty of their new location. As soon as whatever Crombie had done stopped, she dropped to her knees and retched.

"Don't worry, it'll pass. That happens to everybody the first few times."

Lina lifted her head as she wiped her mouth, tears streaming down her face as she glared up at the smirking fae. Rage burned through the last of her nausea, flooding her with energy as she gracelessly pushed to her feet and rushed Crombie.

As far as plans went, she had none. The only thing on her mind was wiping that shit-eating grin off of his face by whatever means necessary. She figured gouging out his eye or ripping off his lips might do the trick. Maybe she'd go for his arm instead so she could beat him with it. Lina wasn't feeling particularly picky. Whatever she could get her hands on first would do. But as she slammed into him, the jarring impact robbed her of breath.

She stumbled back.

"Trust me, you don't want to do that."

Lina bared her teeth in a feral snarl and lunged again, this time swiping at his face. As her nails cut into his cheek, she felt the sting of tearing flesh on her own. She hissed at the unexpected pain. From what she'd gathered in her short time as a berserker, pain usually spurred her bloodlust on, but this was unexpected enough to give her pause. There was no reason *she* should be feeling anything.

Crombie tsked. "I did try to warn you, sweetheart. It's not my fault you chose not to heed me."

Her eyes shot to his cheek . . . his perfectly unmarred cheek. If her berserker were an animal, she'd say it whined in confusion. She could feel the need to strike and destroy pushing at her, but uneasiness swirled through her as well.

"What did you do?"

"Me? I didn't do anything. Well, not in this exact moment." One side of Crombie's mouth twitched up as he watched her. "Yes, I can see you're finally starting to put it together, but let me save us both the headache of you testing your theory and spell it out for you. Our bond makes it impossible for you to hurt me without experiencing the consequences yourself. So I'd be very careful about what you try to do with all that rage I see blazing in your eyes."

She desperately wished she could refute it, but the truth of his words echoed in the burn of fresh scratches down the side of her face. She couldn't touch him. Not without harming herself.

Lina eyed Crombie warily, wondering what other limitations might exist between them due to her bloodsworn promise. Nord had warned her things would only grow worse for her with time, but naively she thought Crombie wouldn't use the bond against her.

They were supposed to be friends . . . of a sort, anyway. Allies, at the very least.

Her jaw clenched. *So much for that.*

Crombie continued to study her, his expression a combination of amusement and curiosity, as if he enjoyed watching her squirm and couldn't wait to see what she'd attempt next.

Lina cried out in frustration as her berserker paced restlessly inside of her. She needed an outlet for her rage, but unless she wanted to risk crippling herself, it wasn't going to be him.

Forcing herself to take full, deep breaths, Lina glanced around and searched for a safer target. She might not be able to hit him, but she needed to hit *something*. If she didn't, the bloodlust boiling in her veins might force her to lash out against him anyway and ruin any possible chance of her getting out of this in one piece. Survival needed to be her priority right now. Making Crombie pay for his tricks would come later.

In the meantime, she'd just have to pretend whatever inanimate object she wailed on was him . . . or better yet, use her magic and turn it into him.

"What are you plotting?" Crombie asked, his head tilting and his eyes sparkling with interest as he watched her take in their surroundings.

Lina wasn't sure whether her intentions were telegraphed by her expression or if he could now read her thoughts to some extent. Since he asked the question, she could only hope it was the former.

She tossed him a smug smile of her own. "You'll see."

"I can't wait," he said as he slid his hands into his pockets. The unhurried act belied his words. Crombie didn't appear to be in any hurry now that they were here.

Wherever here was.

The garden was like none she'd ever seen. Not just because she didn't recognize a single tree or flower, but because of the wild, dangerous quality it exuded. Much like the man who currently tracked her every move.

Glancing up at the sky above and the unfamiliar constellations that twinkled there, Lina realized the garden had been designed specifically with night in mind. All the flowers, without exception, were in bloom. And unlike the bright, vibrant species she was used to seeing, these blossoms were muted. Their palette ranging from white, to gray, to the deepest plum. As if someone had cataloged the exact colors of midnight through the very first blush of dawn and recreated them in this space.

It's a tribute. Anything crafted with this much loving detail couldn't be anything but.

Eyes narrowed; Lina wondered why Crombie had brought her here. It was obviously a sanctuary, but was it his? And if so, did he realize how much it revealed? If the night garden was, in fact, Crombie's, it might be the most personal thing he'd ever shared with her.

Despite the anger roiling inside of her, Lina couldn't help but be drawn to the garden and its occupants, curious what secrets she might uncover about its owner.

Taking a few tentative steps forward, she leaned closer to the nearest flower bed, catching a hint of its heady scent. She was careful not to breathe too deeply, lest the flowers had tricks of their own. The last thing she needed was to get dosed by a territorial tulip or poisonous peony and end up passing out at Crombie's feet.

Her eyes fluttered closed as the fragrance filled her nose. It was impossible not to appreciate the unique combination of musk and spice that called to mind the sorts of things that only ever happen under a veil of moonlight. As she inhaled a second time, the images in her mind coalesced into one very explicit example. The mental picture was so vivid that Lina lost herself to it for a time until some sense of self-preservation pulled her back.

Cheeks flooding with heat, Lina straightened and took a hasty step away. *Wasn't I looking for something?*

She blinked, trying to remember what she'd been in the middle of doing before the flowers distracted her, but the task was gone, along with any sense of urgency she might have had about it.

Perhaps it should have worried her, but at the moment, all she felt was mild frustration she'd made such an easy target. Even though her instinct cautioned her against the inhabitants of the garden, she'd still fallen under their spell. This place might be lovely, but it was far from safe.

Lina stepped firmly back and turned away from the flowers. Spotting Crombie, she headed in his direction. As she did, he brushed his jacket back and sat down on a white stone bench that was set in a little alcove just to the side of a bubbling fountain.

His movements were languid, but she knew they were part of a carefully cultivated performance. The intensity of his stare as his eyes trailed her gave him away. He was far too invested in her response to his sanctuary for anything he did to be truly casual. It was obvious he was trying to put her at ease, using his calm demeanor and their tranquil setting to lure her into a false sense of safety.

More like trying to trick me into forgetting he brought me here against my will, she thought with a snort. *But why do something sure to piss me off, only to turn around and try to win me over again?* Lina's gaze met his as she reached the fountain. *What game are you playing, Crombie?*

He held her stare, his stormy eyes giving nothing away.

For a second, she was tempted to ask him outright, but then his lips curled up in that knowing way of his, and she checked the impulse. Lina wasn't feeling particularly inclined to give Crombie anything he wanted right now. And since what he wanted, so far as she could tell, was her attention and her questions, she'd give him neither.

Her eyes cut to the fountain. Up to this point, she hadn't given it more than a passing glance, but now that she actually looked, she was struck by its sheer majesty. The night garden's centerpiece was truly a work of art.

Instead of something traditional, such as a fish or mermaid, the water spouted out from three figures locked together in battle. The largest of the three was a beautiful winged male. Lina could only assume he was an angel. Though, the violence radiating from his sculpted face made her think he was likely a fallen one. He was dressed for battle, his armor and sword so intricately detailed she could almost believe they were real. Same for his feathered wings, which were flared wide, one protectively curling around one of the other figures. Water poured off of them, creating the illusion of rain falling down upon the three intertwined figures.

Her gaze moved down his body to the place where one of his legs was caught in the mouth of a dire wolf. The beast's ears were low back on its head, its eyes narrowed with the promise of a bloody death. Water trickled out of its maw in what could only be a symbolic representation of blood.

Between the wolf and angel was a woman half-hidden by the angel's wing. Her hands were outstretched, one placed on the chest of the man who hovered above her, the other on the foreleg of the wolf crouched below. Her hair was a nimbus around her, like she'd just whipped her head around in time to catch the angel deliver a fatal blow. Water dripped from her eyes as she cried endless tears for the wolf's fate.

"It's the Battle of the Stars," Crombie supplied. "When Solaris and Lupus fought for Nocturna's hand."

It's beautiful, she thought. Though to Crombie, she said, "It's depressing."

He laughed. "Most fae tales are. Would you like to hear it?"

Yes.

"No."

His lips twitched. "Perhaps just the highlights then. After Lupus was slain, Nocturna turned her back on Solaris, unable to bear the sight of him. Thus began the Lord of Daylight's eternal quest to rejoin the Lady of Night. Though to this day, she continues to elude him. Or so the tale goes," he added with a shrug. "Story aside, Nocturna's known as the mother of the Twilight Realm and first Queen of the Night Court."

"Your court?" Lina asked, recalling a rumor Quinn had shared with her.

"Once upon a time."

"For someone who wants nothing to do with his past, you sure seem to have put a lot of effort into this place."

"It wasn't the land I despised."

The meaning in his words sat heavy between them. But before Lina could ask who he'd despised enough to leave everything he'd known behind, Crombie asked her a question of his own.

"Feeling better?"

The way he studied her as he asked set alarm bells off in her mind. "Better how?"

He waved a hand. "Oh, I don't know. Less punchy, perhaps?"

As soon as he mentioned it, her complete lack of rage became frighteningly apparent. How the hell had she forgotten how pissed she was with him?

Lina immediately reached for her berserker but came up empty. The fact that she couldn't seem to summon any feeling stronger than annoyance at the discovery only added to her confusion.

"What. Did. You. Do?"

"That's the second time you've accused me of foul play since we've arrived. My answer now is the same as before: *I* haven't done anything. Aside from bringing you here, of course."

Lina cast a suspicious glance around. When her eyes found the flowers she'd stopped to enjoy, her sudden lack of rage, or any extreme emotion for that matter, made a disturbing amount of sense. She'd been sedated.

Worse, she'd practically done it to herself.

"I knew nothing this beautiful could be trusted." She sent Crombie a baleful stare. "You're proof enough of that."

He grinned, her irritation only increasing his amusement. "I can't help it if you succumbed to the garden's tranquil allure."

"Right. Because you definitely didn't bring me here for that exact reason. Especially once you realized I'd become a berserker."

Crombie clasped his hands together in his lap, his lips tilted in the barest hint of a smile. He couldn't have looked guiltier if he tried. Dropping his voice to a conspiratorial whisper, he asked, "How did that come to be, by the way?"

"None of your business."

Crombie raised a brow as he held her challenging stare. Instead of pushing for an answer, he surprised her by laughing out loud. "I must admit, while I was hopeful you would not be immune to the garden's magic, not even I anticipated a berserker mid-rage would stop to smell the flowers."

Lina fought hard against a laugh but ultimately lost the battle. It was a rather absurd mental image, now that he pointed it out.

"For what it's worth, I still want to punch you."

"Do you?"

"That surprises you? I can't imagine there are very many people who have met you and *haven't* wanted to hit you in the face."

Crombie's lips twisted. "Yes, well, be that as it may. Generally, the euphoria brought on by the garden tends to supersede such violent inclinations."

"I wouldn't say I'm feeling euphoric, exactly. Just . . . mellow."

"Stay here long enough, and you will."

Great, something to look forward to.

"Just because I can't seem to muster up the appropriate amount of anger anymore doesn't mean I've let you off the hook. You kidnapped me, asshole. That deserves a knee to the balls, at the very least."

Crombie rolled his eyes. "You're being dramatic. All I did was bring you to a place where we could discuss the terms of our arrangement without interruption. I could hardly have a rational conversation with you in the state you were in. Or with that Neanderthal of yours beating on his chest. So I did what I had to do. You're my guest, Lina, not my captive. Though I'd be happy to tie you up, if you'd prefer?"

Heat unfurled in her belly. She might be in love with Nord, but there wasn't a woman with a pulse who wouldn't react to an offer like that when delivered in Crombie's sensual croon.

"Or maybe I'll tie you up," Lina said, snickering as the image of Crombie dressed in a baby pink negligee and his hands bound behind his back solidified in her mind. He'd be pissed, but it'd be worth it for the pictures alone. She'd give him some of those fuzzy pink handcuffs to match.

Mind made up, Lina called on her power, intent on making the image reality. But as soon as she made the attempt, her magic fizzled.

"I'm sure you had something delightful in mind, but you can't do that here either." Crombie pointed to the constellations, which seemed to shimmer as he did. "Those prohibit anyone but me from using magic."

Lina's shoulders slumped as all the joy trickled out of her. "I can't hit you. I can't humiliate you." She shuffled over to his bench and sat down with a huff. "I can't even feel upset enough to yell at you about it."

Crombie laughed. "It would take more than a couple of ropes to humiliate me."

"You only say that because you don't know what I was going to make you wear."

"Sweetheart, you get me my treasure, and I'll wear whatever the hell you want."

A laugh bubbled up as she stared at him, her mind racing with ideas. "Seriously? Just like that?"

"I never joke about business."

She had to admit, the sheer possibilities alone made it an appealing offer. She might have agreed to help just for the chance if she wasn't already bloodsworn and forced to follow through anyway.

Crombie slung his arm on the back of the bench, angling his head down so that their faces were closer together. So close, in fact, she could count the number of eyelashes framing each of his eyes. Her breath stuttered when he pinned her with the full intensity of his stare.

"So, are you ready to uphold your end of our bargain?"

"Do I have a choice?"

"There's always a choice, Lina," Crombie answered. "But every choice has its consequences."

A shiver slid down her spine as his meaning sank in. Things were only going to get worse for her until this matter was resolved between them. So while she technically had a choice, there was only one answer, because she couldn't afford to be weakened by their bond when going up against the Drakes.

"I'm ready."

CHAPTER 5
LINA

"Do you know why I deal in artifacts, Lina?"

She cocked a brow and let out a humorless laugh. "I think we've established that when it comes to you, Crombie, I don't know jack."

He lifted a hand and brushed it over his mouth, but not before Lina caught his smirk. "Well then, allow me to let you in on a little secret."

Curiosity well and truly piqued, Lina turned, pulling one of her legs up so that she could face him fully. Then she propped her elbow on the back of the bench and rested her head on her fist. "I'm listening."

He eyed her pose with amusement. "I see that got your attention."

"You divulging secrets freely? Yeah, that's a surefire way to guarantee I'm paying attention."

"Good to know. But don't get too excited; thanks to our bond, you won't be able to repeat a word of what I'm about to tell you." Crombie's grin stretched as hers faded. "Oh, don't look so disappointed. You didn't really think I would give you anything you could turn around and use against me, did you?"

Lina wasn't sure if she was offended or annoyed by the implication. She'd never been a gossip. In her world, that sort of thing got people killed. On the other hand, being able to share crucial information with her friends was one of the reasons they'd managed to stay alive this long.

"For your information, the thought hadn't crossed my mind."

Crombie's eyes swept over her face. "Interesting."

"What is?"

"You're telling the truth."

"Of course I am."

Then his words registered, and she straightened. If he could tell whether or not she was lying, she'd have to tread very carefully. Not that Lina could recall a time she'd lied to him outright, but still. That didn't seem like the sort of thing he'd let go unpunished.

"Is there anything else I should know about our little connection before we continue?" Lina grumbled.

His expression turned playful. "Probably."

"You're not going to tell me, are you?"

"Where's the fun in that?"

Lina groaned. "You are such an ass."

"Just don't try to do anything to actively harm me, and you should be fine."

"Does that work both ways?"

Crombie's eyes glittered dangerously. "What do you think?"

She let out a gusty sigh. "I feel obliged to warn you, the second I fulfill my promise, my fist has a date with your face."

He laughed, not remotely concerned. "As far as threats go, that might be the cutest I've ever received."

"You won't think so once I make good on it."

Crombie leaned closer, bringing their faces within inches of each other. "Just to prove how little that worries me, I'll give you one free shot once our arrangement comes to an end."

Lina narrowed her eyes. "Free or not, I'm taking it and however many more you earn between now and then."

His lips twitched. "I'll keep my healer on speed dial."

One day, people were going to start taking her seriously. Today, apparently, was not that day.

"Get on with spilling your secrets, Crombie. I don't have all night."

"Somewhere else to be?"

"Literally anywhere you're not."

"Ah, Lina, you wound me," he said, his hand lifting to his chest.

"Liar."

"You and I both know I'm many things, sweetheart. But a liar is not one of them."

"The fae may not be able to lie outright, but you certainly take liberties when it comes to the truth."

Crombie ran his fingers lightly down the side of her face. "That's not all I take liberties with."

A shiver worked its way down her spine, though whether it was in response to his touch or his words, she couldn't say.

"Eventually I'm going to get out of this garden, Crombie. And while *I* may not be able to do anything to you, we both know someone who can. Be careful what *liberties* you try to take." The lack of intense emotion somehow made her words sound more threatening. As if their casual delivery resulted from an intimate familiarity with violence and bloodshed rather than an inability to access the full depth of her anger.

For a second, Lina thought Crombie was going to call her bluff. She held her breath as his eyes dropped to her lips. When his gaze lifted, he held her stare for several heartbeats as his fingers resumed their trail down her cheek to her neck, only to pull away. Her breath flowed out in a rush as he sat back and gave her his profile.

He was silent for a long moment, and then he murmured, "Black as my soul may be, there are lines even I dare not cross."

"I know," Lina whispered.

And she did.

There was a reason fear wasn't one of the things she'd felt when he'd brought her here. Back when she could feel, that is. Whatever else he had planned, hurting her—really hurting her—wasn't one of them. She'd sensed his odd duality more than once. Crombie might be a villain, but he had a moral compass, even if those morals were more skewed than most.

He must have heard something in her voice because his eyes darted to her face before returning to the fountain. "Don't make me into some sort of tragic hero."

"I'm not."

His lips quirked. "Lie."

Lina pressed hers together, biting back a curse. That little trick was going to get real old, real fast. "Actually, the word that came to mind was villain, so you might want to double-check your lie detector. It must be faulty."

"Impossible."

She sighed, thinking for the first time the contact high from Crombie's flowers might actually be a blessing. There's no way she'd make it through this conversation without a raging migraine or covered in blood otherwise. "*You're* impossible."

"True."

"Oh my God," she groaned. "I hate you."

Crombie opened his mouth, his eyes flashing with humor.

She pointed at him. "So help me, if you tell me that's a lie, I'm going to take my chances with that punch to the face. Even if it knocks me out instead of you, at least I'll be unconscious and not have to deal with this bullshit anymore."

He laughed. "Apologies. I can't help that you're so easily riled. Or how much fun it is, but I'll be on my best behavior from here on out."

Lina snorted. "I'll believe that when I see it."

"What about if I pinkie swear?" he asked, holding up his finger.

He looked so ridiculous, decked out in his pristine three-piece suit, his hair an artful tumble around his perfect face, and his little finger extended toward her. She shook her head, trying not to laugh. "Swearing with you last time didn't work out so well for me."

"Ah, but this time I'm the one making the promise."

"True, but I rather keep my pinkies to myself if it's all the same to you."

He dropped his hand, a small smile still playing about his lips. "Suit yourself."

"You owe me a secret," she said when the laughter faded and the silence had settled comfortably around them.

"So I do, and I've always been a man of my word." He stretched his legs out, his attention trained on the tips of his shoes, his hands clasped in his lap. "Of all the items I've acquired, I've never once taken something from its rightful owner."

Lina raised a brow. "What about—"

His eyes lifted to her face, and the intensity of his silvery gaze robbed her of words.

"I've *never* stolen something from its rightful owner."

"O-okay," she managed. "So you're what? Robin Hood? Stealing from the rich?"

"Hardly," he said with a chuckle. "I've never given a single thing away for free. And what I do has nothing to do with helping others. The only person I serve is myself."

"Okay," Lina said again, not sure where he was going with this.

"The way I see it, it's a victimless crime since it was never theirs to begin with."

"Well, that's debatable."

Crombie grinned but remained silent.

"So if you only take what's already been stolen, why not return the objects to their true owners?"

He shrugged. "If they truly cared, they should have made it so their possessions were never lost in the first place. Besides, if I'm able to recover them, what's stopping them from doing the same?"

The man had a point.

"All right, I suppose that's fair." A lightbulb went off in Lina's mind. "And the object you want me to acquire from the vault, was it also stolen?"

Crombie's face twisted with the first sign of genuine anger. "The Mobius Council has made quite the name for themselves taking what does not belong to them."

Lina stiffened. "In almost every case I know about, they only stash an item in the vault when it's too dangerous to remain in the world."

Thunder rolled in the distance, and Lina warily eyed the starry, cloudless sky. Beside her, Crombie's knuckles turned white.

"And who are they to decide?"

Lina opened her mouth but shut it again at the sight of the barely controlled fury on his face. It was easy to forget who she was dealing with when he flirted with and teased her. This wasn't Crombie, her sometimes friend and ally. This was the fae prince—no ex about it.

And he was pissed.

"Crombie . . . this item you want me to retrieve. Did it—*does* it— belong to you?"

When his eyes met hers, she would have sworn she saw lightning flash in their depths.

Well, that answers that.

"The Council, they stole it from you?"

"Not exactly," he admitted, his posture relaxing slightly. "Though they may as well have since they refuse to give it back."

Lina blew out a breath. "You've already petitioned them."

Even though it wasn't a question, Crombie nodded once.

She frowned, wondering how the Council could justify not only the initial theft but the subsequent refusal to return it. Unless . . .

"Is it a weapon?"

Crombie barked out a laugh. "No."

"Then I don't understand. Why did they take it?"

"Just because it's not a weapon doesn't mean it isn't powerful."

"Even so, the high-handedness you're describing seems more befitting of the Brotherhood than the Council. The relics Mobius confiscates are just that. Relics. Objects of power from ancient or extinct people. We don't make a habit of stealing things that don't belong to us. Or at least we didn't. But what do I know?" She laughed without humor. "Clearly I'm out of the loop. Not only have members of the Council flat out lied to me, my own father conspired to have me killed."

She could feel Crombie's gaze on her, but she refused to meet it. She didn't want to see his sympathy, or worse, his pity.

"Seems our fathers have something in common."

Her eyes snapped to his face, but he was no longer looking at her. She started to reach out but hesitated, her hand hovering just above his knee. "Is he still alive?"

"Unfortunately."

The thought that the man responsible for her death was still out there somewhere, that she could run into him at any moment, was its own sort of torture. "I guess that's something I have on you, then. My pathetic excuse of a sire is at least dead."

Crombie's lips ghosted up. "Lucky girl."

Lina snickered. What a strange world they lived in, where the death of a parent made one luckier than another. "So what did the Council take from you, anyway? Don't I get to know what it is I'm supposed to go searching for?"

"That's actually the real reason I brought you here. So you could see for yourself." He gestured once more to the fountain. "Outside of Faerie, this fountain contains the only replica of Nocturna's jewelry."

Nocturna . . . the first queen.

Holy shit.

Lina's eyes fell closed. The Mobius Council didn't just steal from Crombie. They stole the equivalent of the Crown Fucking Jewels from a ranking member of one of the Faerie Courts. No wonder he was pissed. People had declared wars over less.

She knew there was more to it than what he was telling her. Like how Mobius had gotten their hands on a royal artifact, for starters. Or why no one from the Night Court seemed inclined to do anything about it. In the end, the hows and whys didn't really matter. She was bound to help him, regardless. Though, if she was being honest with herself, she would have helped him anyway.

Standing, Lina moved over to the fountain. Crombie stood to follow her, but a muted chirp made his steps falter. She glanced over her shoulder in time to see him reach in his pocket and pull out his phone. His expression darkened as he tapped the screen and accepted the call.

"This better be—"

A sudden boom of thunder was Lina's only warning that whatever the caller was telling Crombie was far from good news.

"I'll be right there," he said, clicking off his phone. He glanced at Lina, his eyes wild in the half-second it took for his mask to slide back into place. "You'll have to excuse me; something's come up. You'll be safe here in the garden until I get back." His eyes warmed the slightest bit as he added, "Just watch out for the flowers."

Lina didn't even get the chance to protest being left alone because Crombie was gone as soon as he finished speaking.

"It's a bit late for that," she muttered with a shake of her head.

With nothing else to do, she turned back to the crying woman immortalized by the fountain, this time paying close attention to the crescent moon pendant hanging from her neck. Lina had just started to study the thick band of swirling stars on the woman's ring finger, idly wondering if it mattered that Nocturna had been depicted with it on her left hand, when the scuff of a boot over stone sounded behind her.

"Back so soon?" she asked, whirling around.

But it wasn't Crombie that stepped from the shadows.

Lina blinked, not sure she could trust her eyes as the boulder of a man came into view. She knew exactly two people who shared that swollen build, but the scar bisecting this one's eyebrow identified him easily enough.

"Zilla? How did you get here?" Lifting her hands to her hips, Lina cocked her head and narrowed her eyes. "Did Crombie send you to keep an eye on me?"

The half-giant gave her a lopsided grin. "Not quite. I'm here to rescue you."

She straightened, his answer taking her by surprise. "Rescue me? Is that even safe—for you, I mean?"

His black eyes softened with affection. "There you go worrying about everyone but yourself again."

"Well, garden prison or not, I'm pretty confident my safety is assured for the moment."

Zilla glanced around, his expression unreadable. "I wouldn't be so confident if I were you." Before elaborating on his cryptic warning, he added, "We should go before he gets back."

Lina moved toward him, unable to keep herself from giving voice to the questions running rampant in her mind. "How did you know where to find me? Or that Crombie took me? Where are we, by the way? Bell Falls? Somewhere else?"

"No time to explain, I'm afraid. They're waiting for us."

"They?" she repeated curiously, but the answer came to her without aid. This had Quinn written all over it. Realizing they couldn't get to her, Quinn would have sent in the cavalry, and Nord was probably losing his shit about the fact he had to rely on someone else to get her out. Finley, as a result, likely had his hands full keeping Nord from going on a full-on rampage. Her heart went squishy at the thought.

"Do you trust me?" Zilla asked, holding a scarred hand out to her once she was just a few steps away.

Lina didn't hesitate to accept it. "Of course I do."

The smile that broke out across his face when she slid her hand into his made him appear almost boyish.

"Then hang on, sweetness. It's gonna be a rough ride."

CHAPTER 6
NORD

"Where are they?" Nord growled, raking his hands through his hair as he restlessly paced a few feet away from the ward that separated him from the heart of Crombie's estate. "They should have met us by now."

"Easy there, tiger," Quinn murmured soothingly. "They'll be here. Zilla won't let anything happen to her."

A growl rumbled in his chest as he glared in the direction of Crombie's house. It wasn't the bouncer he was worried about.

"We should at least be inside so we can reach them if something goes wrong," he gritted out.

"So you've said," Finley replied dryly. He'd been leaning against a nearby oak tree—well out of Nord's reach—ever since he'd refused to breach the ward.

Smart man.

"Only about a thousand times," Quinn agreed beneath her breath.

Nord gripped the sides of his skull, squeezing hard. He knew his rage was barely in check. Because of it, he walked the razor's edge between madness and sanity.

Under ideal circumstances, when triggered, the berserker's lust pushed him to extreme acts that rarely, if ever, fell under the umbrellas of 'safe' or 'sane.' This was nowhere near an ideal situation. To say he was barely hanging on was a massive understatement, if not an outright exaggeration. He was already in free fall. Madness loomed closer every second.

Even so, Nord couldn't help but feel like he was the only one processing Lina's capture rationally. She was in danger, and they were out here standing around like a bunch of useless assholes, putting not only her safety but her life in the hands of a relative stranger.

Berserkers were quite literally born for situations such as these. Impossible ones where death, or at the very least serious maiming, was assured. The bloodlust not only enabled them to perform feats normal men would never dare, it encouraged it. If ever there was someone who should be risking themselves to free Lina, it was him.

So why had he agreed to this? Why was he waiting on the sidelines and leaving his future happiness up to a man he barely knew?

It was absolute insanity. Proof he was nowhere near sane.

In Nord's defense, the plan had seemed sound when Quinn laid it out for him and Finley, but as the seconds slipped by without sight of the woman he loved, Nord cared less about things like rationality and logic. Now he was starting to see the plan for what it was: bullshit.

"You know that I'm right. We can't do a damn thing for her outside the ward. What if they get caught?" he asked, swinging an arm out to encompass the sprawling grounds. "Crombie could catch on at any second. If he does, if he spots them . . ." Nord couldn't make himself finish the sentence. "They're alone in there, without backup. Lina doesn't need a stranger. She needs *me*."

"No, she needs us. All of us. Which means we're exactly where we're supposed to be. If we cross the ward, we risk capture ourselves. Crombie isn't exactly one to roll out the red carpet for his enemies.

What do you think he'll do to us—to you—if he catches you trespassing?"

"You think I care what he does to me?" Nord shot back, his voice rough with emotion. "I would trade my life for hers a hundred times over. There is nothing he could do to me that I would not willingly endure for her safety."

Quinn stared at him, her face soft with understanding for all of a heartbeat before she hit him with her signature sass. "Are you a masochist?"

Nord's steps faltered, his temper flaring at her direct provocation. "Excuse me?"

"Quinn," Finley whispered. "I don't think this is the right time for your brand of tough love."

If he'd been thinking clearly, Nord might have realized that's exactly what she was doing and appreciated how she trusted him enough to purposefully bully him back into his right mind. It was a tactic he'd watched her successfully employ against Lina a number of times, but he was too far gone. And as he'd already decided, logic had no place here.

"No," Quinn said, slicing her arm through the air without looking away from Nord, her palm facing Finley. "I mean it. Do you get off on pain or something? Because it's the only reason I can come up with for why you'd insist on doing something so goddamn stupid."

"Stupid?" Nord repeated, his eyes narrowing. "You think wanting to save her is stupid?"

"Get a fucking clue, Viking," Quinn said with a dramatic roll of her eyes. "How useful are you going to be to Lina if you're locked up? Hmm?"

Nord clenched his fists. *She doesn't understand.*

"You didn't like that question? Okay, how about this one? Have you already forgotten what she sacrificed to free you the last time? Or that the last deal she made trying to rescue you is the exact reason we're in this mess right now? Come on, Nord. Wake up. We both know the second you trade yourself for her, she'll just turn around and march her happy ass back to Crombie to negotiate your freedom. *Again.* Do you really want Lina to make another deal with him? Because that's where things are heading if you don't get your shit together."

The berserker rattled in his chest.

"Jesus, Quinn. Are you trying to set him off?" Finley sputtered. "Give the guy a break. He's worried about her. We all are."

Quinn tossed him a dirty look over her shoulder. "Oh, bite me. I don't see you trying to talk any sense into him—which is Best Friend 101, by the way. So unless you're going to grow a pair and help me out, shut up."

Nord glared at them both, his body vibrating with fury.

When Finley's sole response was to press his lips together and remain silent, Quinn spun back to Nord. She gave him a quick once-over, sighed, and gripped his forearms. The strength of her grasp surprised him enough that he didn't fight against it.

"Lina is going to be *fine.* I promise you, Nord. My track record of looking out for her should speak for itself. I would never have made the call if I thought it would lead to additional risk. You need to trust me, even if you can't trust anyone else."

There was something about the intensity of her gaze which prevented him from looking away. The tightness in his chest eased as her eyes searched his. Without conscious thought, Nord took a deep breath in and then slowly released it. When he did it a second time, Quinn nodded, her hands briefly squeezing his arms before she let go.

"What did you—"

The rest of what he'd intended to say disappeared as a flash in his periphery caught his attention. He snapped his head to the side, his eyes intently scanning the horizon.

There.

A shadow crept around the side of Crombie's estate, looming closer. From this distance, it was hard to make out any details, but

Nord would have recognized the soft gold of Lina's hair anywhere. Instead of relief at the realization, a niggling sense of unease filled him. Something wasn't right.

It took the shadow moving closer for what he'd already instinctively sensed to become clear. Her hair wasn't in the right place. Namely, the flashes of it he could see were far too close to the ground. Thoughts became fragmented after that, as the berserker took control.

The transition was nearly instantaneous, which wasn't surprising given how long he'd straddled the line between the two parts of himself.

With a wild shout, he raced headlong for the ward, no longer in any state to be concerned with things such as alarms or capture. The only thing the raging beast cared about was finding out why the woman he loved wasn't walking on her own.

A hand fisted in the back of his shirt, but whose, he didn't know. He twisted away, the sound of tearing fabric less than a blip on his radar as he kept moving, singular in his purpose.

Nord was a millisecond away from crossing the barrier when he felt it. A tiny fluttering in his chest, like thousands of tiny bubbles floating to the surface. He hadn't felt Lina's emotions since she'd been taken, but now that she was in range again, he knew without a doubt what he sensed came from her.

Even if he hadn't recognized it, the fluttering was accompanied by a wash of warmth that was distinctly Lina. As unique as a fingerprint and as intangible as the breeze ruffling your hair. You knew exactly what caused the movement, even if you couldn't see it.

The berserker lost his hold as Nord realized what the bubbling in his chest was.

Laugher.

Her laughter. And if Lina was laughing, she wasn't hurt. She was okay, more than okay. She was . . . happy.

Nord lifted a hand to his chest as the breath stuttered out of him. The sudden shifts from berserker and back, in addition to the extreme emotions that accompanied them, left him reeling. His knees buckled.

Finley was there in an instant, his arm banding beneath Nord's shoulders to help steady him. "You okay?"

Nord pushed his friend away and sat down hard at the edge of the barrier. He sucked in a lungful of air and ran a shaking hand through his hair. "I just . . . need . . . a moment."

Finley gave his shoulder a squeeze and stepped to the side, which Nord appreciated since it offered him the illusion of privacy while he struggled to get himself together. He was feeling too many things, not all of which came from him. It was a lot to process in his current state.

In an effort to regain control, he focused on the blurred shape racing their way. Breathing became easier as the distance between them closed, although Nord continued to track their progress as if his salvation was reliant upon their success. Which, in a way, it was.

When they were about halfway between the house and the magical barrier, Zilla crossed into a small patch of moonlit ground, and the details hereto concealed by the darkness finally revealed themselves.

The half-giant ran with Lina tossed over his shoulders in a fire-man's carry, her limp body bouncing with each running step forward. If not for the white-knuckled grip Zilla had on her limbs, she would have toppled off.

Nord must have made some sort of distressed noise because Lina's head snapped up, her eyes immediately finding his. She squirmed in Zilla's arms. At first, he ignored her and kept running, but then she poked him in the cheek and Nord watched her lips move as she uttered something he couldn't hear.

Finley let out a low laugh, having no issue catching what she said due to his Guardian-enhanced senses.

"Mind sharing the joke with the rest of the class?" Quinn asked.

"Lina just threatened to revoke his knighthood and lifetime membership in her harem of badasses if he didn't put her down."

"That's my girl," Quinn murmured, a smile evident in her voice.

Apparently, the threat worked because Zilla carefully lowered Lina to the ground not even a second later. She paused just long enough to untangle herself from their co-conspirator's hold and press a quick kiss to his cheek. Then she took off, her arms pumping and her golden hair streaming behind her as she raced to Nord.

It took everything he had not to surge forward through the ward and meet her. He needed her in his arms more than his next breath, but he hadn't waited this long to alert Crombie to their presence at the most crucial moment.

"Get the portal ready," Nord ordered in a low voice as he pushed back to his feet. "I want us out of here the second she crosses the ward."

"Already on it," Finley answered.

Time grew unbearable as Nord waited for Lina to reach him. In reality, it probably took her a minute at most, but each second stretched painfully, and Nord experienced each and every one like a dagger to the heart.

Once she was close enough to touch, though still on the other side of the ward, her name left him in a tortured groan. "Lina."

She took two more steps before she was airborne, her body crashing into him at the same time her lips found his.

He caught her easily, one arm sliding beneath her thighs, the hand of his other tangling in her hair. Lina groaned and melted into him, her legs hooking over his hips, her arms wrapping around his shoulders.

Nord angled them in the direction of the portal, still kissing her as he took his first few steps. Then he pulled away, just far enough to meet her gaze.

"Brace yourself, Kærasta. I have no intention of letting you out of my sight, or my arms, any time soon."

Lina's laughter washed over him. "What a hardship. How ever will I endure it?"

His lips tugged up at the sight of her smile, though he could still feel a tremor working its way down his arms. It would take more than a single kiss to help him recover from the night's events.

Nord took another step toward the portal, eager to be away, but halted to address the man talking quietly with Quinn from the other side of the ward.

"Words seem paltry after what you have done for us, but for now, they are all I have. Thank you, truly."

Zilla waved him off. "No thanks necessary. I meant it when I told her I had her back at the District. Your lady is a special one. Anyway, I should get back before I'm missed." His face was as expressionless as ever, but there was a definite affection as his gaze landed on Lina. "Get home safe and try to stay out of trouble, yeah?"

Lina snorted. "It's not my fault trouble always seems to find me."

Everyone except Nord burst out laughing.

"What's so funny?" Lina asked, looking around. "It's true."

Nord shook his head. "You run headlong toward danger, Lina. I don't think you know how to avoid it."

She raised a brow. "Well . . . so do you."

Unable to deny it, Nord ran his nose along hers. "I can't very well have you running off alone, can I?"

Lina tightened her arms around his neck and snuggled closer, bringing the scent of jasmine and something else with her. Nord pressed his nose into her hair, trying to place the vaguely familiar fragrance. It was too floral to be vanilla, but it contained the same seductive warmth.

The urge to get her home returned with a vengeance.

Nord forced himself to pull away. Looking back at Zilla, he called, "If I can ever return the favor, all you need to do is ask. If it is in my power to give, it's yours."

Zilla gave Nord an appraising look and then surprised him by smiling. "I appreciate that, berserker, but you owe me no debt. It was my pleasure. Now you all really should get going."

"We'll be in touch," Quinn said softly, giving Zilla a smile before rushing off. Finley remained silent but offered him a slight nod as he followed behind her.

Having already said what he'd needed to, Nord simply started for the portal. Lina leaned over his shoulder to blow Zilla a smacking kiss. "Consider yourself promoted, hot stuff!"

Nord could still hear the other man's roaring laughter as he carried Lina across the threshold into the penthouse.

CHAPTER 7
LINA

Nord hadn't stopped touching her since they escaped. Not that Lina was complaining. Since she'd also been an unwilling participant in the 'your partner is being held captive' dance, she knew the exact taste of the terror it induced. And not just because she could feel the remnants of Nord's fear, though she definitely could. It buzzed beneath her skin like an angry wasp.

But even if that hadn't been the case, she would have understood the quasi-obsessive need for physical reassurance. Once you experienced that particular brand of torture, it wasn't the kind of thing you'd ever fully forget.

No matter how desperately you wished you could.

"Cuppa, anyone?" Finley asked, seeming almost giddy as he walked into the living room with a loaded drink tray in his hands. Since their Scotland hideout was no longer much of a secret, they'd opted to return to the penthouse, and Finley, for one, could not be more pleased. Lina supposed that had to do with the fact he was home and could sleep in his own bed versus a couch or floor for the first time in weeks.

He offered Quinn a steaming mug as he passed her, which she

accepted with a soft thanks. Then he glanced at the others as he moved to the center of the room and set the tray down on the coffee table.

"What'd I miss?" he asked, taking a seat on the sofa across from Nord and Lina.

"Well," Quinn said as she carefully positioned her cup of tea on the mantle. "Apparently, Crombie's claiming the only reason he took Lina to his 'special fairy garden'"—she rolled her eyes and made air quotes—"is because he wanted to show her a statue of the first Queen of the Night Fae and her rejected lover. Oh, and the item he's got a massive hard-on for is actually a fae heirloom that supposedly once belonged to her." Quinn turned to Lina. "Do I have all that right so far?"

The best Lina could manage was a half-hearted mumble of assent.

Between the lingering influence of the night garden and the drugging brush of Nord's lips along the side of her neck, it took more willpower than she currently possessed to focus on the conversation. Quinn had been peppering her with questions for the better part of an hour, and Lina hadn't done a great job of answering them.

Experience told her Quinn wouldn't tolerate her lack of attention for much longer. To be honest, the fact that she'd allowed it to go on for this long was telling in itself, but that was a future Lina problem. Right now she had a delicious Viking curled around her, and she couldn't be bothered with much else.

She'd be willing to bet few women lucky enough to find themselves in a similar position would, Quinn included. And who could blame them? Vikings were hot. They were also incredibly attentive lovers, or, at least, Lina's was.

She smiled smugly at the thought. She could practically hear the shouts of jealous women everywhere, demanding to know where they could get one of their own.

I should talk to Astrid about opening up the gateway to Novasgard and offering a Viking matchmaking service. Sort of like a mail-order hunk kind of deal, but without the mail. Oh, maybe we could host a bachelor auction. We'd make a fortune. Lina snickered at the thought of Søren or Björn being auctioned off to the highest bidder.

"Are you even listening to me?" Quinn asked, exasperation heavy in her voice.

Oops. Definitely wasn't.

Lina's guilty look must have spoken for itself because Quinn snapped, "What is wrong with you? It's like you don't even care that Crombie body snatched you—"

"I don't think that's what body snatch—" Lina winced at the glare Quinn shot her way and quickly apologized, "Sorry."

"This is serious, Lady B."

That's a new one.

A part of her, albeit a very small, distant part, acknowledged Quinn was right. She should be more concerned about coming up with a game plan to retrieve Crombie's artifact and get out from under the hold of the vow. But the rest of her was more interested in deciphering her newest nickname. It wasn't that she didn't take their predicament seriously. She just couldn't seem to focus on it, or anything for that matter, for longer than a few seconds at a time.

Ever since escaping the garden, her thoughts had felt like a gaggle of unruly children playing tag. That is to say, impossible to corral. As if the effects of the garden were somehow magnified outside of its borders. Lina wouldn't be surprised to learn that Faerie magic was more potent in the mortal realm. That seemed like some typical fae assholery.

"Lady B?" Lina echoed under her breath.

"I think it's supposed to stand for Lady Berserker," Finley supplied, leaning forward to pick up his cup of tea.

She shot him a thankful smile. "Does that make Nord a Lord?" Lina couldn't help but giggle at her unintentional rhyme.

"It stands to reason," Finley murmured.

Behind her, Nord's chest rumbled with silent laughter. "Careful, Kærasta. I don't think she's amused."

"When is she ever?" Finley asked, giving Lina a conspiratorial wink as he took a sip. He wrinkled his nose, set his cup down, and pulled a flask out from his jacket pocket.

Lina grinned as he uncapped it and poured a liberal splash of whisky into the cup.

Once the flask was empty, Finley returned it to his pocket and took another sip. This time, he sat back with a satisfied sigh. "Much better."

Quinn watched all of this play out with a scowl, her eyes flashing with purple fire. "Are you quite finished?"

"I'm sorry, I'm listening," Lina said, attempting to school her expression into something appropriately somber. "Scout's honor," she added, holding up two fingers.

Nord brushed a kiss to her knuckles and readjusted her hand so that three fingers were raised. "I take it you weren't a Girl Guide?"

"No, but I had a massive crush on a Boy Scout." The arm wrapped around her waist tightened warningly, and Lina laughed as she glanced back at him. "What do you know about the Scouts anyway?"

"I know all sorts of things."

Quinn threw up her hands. "You know, I expect this from him," she said, pointing at Finley, who raised his brows in mock affront. "But not from you."

Nord's smile dimmed.

"Were you, or were you not, prepared to tear the world apart with your bare hands not even an hour ago?" Quinn demanded, placing her hands on her hips. "What happened to that guy? Can I get him back? He may have been more beast than man, but at least he seemed prepared to take things seriously."

"Do not mistake my relief for disinterest," Nord softly cautioned.

Quinn met his stare without flinching. "Could have fooled me. All you've done since we got back is sit there with Lina in your lap like a love-struck teenager."

Only Lina was close enough to pick up Nord's warning snarl. He may appear outwardly content, but Lina could feel his seething emotions. The berserker was not far from the surface, and it would take very little to set him off. Quinn may not appreciate it, but Nord was distracting himself the only way he could to protect them from his rage.

"Give it a rest, Satori," Finley said, coming to Lina's rescue once more. "You're lucky you've got this much out of her."

"Excuse me?"

"Look at her pupils," Finley said, gesturing at Lina. "She's high as a kite. No one in that condition would be able to focus, let alone provide reliable intel. Might as well call it a night and try again in the morning once the effects of whatever Crombie gave her wear off."

"Crombie didn't give me anything," Lina corrected without thinking. She lost some of her bravado as three sets of eyes turned her way and mumbled the rest, "It was the flowers."

"Flowers?" Quinn repeated.

Lina nodded, deciding to keep the part where she'd basically drugged herself quiet. No need for the others to know just how colossally she'd messed up. She seemed to be in enough trouble as it was. She waved a hand. "You know what, it doesn't matter. Carry on."

Quinn shook her head and turned her attention back to Finley. She didn't look completely swayed by his argument. "Lina could know something important. This hold Crombie has over her is only going to get stronger. We need to steal his trinket and be done with him."

"I agree," Nord said, "but not tonight. A few hours won't make a difference. Besides, regardless of the details, the first thing you need to figure out is how she's going to get into the vault. Crombie wouldn't know much about that, but as an heir of Mobius, you should."

"I have to take my place on the Council," Lina blurted, as if it was obvious.

Quinn's gaze shot back to her. "You are high."

Nord's body went rigid, his arm tightening around her once more. "Absolutely not."

"There he is. Thank you for finally showing up," Quinn said. To Lina, she added, "I'm with him."

"Isn't that akin to walking right into Mikel's trap?" Finley asked. "If he controls the Council, shouldn't you stay far, far away?"

That was certainly the safe and logical thing to do. But safe and logical weren't going to get things done.

"Probably, but there's no way around it. If I want in the vault, I have to get access to all things Mobius, and the only way to do that is to rejoin them."

"For the record, I didn't like that plan the first time you suggested it, and I like it even less now," Quinn muttered. Then she closed her eyes and sighed. "But you're right. It's the only way. No one, save the Ascended, has access to the vault. If Lina wants in, she's going to have to reclaim her seat on the Council."

"Am I the only one who thinks this sounds like a terrible idea?" Finley asked.

"No," Quinn replied, "but we have no choice. Crombie totally fucked us by making Lina swear his bullshit vow. We need her free of it if we have any hope of facing off against Mikel. His entanglement in our lives is a wild card we cannot afford."

The events of the night already proved that. Crombie would continue to be a pain in her ass until she upheld her end of their deal. It was bad enough he knew exactly where she was at any given moment and could reach her in the blink of an eye if he so wished. Actually, that wasn't bad so much as annoying. Though, the fact that she couldn't physically defend herself against him if needed was definitely problematic. As was his ability to tell whether she was lying. Especially since he took so much pleasure in calling her on it.

If those new developments were just the second phase of being bloodsworn, how much worse were things going to get?

As worry tried to push its way to the surface, Lina was thankful for the suppressive effects of the garden. Emotions could be helpful, but they had no place in this kind of strategic planning. The facts were the facts. She'd sworn the vow, and the only way out of it was by getting into the vault. Her path forward was clear.

Resolved though she was, her thoughts scattered as soon as Nord bit down on the side of her neck. It didn't hurt; he didn't bite nearly hard enough for that, but there was no mistaking the act of dominance or demand for her attention. As soon as he released her, she shifted in his lap so that she was facing him.

"Can I help you?"

"You're not setting foot in that viper's den without me."

She opened her mouth, but he silenced her with a kiss, waiting until she melted into him to pull back and whisper against her lips, "This is not up for debate."

"The Council doesn't exactly roll out the welcome wagon for outsiders," she warned him.

"I'm not an outsider."

Lina was about to protest again when his meaning sunk in. She let out a soft chuckle. "No, I guess you're not. The Transference saw to that, didn't it?"

"According to the laws and traditions of your people, I have as much right to be there as you do."

"I thought they were our people," Lina replied with an arched brow.

"They are, but I'm sure they'll search for a loophole once they find out."

"Good thing it doesn't matter what the Council thinks. The Ancient Ones have spoken."

"I'll be the first to admit I'm no expert on the ways of the Animagi, but I was under the impression that the Transference was extremely rare," Finley said, his brows veeing down with concern. "Is it wise to reveal you know how to perform the ritual? Mikel seems a power-hungry sort. Won't that be like waving a red flag in front of an already pissed-off bull? Do we really want to draw more attention to ourselves right now?"

"It's a risk we'll have to take," Nord said, his tone leaving no room for argument. "Mikel is gunning for us one way or another. If the only way the Mobius Council will allow me through their door is for me to declare myself an Animagus, then it's a wild card I'll gladly play. Lina shouldn't have to face them alone—"

Quinn made an annoyed sound Lina easily translated as, *"Hello, what am I?"*

"—when I have a legitimate reason to be there and can watch her back," Nord finished.

Finley exhaled loudly and sat back in his seat. "As long as you're aware of the risks."

Lina couldn't help but laugh. "These days, there are nothing but risks."

"True, but some risks are best avoided when possible," Finley pointed out.

Lina shrugged and rested her head on Nord's shoulder, happy to let the others continue to plot and scheme around her if it made them feel better. And by better, she meant more in control. For her part, she'd already made peace with what came next.

Quinn chewed on her bottom lip, looking torn. "Mikel is smart enough to figure out that performing the ritual means we have access to a Codex. He'll absolutely up his game to get his hands on it. But Lina's going to have to prove herself to claim her seat, regardless. So whether we admit it upfront or not, the secret's coming out. There's no way to hide she's unlocked her line's full power, not from the other Council members."

"So it's a calculated risk then. We willingly reveal our hand early and hope to gain some brownie points with the rest of the Council by being transparent," Finley said, running a hand over his jaw. "I can work with that. If the info's coming out anyway, best it's on our terms and when it'll give us some sort of upper hand."

"Agreed," Nord said.

"So we're sure about this?" Quinn asked, looking around at each of them for confirmation. "There's no turning back once we pull the trigger."

Lina didn't bother nodding. She'd already made it clear what she intended to do. The others must have given Quinn some sort of confirmation, because there was a soft clap of her hands.

"All right," she said, sounding all business once more. "I should call my mom and give her a heads-up. She'll take care of the arrangements and let us know when and where to meet."

Lina lifted her head in time to see Quinn exiting the room.

"Tired?" Nord asked, pulling her attention back to him as he ran a warm hand along her rib cage.

She gave him a slow nod, her eyelids already drooping. "I think the buzz is finally wearing off."

"Let's get you to bed then," he said.

"Yippee," she whispered, feeling marginally more energized.

Nord's lips twitched. "To *sleep*."

"Mmhmm," she murmured. "Sleep. Riiiight."

One side of his mouth lifted higher as he set about adjusting her arms around his neck. "I mean it," he said, tightening his hold on her as he stood, "you need to rest."

Lina waved goodnight at Finley, who raised his cup of tea in a silent toast. Then she tilted her chin so her lips were at Nord's ear. "Thankfully, I happen to be an expert on what I need, and wouldn't you know it, right now, sleep's number two on the list."

"What's number one?" Nord asked in a warm rasp, already carrying her in the direction of her bedroom.

"You. Always you."

"Thank fuck."

CHAPTER 8
NORD

Lina made a soft sound of protest as Nord set her down in front of her dresser. "This isn't the bed."

She leaned back into him as he placed his hands on her hips and dropped a kiss to the top of her shoulder. He lifted his eyes to meet hers in the mirror.

"Pajamas. Now."

"You're a real clit tease, you know that?"

Nord laughed. "How can I be a tease when I have promised nothing but sleep?" He watched Lina's eyes travel down his reflection before lifting back up to meet his steady gaze.

"You don't have to *say* anything. You're like a walking advertisement for mind-blowing sex, and I've already bought ten of whatever else you're selling. So gimme."

"I'll give you anything you want," he promised, his voice low, his eyes holding hers. Then he gave her a wolfish grin and brushed the soft fall of her hair to the side so that he could press another soft kiss to the back of her neck. "After you sleep."

Lina's decidedly heated gaze turned sulky. "Since when do you want me to wear PJs to bed anyway? Aren't you king of the 'lingerie just gets in the way' club?"

Nord chuckled as he ran his knuckles down the side of her arm. "If you're in the mood for stockings and garters, Kærasta, by all means. I don't care what you wear, so long as you're prepared to sleep in it."

Tugging open one of her drawers, she grabbed a balled-up item without looking and chucked it at his face. "Spoilsport. I'm not about to waste my good underwear on sleeping."

He knocked the scrap of lace aside and leaned forward, peering over her shoulder into the open drawer. "You have good under-wear?" he asked with a raised brow. "Have you been holding out on me?"

"Hey!" She turned and punched him in the arm. It hurt far more than it would have a few days ago but still wasn't enough to faze him. "My underwear is awesome, thank you very much. I certainly haven't heard any complaints."

Nord couldn't resist leaning forward and kissing the pout off of her lips. "That's because there aren't any. You're temptation itself, no matter what you're wearing."

She narrowed her eyes playfully. "Yeah, you better say that." She poked him in the chest. "Otherwise, I might do something drastic like only wear granny panties and sports bras, which are way more comfortable than the silk and lace numbers I usually wear for you. Which you don't even appreciate. And for the record," she added, really getting into her rant, "you never let me leave anything on long enough to make an event out of it. Why go through all that effort if you're just going to, quite literally, rip it off not even two-point-five seconds later?"

Nord tried hard not to laugh at her not-completely-inaccurate description, knowing it would only spur her on. Though, if he was being honest, she was something else when she was all riled up. That could be the berserker talking, but still, the man in him couldn't help but agree. He knew exactly what all that fire translated into.

"But those two-point-five seconds"—he kissed his fingers—"perfection."

She eyed him, clearly unsure whether or not to believe him. "Uh-huh."

He leaned closer and whispered, "What do you think I'm picturing when I lose myself inside of you?"

Her cheeks filled with color, and her eyes went hazy. "Oh . . ."

He laughed. "Get dressed, and then get into bed. I'll meet you there."

"For the Nord special?" she asked hopefully.

"Dare I ask?"

"Orgasms, Nord. I'm talking about orgasms. A lot of them. You're like the vagina whisperer. You can practically make me come with a single look or growly word. You can't just give me all of that, get me addicted, and then cut me off cold turkey." Lina made a face. "It's cruel and unusual punishment, and haven't we both been punished enough today?"

Nord crossed his arms. As far as convincing arguments went, it was one of the best he'd ever heard. Though he enjoyed watching her pull out all the stops, what Lina didn't seem to realize was that he didn't require any convincing. He and his body were more than willing to indulge her. Not only willing, aching for it.

If not for the dark smudges of fatigue beneath her eyes, and the handful of poorly stifled yawns he'd already overheard, he'd already be buried inside of her. But, as always, the need to take care of her trumped all others. When it came to that, there was little, if anything, that would sway him from his path.

"Seriously," she went on, completely unaware of his internal musings, "if you're so set on making sure I get a good night's sleep, a couple of Os would go a long way."

Wasn't that the truth.

"I'll make you a deal—"

Lina gasped, one hand fluttering dramatically to her chest. "A compromise? Am I dreaming?"

Nord raised a brow. "I'm sorry. I thought you wanted to come tonight. My mistake." He made as if to turn away, but she snatched his arm and gave it a tug.

"Not so fast, mister. What were you going to say?"

It was hard not to smile as he teased her. "I'm not sure you deserve to know."

She couldn't have looked more earnest as she said, "If it has anything to do with you throwing my legs over your shoulders and making my eyes roll back in my head, then I can promise you, there's no one more deserving."

His lips twitched up. "Is that so?"

"Mmhmm. Pretty sure it's a scientific fact."

This time there was no stopping his grin. "Well, in that case. I was going to say that if you're still awake by the time I finish with my shower, I'll see about giving you the, what did you call it? The Nord special?"

Lina lifted both her arms in the air and let out a victorious whoop. "Done and done!" She began to strip, pausing as she tugged down her pants to laugh and shake her head. "I can't believe you just said that."

"Neither can I. You must be rubbing off on me."

"Hopefully, in about fifteen minutes, you'll be rubbing off on me," she shot back with a suggestive lift of her brows.

A sound that was half-groan, half-laugh escaped as Nord shook his head. "What am I going to do with you?"

She crossed her fingers. "Fuck me stupid, hopefully."

Nord's shoulders shook as he ran a hand down his face. "For the love of . . . just get in bed. I'll be right out."

"I'll be waiting," she singsonged, tossing him a grin over her shoulder as she began rifling through her drawer.

He made his way toward her bathroom but stopped dead at the odd tickle in his chest. It took him a second to identify the sensation as a combination of surprise and confusion, and then another to place it as Lina's.

"What's wrong?" he demanded, all trace of their prior playfulness gone.

His blood ran cold as Lina held up a familiar black piece of stationery. For a single heartbeat, he saw nothing but red as his rage, hereto banked by Lina's return, came roaring back with a vengeance. That motherfucking fae had snuck past their ward and left a note for his mate in her fucking underwear drawer without any of them being the wiser.

"That son of a bitch," he growled, plucking the note card from her hand.

His fury spiked to dangerous levels when he realized the silver symbols were utter gibberish. The implied insult couldn't have been more obvious. It wasn't enough that Crombie sullied such an intimate space. No, he had to go the extra mile and rub salt in the wound by ensuring Nord had to ask what the note said.

"Can't read it?" Lina guessed, only half-correct in identifying the source of his anger.

Nord shoved the card back in her hand. "What's it say?"

She eyed him carefully before glancing back at the card in her hand. "I'd rather not tell you."

"Lina . . ."

She bit her lower lip. "It's just going to piss you off."

There was no keeping the snarl out of his voice as he said again, "Lina . . ."

She sighed. "All right, fine. But don't say I didn't warn you." She glanced back at the card, her eyes skimming side to side as she read, "'Pretty thief, you stole something that belongs to me. It only seemed fair I stop by to return the favor. And while I appreciate a clever trick, don't for a second think this matter is resolved. Eventually, you'll pay for what you've done, one way or another. For now, you and I have more pressing matters to attend to. I'll be in touch. P.S. . . .'" Lina's mouth kept moving, but her voice cut out until she concluded with, "'Give the big guy my regards. Crombie.'"

Nord's eyes narrowed, violence pulsing through his veins. "Why did you go silent for that one bit?"

Lina's expression tightened with confusion. "What?"

"The postscript. Your mouth was moving, but you weren't speaking out loud."

"Yes, I was," she insisted, her eyes wide.

She was telling him the truth, or at least believed she was. He gently placed a hand on her arm. "No, Lina . . . you weren't."

"Motherfucker," she swore, her expression fierce for all of a heartbeat before her shoulders sagged and she let out a heavy sigh. "He, uh, might have mentioned that I can't share information about him which he considers sensitive."

Nord blinked. "Come again."

"It's part of this stupid bloodsworn thing. I can't hurt him. Can't share his secrets. Can't lie to him." She groaned, looking thoroughly put out. "He did it on purpose, didn't he? That ass. He knew I'd try to tell you and just loves that I can't."

Ass, indeed. It was the same sort of mental game Nord would play had their roles been reversed. Usually he'd be able to acknowledge a hand well played, even by one he considered an adversary. But this was Crombie they were talking about, and everything about the smug bastard grated. He wasn't about to give him credit for anything but being a piece of shit.

Nord grabbed the card and crumpled it in his hand, tossing it in the direction of the wire wastebasket in the corner without looking to see where it landed. Then he tugged on his power and set the damn thing on fire.

Lina's eyes went wide as she took in the controlled blaze. "You're not going to burn down the room, are you?"

A minute ago, the question would have made him laugh. Now, overcome with wave after wave of relentless fury, she wasn't entirely out of line for asking.

Lina's room felt polluted, as if Crombie had tainted what should have been their sanctuary with his mere presence—which, given the pointed taunts, had been the bastard's intent. The need to cleanse the room and rid it of Crombie's filth tore at Nord, overriding all other coherent thought. Though overkill, fire was an excellent purifier. Had he access to a priest, Nord may even go so far as to insist on an exorcism. But since both of those were out, and something as basic as sage was nowhere near powerful enough to get the job done, there was only one other thing Nord could think of to chase away the bastard's lingering presence and reestablish their ownership of the space.

Grasping Lina about the waist, he tossed her up and caught her over his shoulder.

"Nord . . ." she gasped, though she didn't sound like she was complaining. "What happened to the shower?"

"Change of plans."

Lina's palms pressed against his back as she arched her neck up, likely to see where he was taking her. Her next question not only proved him right, it proved just how well she knew him. His fury retreated at the reminder.

"What are you planning to do? Fuck Crombie out of my room in some kind of alpha male display of territorial marking?"

"You have a problem with that?"

"Well, no. But if you're trying to make a point of taking back what's ours, so to speak, don't you think we should do it on the dresser instead of the bed since that's like ground zero?"

Nord paused, considered, and then turned. "Good idea. We'll start there."

"Start?" Lina squeaked, her breath leaving her once more as Nord planted her on the dresser and spread her thighs in one seamless move.

"It may take a while to get the job done. I intend to be very, very thorough."

Lina's cheeks were flushed, her eyes already bright with arousal. "If I would have known searching for a nightie would have got me what I wanted in the first place, I would have done it sooner."

"Guess that'll teach you to listen to me," Nord said, his hands sliding down her thighs to hook under her knees and pull her to the edge.

Lina wove her arms around his neck, bringing her lips to within a fraction of an inch from his own. "Don't hold your breath, berserker."

Nord brushed his thumb over the center of the damp lace separating him from her core. She shivered and rocked into the caress, seeking more with a breathless whimper. Desire shot through his veins, amplified by the echo and evidence of hers.

Huffing out a purely masculine chuckle, Nord whispered, "You either."

She made a soft sound, but he captured whatever she was about to say as he claimed her lips in a soul-searing kiss. One hand worked its way into the tangle of her hair while the other made short work of ripping a hole through the lace barrier.

"Hope that wasn't one of the 'good' pairs," he breathed.

"Who the fuck cares?" Lina groaned, grounding her hips against the blunt tips of his fingers circling her entrance. "I'll make more. Just get inside me already."

"Fingers, tongue, or cock, Kærasta?"

His thumb teased her clit while he continued to make lazy circles with his middle finger. Lina's eyelids fluttered closed, and her breaths came out in shallow pants as he worked her.

"Answer the question, Lina."

"There was a question?"

"Fingers," Nord said, as the tips of two of his fingers just barely crested her opening. "Tongue"—he ran his tongue along the edge of her ear—"or cock?" He took her hand and pressed it against the denim straining to contain him. She grasped his length, working him instinctively. He bit down on her earlobe when she still didn't reply. "What's it going to be?"

"C-cock," she moaned brokenly as he slid his fingers deeper.

"That's what you always pick," Nord said, trailing his lips down the side of her neck as he disentangled his fingers from her hair to tug his zipper down.

"Then why do you insist on asking me if you already know my answer?" she asked, leaning forward to chase his lips with hers.

He couldn't help but grin as he admitted, "Because I love to hear you say it. You blush every time."

"I do not."

"You do, Kærasta," he insisted, taking her hair in his fist and giving it a quick tug, "and it's fucking gorgeous."

She melted into him, one of her hands pulling him free while the other braced behind her. As she guided him to her center, he grasped her ankles and eased her legs up until her heels rested on top of the dresser, leaving her wide open to him. He pressed a hand to the center of her chest, pushing lightly until her upper body rested against the mirror.

"Comfortable?" he asked, running his swollen tip through her slick folds.

She moaned and lifted her hips in a silent plea for more.

"I'll take that as a yes." He pressed in, the hand at her chest dropping to grip her hip. Her name left him in a whispered groan, "Lina."

Her head fell back with a soft thud as it hit the mirror. "God, Nord. Is it just me, or does this feel even better than usual?"

It wasn't just her. His senses were heightened, each soft pant of her breath or brush of her skin enhancing his need for her. They'd barely begun, and he already felt like he was about to come apart.

"Do you think it's a side effect of the flowers from—"

Nord stopped her with a savage kiss. "You better not be about to say another man's name while I'm inside you," he warned her.

Her laugh turned into a moan as he moved deeper. "You feel amazing," she said in a throaty whisper, her nails dragging across his back.

He wanted to disagree. To tell her it was her, not him, who felt like the answer to every fucking prayer he'd ever had as she clenched around him, her body urging him deeper. But he took his time, resisting the urge to drive home so that he could draw out the moment and savor the feel of her wrapped so perfectly around him.

She looked like a damned goddess with her lips parted and her sparkling eyes hooded. Her hair was wild, her skin flushed and covered only by a thin band of pink lace around her hips. His eyes dipped, watching the place where they were joined as he slid in that final inch.

The wood groaned as Lina's hands clenched around the dresser's ledge. "Fuck, yes."

He slowly withdrew, eliciting another of her wanton moans he felt straight in his groin. "I love how greedy you are. How you grip me like you're never going to let me go," he rasped, his balls tightening in anticipation as he drove back in to the hilt in a single hard thrust.

"Yes! Just like that."

He grinned at her breathless demand, more than willing to obey. So he withdrew and thrust again. And then again. And again. Lina's answering moans almost—but not quite—eclipsed the bang of wood against the wall as each powerful drive of his hips sent the back of the dresser and its mirror crashing into drywall. Not wanting to temper his thrusts, Nord used his power to hold the piece of furniture in place as he continued to buck into her wet heat.

Lina's head thrashed side to side, her pulse fluttering wildly at the base of her throat. "I'm so"—her breath hitched—"close."

"That's it, Kærasta. Come for me."

Lina reached between her legs, her fingers briefly curling around the root of him before moving up to rub furious circles over her swollen nub. She was crying out his name within seconds.

Nord's hands were already at her hips, pulling her forward and off the dresser and then spinning her around so that her chest was pressed against the edge. Her thighs were still quaking with aftershocks from her first orgasm as he drove back in.

Lina slammed her hand against the mirror as he pulled back and plunged in once more, picking up momentum with each consecutive thrust.

"Ohmygodyesjustlikethat."

Her words were hardly coherent as they came out in one breathless rush, but since he could feel her desire spiraling up once more, he didn't require any help translating.

Wanting to see her face as she fell apart, Nord glanced back up to the mirror. Her eyes were clenched shut, her mouth open on a soundless cry. He'd taken her more times than he could count at this point, but Nord knew this moment would be one he returned to often. For him, there was nothing sexier than the sight of Lina losing herself to her pleasure. Pleasure he, and he alone, gave her. His breath grew ragged and his control slipped, his fingers digging into her hips as his thrusts grew wild.

The dresser trembled from the onslaught, shuddering in time as he fucked her. Not about to stop, not even for a shattered mirror, Nord sent another wave of magic to reinforce the dresser and hold it in place as he continued his relentless thrusting.

Lina's inner muscles started to convulse, signaling the approach of a second climax.

"Again, Lina. Come for me."

"But—"

"Now."

He reached around and pressed his fingers over her clit, barely needing to do more than touch the slick bud before she was crying out again and slamming her hand against the mirror, her palm sliding across it with a loud screech.

This time, Nord came with her, leaning forward and biting her shoulder to drown out his own cries of pleasure.

Her legs continued to shake as he slowly pulled out. Without a word, he bent and lifted her, angling them both toward the bed. As he took his first few steps, he dropped the hold on his power. There was a groan and then a loud crash as one of the dresser legs snapped and the entire thing tipped forward.

Lina gaped in shock while Nord's shoulders shook with suppressed laughter.

"I mean . . . that's one way to redecorate . . ." she murmured.

"Don't worry. We'll go on a rescue mission to salvage your good stuff later. After round four or five."

She snickered. "Four or five? Are we talking orgasms or broken pieces of furniture?"

He stopped by the side of the bed and tipped his chin so he could meet her gaze. "You should know by now that if we were counting in orgasms, the number would be much higher."

"Well, yeah. But you seem to be a man on a mission. Don't get me wrong, I'm not complaining—at all—I'm just not sure what point you're trying to make."

"Am I? You're the one who demanded orgasms, Lina. I'm just giving you what you asked for."

"Sweet Mother of God, I love it when you talk like that."

"I've noticed." He dropped her on the bed with a laugh, taking a second to remove the remains of her underwear before pointing to the headboard. "On your knees, face the headboard, legs spread."

She shot him a curious glance over her shoulder as she made to obey his orders.

Nord allowed himself to enjoy the beautiful picture she painted as she crawled up to the top of her bed on her hands and knees, ass in the air, skin rosy from pleasure. As she took the position he'd requested, she looked over her shoulder again, her hands resting lightly on the top of the wooden frame, her hair falling down her back in a golden waterfall. "Like this?"

"Just like that."

He peeled off his clothes and joined her on the bed. It was clear she expected him to take her from behind again because she arched her hips but looked down in surprise when he rolled onto his back and scooted his way up so his shoulders were between her legs.

"What are you doing down there?" she asked, peering down at him.

Nord grinned, running his hands up the sides of her legs and resting them at her hips. "We've taken care of getting you off with my cock and fingers. Time for the tongue."

Applying some pressure, he pulled her down until she was close enough that he could press a kiss directly on that sensitive bundle of nerves. Lina's eyes widened for a second before she let out a loud moan. He took that as an invitation to continue and applied more pressure to her hips as his tongue began its sensual tease. She moved with him willingly, her hips already bucking as she proceeded to ride his face. When he bit down and growled, the entire headboard shook from the force with which she grasped it. Nord laughed and did it again.

Then she rose slightly, forcing him to pause.

"Too much?" he asked.

She licked her lips and shook her head. "N-no, I was just . . . just wondering if you planned on leaving any of my furniture standing?"

Nord knew his answering grin was wicked. "Not if we do it right." He nuzzled her inner thigh, tickling her with his beard. "Come on, Kærasta. Time for round two."

CHAPTER 9
QUINN

Phone calls shouldn't feel more dangerous than burglary, and yet, breaking into Crombie's wannabe castle didn't come close to what Quinn felt staring at the screen of her cell. But that was because she knew what was at risk if the Drakes or one of their ass lickers found out about this call. She held no illusions about who the true villain in her life was, and it sure as fuck wasn't a pretentious faerie currently slumming it in the mortal realm.

Just pushing the contact button for her mother's burner phone had Quinn's hands slick with sweat and frenetic energy thrumming through her already overloaded system. Not that she'd ever admit it to anyone if they picked up on it. Appearance was everything when you played the kind of games she did.

"Mon coeur, I had a feeling you'd call me tonight."

Her heart rate returned to something resembling normal at the sound of her mother's greeting. Though the French was unexpected. She'd stopped using it around the time her husband died, stating it was too painful a reminder of what she'd lost. The same feeling warning about the call must have also hinted that her daughter needed comfort tonight.

That, combined with the fact she'd answered almost immediately, went a long way to steeling Quinn's frazzled nerves. Cora Satori had been playing the game longer than Quinn had been alive. If there was a chance taking this phone call would have caused the wrong sort of ripples, she wouldn't have answered. Then again, her gift couldn't be used at will, and while it provided her with powerful insights, she was no prophet . . . even if it felt like it at times.

"Mama," Quinn whispered down the line, giving in to an unexpected wave of vulnerability. So much was revealed by the lone endearment. Things she wouldn't dare say on a phone and couldn't admit regardless. Things like 'I'm scared' and 'What I'm about to ask you might get us all killed.'

Her mother heard—and understood—every unspoken word. "Oh, mon petit chaton."

Quinn's eyes fell closed at the use of her childhood pet name. It had been more than two decades since she'd heard her mother call her kitten.

The Satori women were not prone to self-indulgent fits of sentimentality or public displays of weakness. Not that love was a weakness. One only had to look at Lina and Nord's track record to prove just how inaccurate that statement was. But in a world where relationships were systematically exploited and men often prevailed due to brute strength, Quinn and her mother survived by stripping themselves of all softness. Well, that and being more clever than anyone else in the room.

What they lacked in brawn, they made up for with their shrewd and calculated assessments. The only way to win a rigged game was to make moves no one anticipated until it was too late. The Drakes might have chosen the game and set the rules, but the Satori were the ones who manipulated the pieces on the board.

As her father often reminded her in the too few years they'd had together, sphinxes were part lion. And no one fucked with a lion unless they had a death wish.

It was a mantra she'd built her life and reputation on. Now no one fucked with *her*.

Quinn exhaled and opened her eyes. "We need you to call an emergency meeting of the Council."

"Oh?"

"We're done hiding, Mama. Mikel's reign of terror needs to end. He may manipulate the strings of the other members like a dirty little puppet master, but the Mobius Council was created to protect the last of the Animagi, not oppress them. Our people deserve better than a madman who blackmailed his way into power. He's undermined everything we used to stand for."

There was a long pause. Quinn could only imagine what was going through her mother's mind. Likely the same sense of nauseated horror Quinn had felt when Lina made her declaration.

Mikel was not just any villain; he was *the* villain. Between the power he possessed, the power he craved, and the number of people who owed him money they could never repay or had secrets that would destroy them if they got out, he was not someone you crossed lightly. If ever.

They'd either defeat him or die. Those were the only options. And in the last century since he'd risen to power, there'd been few opponents and a lot of death, so the odds weren't looking good.

Finally, her mother spoke. "Is she ready? Regicide is not an easy task."

Quinn scoffed. "Mikel is no king."

"He may as well be, mon coeur. All he lacks is the title."

"And a crown, and a throne—"

"True rulers only require loyal followers. Look at our Evalina. She's acquired quite the court."

"Right. But she's not a corrupt asshole either. Lina is actually worthy, but even if that wasn't the case, royal blood actually runs through her veins. Anyway, I'm not sure Mikel's followers qualify as loyal. They only sided with him because he blackmailed them."

"Self-preservation is a powerful motivator, and not one that's easily countered." Her mother sighed. "We always knew it would come to this, but there are no do-overs here. If we pull the trigger, we need to be sure we aren't going to miss. So I'll ask you again, is she ready?"

An icy chill crept down Quinn's spine. Was she? Lina said she was, but . . .

Quinn stopped the thought before it could list a dozen different doubts. The time for doubt had passed. Because of Crombie's interference, any wiggle room they'd had in the timeline was gone. It was literally now or never. Delays would only solidify Crombie's hold on her, and if that happened, she'd never be in any state to take down Mikel.

Time was one thing that they'd never had on their side. Quinn could practically feel the grains of sand slipping through the hourglass, and with them, their chance at success.

"She's as ready as she'll ever be," Quinn eventually answered.

"Then let us hope it will be enough."

"It has to be."

They both fell silent. Then her mother's soft sigh came through the speaker, and she said, "I'll call the meeting and send you the details as soon as they're confirmed."

"Thank you, Mama."

"Be careful, mon coeur."

Quinn's heart clenched, but she let out a humorless chuckle. "It's a little late for that, don't you think?"

Her mother's husky laugh filled the line. "In that case, remember who you are . . . and who you serve."

Cora ended the call, leaving Quinn staring at the screen with a furrowed brow. As the words sunk in and their meaning became clear, her lips curled into a slow, dangerous smile.

She was Quinn fucking Satori, and while she'd pledged her allegiance to Lina long ago, there wasn't a single person on this earth she served.

And there never would be.

"Should I be worried?"

She startled at Finley's deep voice, taking care to lock down her expression before looking up at him so as not to give away just what it did to her when he pinned her with those hazel eyes of his. Something about the banked heat she found there made her want to bask in it like a lazy, contented cat.

"Worried?" she repeated, her voice carefully neutral. If ever there was someone she couldn't afford to let see past the surface, it was him.

Mikel may be her greatest enemy, but Finley posed an even larger threat. He was the only man she'd ever known that tempted her to break her number-one rule: one night only. But she'd learned a painful truth at a young age. Loved ones could be used against you, and when you had a gift like hers? It was pretty much a matter of when, not if it would happen. Quinn never wanted to be in a position where she was forced to do something unforgivable or watch someone she loved die. No, there was too much at stake for someone like her to risk falling in love. It may be a lonely road she'd chosen for herself, but she'd travel it gladly if it kept her out of a monster's pocket. Especially one as evil as Mikel.

"When you smile like that, I'm half convinced you just ordered a hit on someone."

Quinn's lips twitched. "In a way, I suppose I did."

Finley gave an exaggerated shudder, his eyes darting from side to side. "Should I sleep with one eye open?"

"In general? Probably. Because of my call?" She gave him her most seductive smile. "We both know I'd do the honors myself, Batman. And I wouldn't make a secret of my intentions."

Finley straightened, his playful expression turning unreadable as he shoved both of his hands in his pockets. "Glad to hear it. So what'd Cora say? Are we all set for tomorrow?"

"She said a lot of things," Quinn replied as she tucked her phone back in her pocket. "But as for the meeting, we are. She'll send us the details of where and when. I expect I'll have those within the hour."

He gave her a considering once-over, which she felt like the rough drag of his palm over her naked skin. It was all she could do to suppress a longing shiver. Given the way his eyes sharpened, she had a feeling he knew it too.

"Nothing left to do then but wait," he murmured finally.

Quinn held his stare, wondering whether it was her imagination or if there was an invitation hidden in his words.

A not-so-subtle crash gave her another jolt. Both their heads craned toward the sound, Finley already protectively angling his body in front of hers. Quinn would have been worried something terrible happened, but the rhythmic thumping echoing down the hall was easily recognizable.

At least one of us is getting laid regularly. Good for you, Lady B.

"So much for soundproofing," Finley muttered.

Quinn bit back a laugh. He sounded so put out, she couldn't help but badger him. "Jealous, Fin? Got a serious case of blue balls?"

"Unless you're offering to suck on them, I don't want to hear mention of my balls coming out of your mouth, Satori."

Quinn blinked, the mental image sending a pang of lust rolling through her. "Are you sure about that?" she purred. She knew she shouldn't goad him. Not when she was already struggling to keep him at arm's length. But it would have been easier to stop a freight train with a feather than keep the question from leaving her mouth. Her eyes dropped meaningfully to the bulge in his pants before lifting back up. "Seems like you enjoyed it."

Finley's eyes flashed, and Quinn's pulse leapt in response. He may be off-limits, but she loved watching the rigid grasp he had on his self-control falter. She desperately wanted to be the one who pushed him over the edge and forced him to give in to what he so clearly craved. Namely her.

Quinn's phone pinged, ruining the moment and saving them both from doing something they'd regret. A quick check confirmed what she already guessed. Her mother worked fast.

"Meeting will be held in the Council's chambers tomorrow at noon," she announced.

There was a beat of silence, and then Finley crooked his brow, his dimple flashing. "Are you going to be the one to tell them, or am I?"

"Not it," Quinn answered immediately.

"Coward," he teased.

She crossed her arms. "I'm not getting in the middle of two fucking berserkers."

"I think you mean two berserkers fucking," he drawled as the relentless thumping down the hall grew more frantic.

They laughed, his joke sending the last of the tension between them scattering.

"It can wait until morning," Quinn decided. "I think they've earned it."

CHAPTER 10
LINA

Lina knew the exact moment the effects of Crombie's magic flowers faded. Between the body aches, overstimulated senses, a head that suddenly weighed eight hundred pounds, and fatigue so strong she might as well have been attempting to trudge through day-old gravy, it was like she'd been hit with the flu and the worst hangover of her life all in one. And that was before she took into consideration the ruthless pounding in her temples, which felt as if the world's tiniest drummer had taken up residence in her mind and was currently performing a drum solo.

She staggered down the hallway into the dining room, where she slumped into her usual chair with a soft groan.

Nord was already seated at the table, looking far more put together than she did, the bastard.

He gave her a sympathetic once-over. "That bad, eh?"

Lina shot him a bleary-eyed glare. "As soon as this vow is fulfilled, I'm cutting Crombie's dick off with cuticle scissors and slapping him with it."

Nord winced, though his eyes twinkled with bloodthirsty appreciation. "If it makes you feel better, I can't remember the last time I woke up with a headache like this."

"You're feeling it too? But how? You weren't even there."

He shrugged. "I must have inhaled some of the pollen off of you. Obviously, its effects were far stronger on you than me, but it does explain why both of us remained calm last night, despite everything that happened."

Lina raised a brow. "You call what happened in that room calm?"

"I call that a good time," Nord replied with a cocksure grin.

Her lips lifted, her lady parts giving a happy flutter at the reminder. "Yeah," she agreed, resting her head on her arms. "It was definitely that."

Nord murmured sympathetically and reached over to rest his hand on top of her head. His thumb stroked lazily over her forehead, each soft sweep seeming to brush away some of the cobwebs in her mind as well as dull the ache.

"Don't stop," she pleaded, her eyes falling closed. "That feels amazing."

Lina forced her eyes back open at the sound of Finley's pained groan. "Please tell me you two aren't fornicating on my table. I would have thought you'd gotten enough of that last night," he said, stepping hesitantly into the kitchen. When he realized they were both fully clothed and clearly not humping like rabbits, he let out a relieved sigh. "Glad to see you two have some restraint after all."

"Fuck off, Fin," Nord softly growled.

Finley's eyes narrowed with concern. "Not feeling well, love?" he asked, taking in Lina's haggard appearance.

"Crombie's weeds pack a punch," she replied, feeling marginally better with each brush of Nord's fingers over her skin. "Thankfully, Nord's touch seems to help alleviate the worst of it."

Finley's eyes flashed silver. "Did you intend to heal her?"

"I'm not healing her," Nord said, his brows lowering in confusion. "I haven't accessed my magic at all."

"Yes, you are, mate. I can see traces of it leaving you."

Lina lifted her head at that, her and Nord sharing a look.

"Seems like this Transference of yours gave you some passive abilities."

"Passive abilities?" Lina asked.

"Things that happen without conscious effort. You were feeling unwell, so Nord instinctively began to heal you," Finley explained.

She sat fully upright, holding her hand up to Nord's face. "Let's see if it works when I do it to you."

Nord leaned forward so that her fingertips grazed his skin. He let out a relieved groan as she ran them across his brow. "Gods, that's nice."

Lina smiled as she linked her hand with his. "Well, that's a nice perk."

Nord nodded his agreement as he picked up the coffee cup sitting in front of him. "Want some?" he offered after taking a sip.

She wrinkled her nose. "No thanks. I'm just going to sit here clinging to you like a half-dead koala until I feel like myself again."

He gave her hand a little squeeze. "Sounds good to me."

The slam of the front door closing had them all on their feet. They relaxed as soon as Quinn called out her greeting.

"When did she get a key to the penthouse?" Nord asked.

"Last night. She refused to leave without one," Finley said as he splashed some milk into his tea.

"Your room will never be safe again," Lina said, sitting back down with a laugh.

"Don't I know it," Finley muttered darkly. "At least the garage is safe."

Quinn breezed in, looking stunning in a sleeveless black dress that hugged her body from her collar bone to just below her knees. It was far more conservative than what she usually wore, but no less stunning because of it.

Lina whistled. "I didn't realize breakfast had a dress code."

Quinn grinned, tossing her hair over her shoulder and executing a little turn. Lina caught a flash of red on the soles of her stilettos that perfectly matched the shade of scarlet painting her lips. "There isn't. This is for the meeting."

"Meeting?" Nord asked.

Quinn arched a brow and shot an accusing glance Finley's way. "You haven't told them yet?"

"I didn't get a chance," Finley protested.

"Told us what?" Lina asked, her gaze darting between them.

"My mom arranged the Council meeting. It starts in an hour."

"Shit, I guess I should go get ready," Lina said, bracing her hands on the table as she pushed to her feet. She blew out a breath. "Wish me luck."

"Getting dressed?" Finley joked. "I didn't realize it required special skill."

Quinn's eyes took an exaggerated trip down his tall frame. "And it shows."

Finley's playful smirk turned into a scowl, causing the rest of them to laugh.

"Want me to make you something to eat?" Nord asked.

Lina pressed her hands to her stomach. "No, I don't think I could keep anything down. Thanks, though."

His warm fingers curled around her wrist and tugged lightly, pulling her down so he could press a soft kiss to her lips. "Everything's going to be fine. I'll be with you the entire time."

She cupped a hand to his cheek, returning his tender kiss with one of her own. "I know."

"Tick tock, Cuska. You can make out with your man later. We've got places to be and dynasties to overthrow." To Finley, Quinn added, "You think they would have gotten enough of each other last night."

"That's what I said," Finley rumbled back, smirking at Lina over the rim of his mug.

Lina blushed, wondering just how much they'd overheard.

"Ignore them, Kærasta. They're just jealous." Nord's hand

wrapped around her hip, giving her an affectionate squeeze. "As they should be."

She grinned, giving him a little wink as she rushed out of the room. As soon as she was alone, the smile slipped from her lips and nerves took over.

The consequences of today's meeting were monumental. It would set the sorts of things in motion that could never be undone. Had she any other choice, Lina may not even set foot down this path, but here she was. Ready to claim her birthright.

With all of that hanging over her, the one question running through her mind was ridiculous by comparison.

What the hell am I supposed to wear?

Lina stood in front of her closet, her eyes running through her options and dismissing them just as quickly. This wasn't exactly a jeans and leather jacket sort of meeting. Today was about making a statement. A lasting one. If Lina was going to demand her rightful place on the Council, she needed to look every bit the confident, powerful, take-no-shit badass she was pretending to be.

No, she mentally corrected. *That you* are.

Releasing a heavy breath, Lina realized the kind of thing she was searching for, she didn't currently own. She'd have to improvise.

Focusing on the message she wanted to send, Lina crafted an outfit in her mind that practically screamed it. Nord was the one who'd told her clothes could be weapons. She didn't want there to be any doubt that's exactly what she was when she set foot in front of the Council.

As the tingle of her magic faded, Lina moved to stand in front of the full-length mirror. Gone was the sleep-rumpled woman from earlier. In her place stood a woman ready to claim her empire.

She'd chosen to wear her family's color, emerald green, in the form of a silk camisole, tucked into a pair of wide-legged, high-waisted black pants. The tips of her stilettos peeked out from the bottom, the snakeskin a perfect accent to her top. Her hair was stick straight and pulled up in a high ponytail that left her arms and back bare. She wanted to ensure that her tattoos were visible. Especially the crest on her upper arm.

Lina lifted her hand up to touch the locket hanging just above her heart. The rest of what she wore was for the Council. This was for her. She didn't need to open it to see the pictures nestled inside. Just knowing they were there, together at last, made Lina feel like she possessed her mother's unyielding strength and her uncle's brilliant wit.

She turned this way and that, studying herself in the mirror with a critical eye. Something was missing. As an idea took shape, her lips curled up in a secretive smile. Wanting to ensure she got the details absolutely perfect, Lina picked up the cell phone Nord left by the bed —because hers was still MIA. A quick search provided the image she needed; her magic took care of the rest.

Lifting her hair off her neck, Lina eyed the tattoo resting at its base with a satisfied smile. "Perfect."

She decided to twist her ponytail up into a sleek bun to ensure that no one would miss her final touch, even if they didn't understand its meaning. While the Helm of Awe was fairly recognizable, Lina doubted anyone on the Council would realize that it was more to her than a Norse symbol of protection. It was a nod to the newest part of her nature and the man she'd given her heart to.

A soft knock at the door caused Lina's stomach to flutter with nervous bats. Butterflies were too delicate a creature for the anxious twisting taking place there.

"Lina?" Nord called, cracking the door open.

"Come in," she answered, keeping her back to him.

"Quinn's getting antsy—"

She knew the second he spotted the symbol because his words cut off, and her name left his lips in a reverent whisper.

"Lina."

As he crossed the room to stand behind her and get a closer look, she allowed herself a moment to appreciate the way he filled out his dress pants. As far as finding something that radiated with 'don't fuck with me or I'll break every bone in your body' vibes, Nord nailed it. Then again, that would be true in anything he wore. For his introduction to the Council, he chose to wear all black, the sleeves of his button-up already rolled up to reveal his inked forearms. In addition to his rings, he also added black leather bands on each wrist and one silver cuff with two hissing serpent heads.

"What's this?" he asked in that same hushed tone, his fingers stroking the southernmost line that flowed down the top of her spine.

"Don't you recognize it?"

"You know I do, Kærasta," he replied, tracing the main circle and sending goosebumps skittering down her body. "I'm just surprised to see you wearing one of the marks of my people."

"It seemed appropriate. My tattoos all represent a piece of my heritage. Today might be about claiming my place among the Animagi, but because of you, I'm also a berserker. And while Odin may not count me as one of his, if this thing really does offer any protection against enemies, I figured it couldn't hurt."

They exchanged smiles that were just on this side of dangerous. "That you are, Kærasta. And I pity the man or woman who forgets it." He leaned forward and pressed a kiss to the center of the tattoo, curving one arm around her lower stomach and holding the other out to reveal the same mark on the inside of his left forearm. "And now we match."

Lina grinned. "Where do you think I got the idea?"

She ran her fingers down his arm and then slid them over the back of his hand until her fingertips brushed the cool metal of his rings. She felt a soft pang as she looked at her own naked fingers. A tattoo she had no qualms using magic for, but she'd refused to recreate something as sacred as her first ring.

Lina's blood simmered as her berserker stirred. Crombie had robbed her of that moment. If not for him, she'd be wearing it right now. Thinking of the sneaky fae reminded her of his note and the fact that he was forcing her to withhold information from Nord and their friends. It was a dickhead move, making her keep secrets. Especially nonsensical ones. The part of his note he'd prohibited her from sharing wasn't even relevant, unless knowing about his musical preferences was the equivalent of a state secret.

Her teeth clenched as his parting shot ran through her mind. *'Nice shirt, by the way. I've always been partial to the Apocalyptic Unicorns, so you'll have to forgive my need to relieve you of it. How did you come by one autographed by the original band members, anyway? Oh, and if you want it back, you'll have to bring me something else from the vault in exchange.'*

She wondered if Crombie would have been interested in the band tee if he'd known she'd borrowed it from Finley. *Does it count as borrowing if I forgot to ask permission first?* Lina bit her lip, unsure if it was a blessing in disguise that she had no way of telling her house-mate his shirt was missing.

Fucking Crombie. It was starting to feel like the prick existed solely to make her life hell.

Nord must have felt her growing fury, either that or he could read the longing on her face as she stared at their linked hands, because he wrapped his other arm around her so that he was hugging her.

"We'll forge your ring, Lina. Your first and each one you earn thereafter, my bloodthirsty berserker. I promise."

She tipped her head up and kissed him just beneath his jaw. "I'm going to hold you to that."

"See that you do. Now, are you ready to go claim your birthright?"

Her eyes met his in the mirror once more, her expression every bit as savage as his. "I am."

CHAPTER 11
LINA

"All right, so where are we going?" Finley asked, rubbing his hands together.

"Downtown," Quinn answered. "As close to the corner of Broadway and Beaker Street that you can manage."

"Beaker? Really?" Finley asked. "Isn't that part of town a little . . ."

"Unsavory?" Lina offered.

"That's a nice way of putting it," Finley said. "I know Mobius is hardly a bunch of upstanding citizens, but I'd have bet money they'd pick somewhere a little less seedy for their hideout."

Lina smirked. "I'm surprised you'd take anything at face value these days, Fin."

He looked confused for a second before his expression cleared. "It's a glamour?"

Quinn wiggled her fingers in a sarcastic imitation of jazz hands. "Surprise." She dropped her arms and rolled her eyes. "We're not a bunch of amateurs, Fin. Who do you think you're dealing with, the Brotherhood? The Council can keep a secret better than just about anyone."

Finley gave her an annoyed huff. "What crawled up your ass?"

"Not you," Quinn said brightly, leaning forward and pinching his cheek, "much to your disappointment, I'm sure."

"Mine?" Finley asked, slowly but firmly pushing her hand away as he leaned down so that their eyes were level, "Or yours?"

Lina was standing close enough to see Quinn's pupils dilate before her friend blinked and let out a delicate cough. "Don't flatter yourself."

Nord chuckled under his breath, and Lina looked up at him to roll her eyes in a conspiratorial fashion. He gave her hand a squeeze and shook his head.

Finley stared at Quinn for another beat, likely to ensure whatever mental message he was telegraphing with his eyes actually resonated with her stubborn bestie, before he straightened and asked Lina, "If the hideout is concealed by magical means, why haven't we detected it?"

Lina shrugged. "Probably because the glamour isn't on the street level? The area itself is exactly what it appears to be, and that's reason enough not to go digging. What's below ground, however . . ."

He looked impressed. "I can't believe they've been right there this whole time. The lads are going to go apeshit when they find out. Guardians have been trying to locate the Mobius base of operations for decades."

"Your Brotherhood isn't the only secret society that excels at spreading misinformation and staying out of sight, Fin," Lina said.

"Apparently," he murmured. Turning to Nord, he asked, "Did you know about this?"

"Why would I know about it?"

"Because you're one of them now?"

"Pretty sure it doesn't work that way, brother. It's not like Animagi are a hive mind. I didn't acquire all their secrets just because I became one of them."

"That would be cool, though," Lina said. "Not to mention useful."

Finley shrugged. "I had to ask. With all the new tricks you can do these days, it wouldn't be the strangest thing to discover your mind contains a veritable treasure trove of ancient knowledge."

"I mean, it does," Nord said with a half-smile. "Just nothing it hadn't already possessed."

"I walked right into that one," Finley said with a soft laugh. "Anyway, I know the area fairly well. I can portal us a couple blocks away."

"What do you mean 'us'?" Quinn asked.

"What part of the pronoun are you having trouble with?" Finley asked, his eyes turning silver as he drew on his power and created the portal.

"Easy, tiger," Quinn said, holding up a hand to his chest. "You're not coming."

"What?" Finley asked, looking genuinely confused. "Of course I'm coming with you. I'm not letting you guys go in there without backup."

"You're the enemy," she reminded him. "If anyone from the Council sees you lurking about, the jig is up. We're supposed to be infiltrating, not raising red flags. And you, my dear Batman, are one big red flag."

The number of emotions that ran across Finley's face would have been comical any other time. But the last time their group split up, one of them wound up dead. Leaving someone behind a second time should have been out of the question. They were safest together. Unfortunately, circumstances were out of their control. This meeting was essential to their plan, and there was absolutely no way a member of the Brotherhood would be welcome inside the Council's chambers.

"If I'm not with you, how are you going to get back?" Finley asked, crossing his arms.

"I'll call you when we're ready," Nord answered, as if it was obvious.

"I'm not some Uber driver for you to summon when you need a

lift," Finley said. His expression was set, a muscle fluttering in his jaw.

Lina was pretty sure this was as close to a pout as she'd ever see from him. Finley had been by their side since day one. Making him sit this one out after everything he'd risked helping them had to be a massive blow to his ego. Even if it was the only option.

"I don't like it any more than you do," Lina said, resting a hand on his arm. "But Quinn's right. You have to stay here. It would be foolish to have you wandering around Drake territory without backup. The penthouse is basically a fortress. It's the safest place for you if we're not together." Lina forced herself to breathe around the sudden ache in her chest as she added, "This meeting is going to be hard enough; I can't be worried about something happening to you while we're inside. I can't lose anyone else, Fin."

His expression softened at the obvious pain in her voice. Finley surprised her by reaching out, hooking his arm around her neck, and tugging her forward until she collided into his chest. Then he pressed a kiss to her temple and rested his chin on top of her head.

"I'd be offended you doubted my ability to take care of myself if I didn't understand exactly how you felt." He blew out a breath. "I'll stay here, but don't expect me to be happy about it."

"What if I promise to help you add to your collection? Will that help alleviate some of the sting?"

Finley let her go so that he could peer into her face. "Are you offering me a bribe or a reward?"

Lina shrugged. "Call it whatever you want."

He gave her a considering look. "Are you going to actually locate and purchase my new acquisition, or are you going to cheat and conjure it?"

She raised a brow. "Does it matter so long as it's shiny, runs, and is all yours?"

He narrowed his eyes, waiting a beat before he answered. "I want it on record that I had already agreed to be reasonable prior to your offer." Then one side of his mouth curved up, causing a dimple to flash. "But, since you did offer, I'll have a list of acceptable choices waiting for you when you return."

"Make sure to include pictures for me," Lina said with a little chuckle.

He held up a finger. "And . . ."

"And? Are you getting greedy now, Fin? What happened to being reasonable?"

"Annnnnd," he repeated, "if you do cheat and conjure my prize, I expect two"—he held up two fingers and wiggled them—"not one new beauty in the garage by the end of the day. I'll clear out the stalls while you're gone."

Lina pretended to consider his counteroffer, crossing her arms and giving him a very Quinn-like stare. Then she ruined the effect by grinning and holding out her hand. "Deal."

Finley was quick to place his hand in hers. "Deal."

Nord shook his head, a smile teasing his lips and his words knowing, "You do realize what you've just done, right? Not only are you an enabler, you just created a monster. Fin's not going to agree to do anything without you 'adding to his collection' from now on."

She frowned, wondering just how many ridiculously expensive cars one man needed. Try as she might, she just didn't see the appeal. It wasn't like he drove them. Mostly, they just sat there collecting dust.

Her expression cleared as she decided it didn't matter. In the past few months, Finley had become like a brother to her. And for someone who could appreciate the distinction between family you were born into and family you chose, there was little, if anything, she wouldn't do for him. So, if it made him happy and kept him out of harm's way, Lina would keep Fin in new vehicles until he was drowning in them. It was a small price to pay for someone who'd given her so much without ever expecting anything in return.

"Guys, we need to get going," Quinn called. "The meeting's going to start soon."

The mood sobered instantly.

"Right," Finley said, returning his attention to the matter at hand. A portal shimmered into being beside him less than a heartbeat later. "Call me the instant you guys are done, all right? You're not the only one who's going to be worrying."

"We will," Lina promised, giving him a quick peck on the cheek.

Even the normally flippant Quinn paused to rest her hand on Finley's arm. She opened her mouth, then closed it, sighed, and said, "If you go and get yourself killed while we're gone, I'm going to find a way to bring you back and kill you myself. Understand?"

Finley grinned. "Is that your way of telling me you care about me, Satori?"

She made a show out of scoffing, but genuine worry shone in her eyes. "More like I don't want anyone else to steal my thunder. If anyone's going to kill you, it should be me. I think I've more than earned the right after putting up with your bullshit for this long."

"Possessive." He dropped his voice. "I like it."

Quinn laughed and rolled her eyes. "Of course that's your takeaway." She made a move toward the portal.

"Hey, Satori?"

She glanced back at him.

"You either, all right? You made me a promise. I expect you to keep it."

"I did?" she asked, cocking her head to the side.

Finley grinned, his eyes heated. "When this is over, you and I are playing Show and Tell."

"Oh. Right." Then to Lina, she said, "When we get back, remind me to make him forget about that, would you?" Without waiting for a response, she stepped through the portal.

Finley held up a warning finger. "Don't you dare."

Lina lifted both her hands in a 'you don't have to worry about me' gesture. "See you when we're done, Fin."

He gave her a tight nod.

She turned, ready to follow Quinn, when Finley's low voice caused her to slow her steps.

"If anything happens to her—"

"I won't let it," Nord replied, his voice leaving no room for doubt.

Finley blew out a breath. "I know. Christ . . . just make sure she comes back to me in one piece, okay?"

Lina bit back a wistful smile, the proof of Finley's feelings for Quinn lighting her up like a Christmas tree. If ever two people needed to get their heads out of their asses and just tell each other how they felt . . . She knew better than most how the universe had a way of ensuring things happened when they were supposed to. Though, in this case, if the universe didn't stop taking its sweet time, she might have to intervene and get the ball rolling. One way or the other, *Quinley* would have their day.

With a full heart and renewed motivation, Lina took the single step that led her from the safety of the penthouse and deposited her straight in the heart of what should have been her empire.

Smoothing the front of her shirt, Lina eyed the crumbling buildings and garbage-strewn streets with the practiced eye of someone intimately familiar with their secrets. A little shiver raced down her back as she noticed the darkened alley to her left. It may not be the actual one where Mataius ran her down, but it could have been.

Crinkling her nose, she turned to Quinn as Nord stepped through the portal. "Is it just me, or is this place an even bigger shithole than it used to be?"

Quinn cast her eyes around. "Seems like the same 'ol shit heap it's always been to me. Maybe it just seems that way to you because you've been gone?"

"Maybe," Lina agreed, silently deciding that her first order of business once they cleaned house and rid the Council of the Drakes' filth would be to bring the rest of the Animagi back into the light. Starting with the headquarters. No legitimate organization would willingly choose to be tied to a place like this.

The Animagi deserved better. And after what they'd suffered at the hands of Mikel, they'd more than earned a fresh start.

Without another word, the three of them took off down the street,

Quinn in the lead, Nord hanging a little back like he was a one-man security detail. Quinn moved fast, the uneven pavement no match for her even wearing six-inch heels. She reached the chain-link fence that marked the hidden entrance a good half-minute before Lina and Nord.

When they caught up, she peeled back a piece of fence for them to duck through. She and Lina had no problem squeezing in. Nord struggled a bit and ended up having to rip off more of the fencing to make the hole wide enough for his bulk.

Once they were all on the other side and the fence back in place, Quinn silently led them to the end of the walkway between two abandoned buildings. At one time, the skyscrapers had been bustling, but now the steel and glass edifices were little more than casualties of an era long-forgotten.

"Where now?" Nord asked in a hushed voice, eyeing the dead end with a raised brow.

"Now we go down," Quinn said, pointing to the circular piece of metal by her feet.

"The sewers?" he asked, his surprise evident.

Quinn laughed. "Don't look so worried, big guy. I didn't think a berserker would care about getting a little dirty. Don't you like, bathe in the blood of your enemies and all that?"

He rolled his eyes.

"It's not a real sewer," Lina whispered.

"I gathered that."

"Hey," Quinn protested, "where's the fun in giving away the surprise?"

"Quinn," Lina said, with a firm shake of her head. "Stop. He's one of us. We're not doing the whole hazing thing with him. Besides, we don't have time to waste, even if we were. Which we are not," she emphasized a second time for good measure.

"You're no fun anymore," she huffed.

"I disagree," Nord said, making them both laugh.

"Well, of course you think so," Quinn snickered. "Would you

mind doing the honors? While the sewer may not be legit, the manhole cover is."

Nord lifted it without issue, leaning the heavy slab of metal against the side of one of the buildings.

"Thanks, handsome," Quinn said, blowing him a kiss as she started to descend the ladder into the darkness below.

Lina went next, suppressing a shudder as she climbed down. She'd always hated having to use the visitor's entrance. As an Animagi, she was immune to the glamour's sensory elements, a fact for which she and her nose were immensely grateful. But there was still something about lowering herself in the pitch-black space that made her think of all the monstrous things that could be waiting for her below. Odd, considering the people she was about to face were some of the worst monsters of all.

The climb was deceptively short, the darkness playing tricks with her depth perception. After only about ten rungs, Lina's heels skimmed smooth concrete. She moved to the left, knowing that once she passed the final, invisible barrier, she'd be surrounded by soft, welcoming light.

Quinn was already standing near a set of smoky gray glass doors, phone in her hand, fingers flying over the screen as she typed out a quick message.

"Cora?" Lina guessed.

Quinn gave a sharp nod. "Letting her know we're here. Just waiting for her all clear before we head inside."

Nord joined them, his eyes taking everything in as Quinn finished speaking. Feeling his ripple of surprise, Lina glanced around the waiting room, with its shiny black tiled floor, white leather sofas, dove-gray walls, and crown molding.

"Not what you expected?" she asked.

"At the bottom of a manhole? Can't say it is."

Lina smirked and slipped her hand into his. "Get used to the dog and pony show, Viking. You ain't seen nothing yet."

"Well, now I'm expecting big things," he said, giving her hand a squeeze.

"Such as?"

"A fire-breathing dragon, at the very least. Maybe a herd of unicorns?"

She laughed. "What do you think this is, a zoo? Also, be careful what you wish for. We're dealing with the Drakes, remember?"

"And unicorns are a bunch of sparkly assholes," Quinn added. "Have you ever met one? Total horndogs. If it's breathing, they'll hump it."

Nord let out a bark of shocked laughter.

"Don't believe me?" she asked with an arched brow. "Guess what you're getting for your birthday."

Lina had to bite the inside of her cheek to keep from laughing. "She's just bitter because a stallion got a little over-friendly when we were younger. So she's decided to take it out on the entire species in retaliation. Total smear campaign."

"So do we like unicorns or not?" Nord asked, his eyes glittering with amusement as he looked between them.

"We do," Lina affirmed. At the same time, Quinn snapped, "We absolutely do not."

"Gotcha," Nord murmured, silently laughing at them.

Quinn's phone gave a little buzz, and she scanned the screen. Then she slid it into her clutch and snapped it closed. "Show time, love birds. You ready?"

Nord and Lina exchanged a quick glance before nodding. With another squeeze, he let go of her hand and moved so that he could hold open one of the heavy doors for her and Quinn. As they crossed the threshold, they stepped into a completely deserted reception area. For larger meetings, Animagi would gather here to enjoy refreshments and mingling before stepping into the formal chambers, which were located at the other end of a long hall to their right.

Their footsteps echoed as Quinn wordlessly led them to another set of doors. These ones matte black and arched, with an ornate M carved across the center. Adrenaline surged with each step they took. Both hers and Nord's. There was no way to know what to expect once they set foot inside the meeting, and as a result, their berserkers were preparing for the worst.

As much as she loved having a secret weapon—two of them, actually—Lina knew she couldn't afford to lose control today. No matter what Mikel and his sycophants threw at her, she had to play this perfectly. She couldn't give the Council any reason to doubt her, which meant there could be absolutely no berserker rages. For one wistful second, Lina wished she had access to more of Crombie's delicate flowers. At least then she could be sure there'd be no slipups.

You've never been one for training wheels. You're a trial-by-fire girl, remember? What better test of control could you hope for?

The pep talk did little to soothe her, so instead, Lina took a deep breath and focused on setting one foot in front of the other. When that didn't work, she stared at the back of Quinn's head and tried to draw strength from the man who trailed behind her. It helped. Sort of.

All too soon, the walk was over, and Quinn rested her hands on the ornate silver handles. She tossed a final, bracing look at them over her shoulder and then flung the doors wide open.

The shock of the room's occupants was palpable, their silence absolute. From her position in the hall, Lina couldn't see Quinn's face, but she knew her friend well enough to picture the smirk lifting her lips.

"What? No hello? I'm hurt, guys. Didn't you get the memo? This is a welcome-home party. Where are the streamers? The balloons? The half-naked go-go dancers?" Quinn let out a dramatic sigh. "Well, perhaps when you see what I've brought you, you'll be a little more enthusiastic about my return." Quinn tilted her chin back. "Lady B, why don't you come on out and meet some old friends of mine."

Lina shot Nord a look over her shoulder. He gave her a slow nod, letting her know he'd be right behind her the entire time. Then she squared her shoulders and sauntered into the room with her chin high and her best 'you don't want to fuck with me' expression.

The people within may not realize it, but the revolution had officially begun. Long live their rightful queen.

And may Mikel Drake burn in hell.

CHAPTER 12
NORD

Forcing himself to stay put while Lina walked into a room filled with potential threats had Nord's berserker straining to break free. He hated everything about this plan, necessary or not. The warrior in him didn't understand why he couldn't just walk in there, slit Mikel's throat, and be done with it.

Knowing the cretin was somewhere in the other room with Lina, still daring to draw breath, was offensive to Nord on the deepest of levels. If something happened, would he even be able to reach her in time from out here? The possibility of being too late sent his berserker howling with rage.

As the doors swung shut behind Lina, the need to surge forward and follow her coiled within him. Only his promise to her checked the movement. She wanted—needed—to do this her way. He couldn't interfere.

Not yet.

That didn't mean he couldn't bend the rules a little. No reason he couldn't take advantage of the Council's ignorance to his presence and see what he could learn about the people whose ranks he'd recently joined.

As a Guardian, he'd excelled at glamours. Specifically, at making people see only what he wanted them to see. Given the similarities between that skill and his new reality-shaping gifts, Nord didn't see a reason he wouldn't be able to do so now. The theory was simple enough: take what was real and change it into what he wanted it to be.

Was it the best idea to try something untested here, where he wouldn't know if it worked until it was too late? Probably not.

Was he going to do it anyway?

Abso-fucking-lutely.

He'd go insane stuck out here otherwise, with only the murmur of voices to clue him in as to what was happening inside.

Nord slid his foot in the way before the door could fully close, leaving himself a sliver of space to peek out of so that he could determine the ideal place to cast his illusion. He couldn't see much, but the room appeared to be circular, with a short, square space leading from the doors to the interior. Meaning the chamber as a whole was shaped a bit like a lightbulb, with the high walls lining the entrance blocking off everything to either side. Since he wanted the best vantage point he could manage, Nord would need to get at least to the other side of the entryway.

Calling on his power, Nord focused on creating a barrier that would allow him to peer out but would seem to be the empty entrance if someone looked in his direction. Essentially, he wanted to create a one-sided mirror. But without the mirror.

Feeling the magic leave him, Nord could only hope it worked. Giving the door a slight push with his shoulder, he eased his way inside and crept forward. When no one immediately took notice of him, he released a breath and moved the rest of the way, as assured as he could be that his presence was concealed.

Despite the bombshell Quinn had dropped on the Council members, the room was dead silent. Everyone was still too busy staring at the resurrected Cuska heir in complete shock. Neither Lina nor Quinn seemed to be in any hurry to fill the silence.

Instead, they stood in the center of what Nord could now see was a small amphitheater. The northern half of the room was reserved for the heads of Mobius and their two chosen representatives, while the southern section appeared to be public seating, which was currently empty. Nord was glad for that. It meant there were far fewer faces for him to memorize.

Like the waiting room, the meeting chamber was predominately black. Black velvet seats for the audience. Ornate ebony chairs with obsidian statues towering behind each of them to represent the family's animal counterpart. In fact, the only color featured in the room's furnishing came from the five vertical banners that spanned the southern wall. Each one mirrored the location of one of the chairs. Nord found it telling that the length of emerald silk with its hissing snake had been moved to the far right, while the ruby one with a roaring dragon hung in the center. All the other banners lined up with their family's position on the other side of the room.

When they'd first discovered Lina's connection to the infamous Council, he and Finley had poured over the Brotherhoods' files regarding its members. Granted, due to their clearance level, there wasn't much they had access to. But the few they could get their hands on contained some photos with names scrawled underneath. That, combined with the information Alistair imparted, certainly came in handy now. Nord had no trouble distinguishing who belonged to which house as he scanned the people perched in the throne-like seats.

Though, to be fair, even if that hadn't been the case, the ostentatious setup made it pretty obvious.

Dog and pony show is right.

Dismissing the people who remained standing for the time being, Nord studied each of the Council heads and their position in the semicircle. At the far left were the Thortons with their soaring thunderbird, meaning the woman seated beneath it must be their matriarch, Natalia. It was hard to pinpoint her age. She looked anywhere from her thirties to late forties, which meant, in actuality, she could have been somewhere in her first or second century. Her sable hair was at least waist length, with two small braids framing her face, and her chocolate eyes were blown wide.

Beside her on the right sat Kristoff Alinari, accompanied by a fierce griffin. Out of all of them, his features had the most in common with his family's animal. His black eyes were beady, his nose hooked and beak-like. His dark hair was slicked back, featuring a prominent widow's peak. And while his olive skin was unlined, his mouth was pulled down in a severe frown.

Across from Kristoff was Cora with the Satori's enigmatic sphinx, and in the far right seat, a slight blond man with a blood-red tie he assumed to be Lina's cousin Nico. Nord's eyes narrowed, wondering if he was reading too much into the Cuska representative wearing the Drakes' colors.

That left only the man in the center. Nord's jaw clenched, his teeth grinding together as his eyes landed on the Drake patriarch himself. His blood began to boil at the sight of the charlatan who dared to sit in Lina's spot below the snake.

Mikel's picture hadn't been included in the Brotherhood's files, though he looked much like Nord expected. Everything about him exuded power, from his perfectly tailored suit and expensive watch to the calculated sheen in his sea-green eyes. His once black hair was peppered with gray at the temples, making him appear the oldest of the group by far. His angular face with its sharp cheekbones was lightly tanned, and there was a deep groove in the center of his chin. Even from his current position, Nord could make out the faded black marking on the backs of his fingers and hands, which held the arms of his chair just a hint too tightly to appear casual.

As Nord studied him, Mikel's lip curled back, making the thin white scar that ran from just beneath his nose to the center of his lip more noticeable. "What kind of game are you playing, Satori?" he snarled, his cultured voice soft but no less of a threat because of it.

Cora's raised brow was the only physical reaction she gave him. "What are you implying, Mikel?"

"I'm not implying anything. You're the one that called this meeting. Clearly, you're party to whatever charade this is supposed to be. Everyone knows Evalina Cuska died twenty years ago. So why parade this impostor in front of us?"

The man's dead eyes fell on Lina, causing Nord's fingers to dig so hard into his palms that he drew blood. He was no stranger to evil, but the sight of this cold-blooded killer staring at his mate with such a complete lack of anything resembling humanity was almost more than he could bear.

She isn't safe, the berserker growled in his mind, urging Nord to give in to the rage so he could do what he'd been born to do. Protect. Defend.

Destroy.

He might have given in too, if not for Lina's ringing laughter.

"Do I look dead to you? Though . . . since it was your son who attempted to murder me, I suppose you would hope never to see me again."

That's my girl. The display of utter fearlessness and brazen bravado made Nord want to burst into applause. A soft smile lifted his lips, and he relaxed slightly, seeing that she had things well in hand.

Natalia audibly gasped, her caramel skin leeching of color. But she was the only member of the Council to react to Lina's declaration. Unless a slight tightening around Mikel's eyes counted.

"Oh?" Lina deadpanned, lifting a hand to her chest. "Was I not supposed to talk about the fact that your son was a murderous bastard? Sorry, I thought that was common knowledge. Though, I guess if it was my heir that shit the bed, I probably wouldn't want to admit to it either."

If he wasn't actively looking for a tell, Nord might have missed the slight twitch in Mikel's eye.

"Cousin?" Nico asked in a tremulous voice, rising out of his chair. "Is it really you?"

Lina's eyes shifted to him and then immediately cut away, dismissing him entirely.

Nord had wondered how Lina would react to seeing one of her last remaining relatives. He hadn't expected a complete lack of response, though it was far more telling than anything else she might have done.

From the look on Nico's face, he hadn't expected it either.

Lina turned to Quinn. "Did I stutter?" she asked in a mock whisper.

Quinn shook her head. "I heard you loud and clear, Lady B."

"Hmmm," Lina mused, looking back up at the stage. "Maybe it's an acoustic issue. Perhaps you all could hear me better if I joined you." Without waiting for anyone's permission, Lina moved for the stage, her hips swaying gracefully as she walked up the short set of stairs and straight toward the place where Mikel sat. "If you wouldn't mind," she said, her voice lowered, but not nearly enough to be actually respectful. "I think you're in my seat."

You could have heard a pin drop as the others waited for some sort of reaction. For his part, Nord was semi-erect watching Lina stare the Drake bastard down without blinking.

One of the two men standing on either side of Mikel growled in warning, but Lina ignored them completely.

Her eyes purposefully lifted from Mikel's granite expression to the statue behind him. "Last time I checked, it was the Cuskas who were the serpents, and the Drakes who were the flying lizards."

Utterly. Fearless. Nord grinned. He might be the only one who appreciated it, but Lina was proving, once again, that while she may not have been born a Viking, she possessed their indomitable spirit.

Mikel's knuckles turned white where he gripped the arms of his chair.

"Your father would be absolutely appalled by the level of disrespect his heir is showing right now," Kristoff Alinari spat.

Lina's eyes slid toward the Alinari patriarch. "One can only hope," she said, crossing her fingers. "It's always been my life's goal to systematically dismantle everything he stood for."

Natalia gasped again, but there was no hiding Cora's approving smile. Kristoff, Mikel, and Nico were less impressed. Nord made another mental note, not remotely hesitating to place one of her relatives on his shit list. Anyone who sided with Mikel was an enemy as far as he was concerned.

"If you're going to lay baseless accusations at my son's feet—" Mikel started.

"There's nothing baseless about them when they're the truth," Lina countered coolly.

"It's a serious offense to accuse any of the Heirs of treason such as you have described," Natalia said, leaning forward. Her husky voice was uncertain as her eyes shifted from Lina to Mikel. "Are you prepared to support your claims?"

Lina straightened. "I have nothing to hide. I'll submit to a reading from one of the Satori, if required."

The offer alone must have been impressive because the mood in the room instantly shifted.

Natalia blanched. "I don't think that will be—"

Mikel glowered. "Ludicrous allegations aside, if your intention is to claim a spot on the Council, you must prove you belong among its ranks. Last I heard, Anatoly died prior to any transfer of power. What makes you think you even deserve to sit among us?"

Lina slowly turned her head back toward Mikel. "Would you like a demonstration?" she asked, her voice deceptively soft.

If Nord didn't already love her beyond reason, he'd have fallen head over heels for her in that exact moment.

Mikel's lips curled as he settled back in his chair, but there was nothing amused or relaxed about it. Nord would bet everything he owned that the other man was internally seething at Lina's reappearance and absolutely unrepentant attitude.

"It's not about what I'd like. Merely what is required. Protocol exists for a reason."

"You want me to jump through a hoop for you? Name the terms, Mikel. I would love nothing more than to *prove* myself to you." Lina's voice was dripping with saccharine sarcasm.

Nord would have taken her right there and then if he could. Fuck the witnesses. He'd never seen her in her element quite like this, and watching her metaphorically grab each one of those pretentious assholes by the balls and squeeze until they were little more than sniveling worms at her feet was doing it for him. Big time.

That was his woman out there. Claiming what was hers. He could not have been more proud.

"Wait, aren't we getting ahead of ourselves?" Nico stood and asked, no longer bothering to pretend to be the concerned cousin. "The Cuska seat is filled. I've more than got it covered."

Quinn pinned him with a narrow-eyed stare. "You and what power, kid?" She rolled her eyes. "Just sit down; the grown-ups are talking."

Nico's cheeks turned a splotchy shade of crimson as his knees immediately bent at her command.

"You dare use your gift on me?" he gasped in outrage.

Quinn blinked. "What, like it's hard? You're a council member in name only, Nico. Now sit down before you hurt yourself." Her eyes blazed with power, and Nico sat down hard.

Kristoff leaned forward, his expression thunderous. "Be that as it may, you don't even have that much, heir. You're not a member of the Council, in name or otherwise."

Cora crossed her legs, waving her right hand lazily. "That's easily remedied. I abdicate my claim."

"You know that's not how things are done, Cora," Mikel said in his dangerously quiet voice.

"The Satori power has already passed to my heir, Mikel. Had Quinn not been in hiding, she would have taken the family seat years ago. Do we really need to go through what is little more than a formality just to pacify some fragile male egos?"

Mikel's eyes glinted with warning, though it was Kristoff who responded, "You forget your place."

"Oh? He's only got the one asshole, Kris. Not all of us can shove our tongues up it at the same time. I'd say you've more than got that covered for the rest of us."

Nord grinned as Kristoff turned a vibrant shade of purple, and the two men on either side of him shifted uncomfortably.

Well done, Cora.

Natalia cleared her throat. "I think we've gotten a little off topic. There are several issues before the Council, though the most pertinent for the moment seems to be the matter of the Cuska seat. If Evalina is truly returned to us, by right, of course, it should be hers. Assuming the Ascension was successfully completed. As for her claims regarding Mataius, seeing as how she is very much alive, they are irrelevant."

Lina managed to keep her expression blank, but Nord could feel the molten surge of anger the statement caused. Even dead, Mataius was still a sore spot for all of them. Nord wondered why Mikel wasn't trying to use his son's death to gain leverage.

Unless . . .

Was it possible they didn't know he'd been murdered? What could Mikel possibly stand to gain by keeping it secret? Nord ran his hand over his mouth, trying to solve the riddle while the conversation continued.

"And what about the Satori seat?" Quinn asked.

Natalia lifted one shoulder in a shrug. "If you can prove the power has indeed passed from your mother to you, then it is, by right, yours."

Mikel let out a low, disbelieving cough. "So we're just in the business of handing seats over now? What about yours, Natalia? Should we expect your heir to turn up today and replace you as well?"

Natalia cast her eyes down. "You know I don't know where my daughter is, Mikel." The man standing to her left placed a hand on her shoulder as she let out an almost inaudible sniff.

"And what if she does, Mikel? You afraid of what might happen when you no longer hold the majority vote?" Lina taunted.

"As if I would ever be afraid of a child such as you."

Lina crossed her arms. "Maybe you should be."

"Now see here," Nico said, his eyes darting briefly to Quinn, who snickered as he pushed to his feet once more. "Don't I get any say in this? What am I supposed to do? Just step aside without so much as a 'by your leave'? The Cuska seat was abandoned, and I was the one selected to take up the mantle. Shouldn't that count for something?"

"All that's ever counted is power, Nico. And everyone here knows you don't have it," Lina said.

"You really think you can best me? Fine. Prove it."

Nico was already rolling up his sleeves and moving toward her before he finished speaking.

Nord caught a flash of the berserker in Lina's eyes as she grinned. "Gladly."

When asked how an heir inherits their family seat, Alistair had informed Nord and Finley that a demonstration of magic was required. Something to indicate the heir had acquired new abilities within their family's purview. But he'd never mentioned what happened when two Animagi fought for the position.

Probably because it'd never happened before.

The Ascension should have done away with any rival claims. So what was Nico trying to prove? He couldn't possibly believe he'd actually win in a test where his magic was pitted against hers.

"First blood?" Lina asked sweetly.

Nico cocked his head. "I'll try not to hurt you too badly, cousin."

A hand ax shimmered into being in Lina's open palm as she gave Nico a bloodthirsty grin. "I can't promise the same."

Nico's eyes widened, but Lina's hand closed around the haft, and she swung before he had a chance to process her words and react. Nord had to swallow back a roar of approval as the blade cut through the skin of Nico's upper arm, damn near severing the limb in two.

Blood spurted, and Lina's cousin dropped to his knees amidst a chorus of breathless gasps as his arm hung awkwardly at his side.

No one had expected Lina to act so quickly. Or with such violent abandon.

"Oh, don't get your panties in a twist," she said as nervous whispers broke out around the room. "You guys wanted proof of my abilities. At least let me show you what I can do." With that, Lina shifted so she was kneeling beside her cousin. He cried out when she reached for him. "Unless you'd like for this to be a permanent change, you should probably let me heal that for you."

He blinked at her, his skin pale and his eyes already glazed with pain.

She studied him for a second before she lifted her hands once more. This time he didn't protest when she laid them on his injured arm. It was a matter of minutes at most before the skin and bone had knitted itself back together. Only the blood staining his shirt and skin remained as a testament to what she'd done.

"My . . ." Natalia said, a hand resting on her chest as her eyes darted between a pristine Lina and her blood-soaked cousin. "That was impressive."

From the looks the rest of the room was currently sending Lina's way, they agreed, though some looked happier about it than others. Cora was openly smiling, as were the two women flanking her. The two Cuska representatives that had stood with Nico were eyeing Lina with no little reverence. And while the Thortons and Alinari seemed more or less excited about the outcome, Mikel was the only one who looked as if he'd swallowed something sour.

"You call that impressive?" Mikel scoffed. "Parlor tricks, no more."

Nord bristled at the insult while Lina raised a brow. "Really? I don't recall my father being able to heal like that."

Mikel waved a dismissive hand. "No, but your uncle could. You haven't shown us anything we haven't seen before."

Lina's expression turned stony. "When has that ever been the rule?"

Mikel held her stare, his voice hard as he replied, "Since I said it was."

Her anger burned inside of his chest, her rising fury calling to Nord's as his berserker reared its head.

"Who cares?" Quinn asked, coming to her best friend's defense like always. "All she had to prove was that she was better than him." Quinn waved a hand toward the still stunned Nico. "She destroyed him in ten seconds flat. How is this even a debate?"

"No," Lina said, laying a hand on Quinn's arm, adopting her regal persona once more. "That's fine. If Mikel wants to be dazzled, I'll indulge him." She turned back to the Drakes' leader with an unconcerned tilt of her head. "So what would you like to see, Mikel? What would impress you?"

"I doubt there's very little you could do that I would find impressive, Ms. Cuska."

"Oh, I don't know about that. In fact . . ." she tapped her finger to her mouth, her eyes sparkling with mischief as they shifted for just a second to the doors Nord stood in front of, giving him a hint as to the direction of her thoughts. He grinned in response, already eager for the confrontation that was coming. "I know just the thing. Nord, darling," she called loudly, "would you be a dear and join us, please?"

Mikel stiffened with outrage. "You dare bring an outsider to our chambers without permission?" he snarled.

Lina's eyes flashed as Nord dropped his illusion and strode into the room, making it to her side in no time. She slid her hand into his, and he gave it an encouraging squeeze.

"Oh, but don't you see, Mikel, he's not an outsider at all. Thanks to me, Nord is one of us."

Every set of eyes in the room shifted to him at her declaration. Every set but one. Mikel kept his icy gaze trained on Lina, his jaw flexing as he glared at her.

Lina dropped her voice and leaned forward slightly so that their gazes were level. "Tell me, are you dazzled now?"

CHAPTER 13
LINA

"You did not!" Finley said on a booming laugh.

"She did," Nord confirmed, a look of unmistakable pride shining in his eyes.

Finley leaned over and held his hand up for a high five. "You might just be my hero, love."

Lina beamed at him as she slapped her palm against his. "It was pretty epic, wasn't it?"

"Undeniably. What I wouldn't give to have been there to see you in action." He shook his head, still smiling. Grabbing his highball glass, he took a sip of his scotch and settled back in his chair. "So, what happened next?"

"There wasn't a whole lot that could happen after that," Quinn said. "Not like Mikel or the others could refute the six-plus feet of hulking Animagi standing right in front of them."

"Well, they tried to," Lina said, "but Quinn's aunt, Sheridan, shut that down. She projected the memory of Nord using his Animagi gift in the alleyway for them to see as proof. No one was really interested in pushing the issue after they saw what happened to the Director."

"What about you?" Finley asked, turning to Quinn. "What hoops did you have to jump through to prove yourself?"

Quinn gave a bored shrug. "I returned a forgotten memory."

Lina couldn't help but smile at the way her friend downplayed it. "To keep her daughter safe, Natalia requested that the memory of where she hid was taken from her. Now that the rest of us are back, Quinn returned the memory so that she could bring her home if she wanted to."

Finley's gaze turned piercing as he stared at Quinn. "You can return memories that have been removed?"

She fidgeted under his regard and couldn't quite meet his gaze as she replied, "Yes. In some cases."

"Such as?" Finley prompted, taking another sip of scotch.

"Who modified the original memory, the method by which it was hidden, those sorts of things," she said, feigning breeziness.

Finley hummed quietly in his throat, his eyes never leaving Quinn's. "Good to know."

Lina raised a brow, certain she was missing something. "Anyway," she said, drawing out the word. "By all accounts, today's mission was a raging success."

Quinn snickered. "I see what you did there. Berserker. Raging. Funny."

Nord chuckled while Lina rolled her eyes.

"Even though phase one went off without a hitch, we can't get complacent. Mikel's not going to be very happy with me after I embarrassed him like that today—not that he liked me much to begin with. And the only reason I was able to pull one over on him at all is because he didn't see it coming. We won't get away with something like that a second time."

"So if phase one was getting on the Council, phase two is . . ." Finley trailed off with a quirk of his brow.

"Paying a visit to the vault," Lina supplied.

"Right. Right. And when do you want to do that?"

"The sooner, the better," she said, the high of her win fading as reality crept back in. "There's no knowing when Mikel is going to strike back, and with Crombie's bond only getting stronger, I can't risk the handicap."

Nord squeezed her thigh. "You just say when, Kærasta. We'll make it happen."

She gave him a grateful smile. "Well, thankfully, the visit itself won't be that complicated. I just need to get the key from Nico. He stormed off before I could ask him for it. But once that's in hand, it's really just a matter of making the trip down there and then seeing how long it takes to find Crombie's treasure."

"Asking for the key won't raise any brows?" Nord asked.

Lina shook her head. "The key's not just for the vault; it provides access to lots of things. Now that he's been replaced, it would be irresponsible to allow him to hang on to it," she said with a devious smile.

"And that's it? You get the key, and we can just waltz right in?" Finley asked.

"Um . . . yeah, basically," Lina said, squeezing her hands together to keep from wringing them and giving herself away.

Quinn gave Lina a pointed look. "You seem to be leaving out some key intel there, Lady B."

"I am?"

Quinn snorted. "Don't use that innocent act on me, Cuska. I'm the one that taught it to you."

Nord cast his eyes between them, his brows lowering suspiciously. "What aren't you telling us?"

Lina bit the inside of her cheek. "It's not that big of a deal."

Nord turned to Quinn. "What isn't she saying?"

"You can't go with her."

"What? Why not?" he asked, his expression darkening.

"The magic that protects the vault prohibits all except the five heads of the Council to go inside. Pretty much every alarm in existence will go off if you tried to set foot in there with her," Quinn said.

Nord scowled at that, clearly unhappy with the thought of having to stay behind.

"Welcome to the bench, mate," Finley said, lifting his almost empty glass in a mock toast.

"Look, you really don't need to worry," Lina said, lifting her hands in a placating manner. "Now that I'm on the Council, Mobius property is basically the safest place I could be."

Nord visibly bristled at her words. Lina didn't require any help translating his reaction. He was offended there could be any place safer for her than by his side. Her heart gave a little twist.

"You know that's not what I meant," she said softly. "It's just that Council law prohibits Mikel from doing anything to me directly. As far as he's concerned, the second I took the Cuska seat, I became untouchable. I mean, you saw how his hands were tied today. For him, appearance is everything. He'd never risk pulling anything on Mobius turf. So you see, even if I have to go in alone, I'll be fine."

"If you're as untouchable as you claim, then why are you so worried about him?" Nord pointed out. When she didn't immediately answer, he lifted both of his brows knowingly. "Exactly. Every rule has a loophole. Hell, the four of us have exploited enough of them. Just because he cannot touch you, Lina, does not mean he cannot hurt you. Alistair is proof enough of that."

She flinched, and something like regret flickered in Nord's eyes, but he did not back down.

"Mikel will not allow anything as mundane as a law to stop him from getting what he wants. If he cannot go after you directly, he will find a way to do it from the shadows. He's a master manipulator; you've said as much yourself. Your title is meaningless in the face of someone such as that, so you'll have to forgive me if I don't place as much faith in it as you do."

"Well, you certainly know how to suck all the air out of the room, dontcha, big guy?" Quinn said, sliding a fresh cocktail in front of Lina, who accepted it gladly.

"No, he's right," Lina said, cradling the icy glass in between her hands. "Mikel shouldn't be underestimated. And I don't underestimate him," she added, lifting her eyes to meet Nord's. "But I'm telling you, getting into and out of the vault is not going to be a problem. I know it's hard for you to cede control, but you're going to need to trust my judgment on this one."

He held her gaze, and she could feel his turmoil gathering in her chest.

"Nothing good ever happens when we're separated."

Quinn huffed out a humorless laugh. "If you want to get technical, the last handful of shitty things happened while you were together, so what does it really matter?" A growl rumbled in Nord's chest, and Quinn blinked at him. "What, too soon?"

Finley reached out and caught the back of her shirt, giving it a sharp tug until she fell onto the loveseat beside him. "That's enough out of you," he said. "Not every conversation requires your cheeky commentary."

"Sure it does." She gave him a dirty look as she straightened herself. "I just say what everyone else is thinking."

One side of Finley's mouth curled up in a smile. "I highly doubt that."

Quinn rolled her eyes. "Fine. I just say what the intelligent people are thinking."

Lina watched their stare down with a small smile. If nothing else, those two could always be counted on to ease the tension.

"Are you mad?" she asked Nord, her voice low.

"What do you think?" he asked, matching her tone.

Lina set her untouched cocktail down and scooted over until their thighs were pressed together. She tilted her chin up and brushed a soft kiss to the hinge of his jaw. "What about now?"

He made a rumbly sound in his throat, so she repeated the move, this time running her fingers through his beard to cup his cheek.

"Now?" she whispered.

He let out a soft groan and wrapped his arms around her,

hugging her tight. "You know it's only my concern for you. I don't doubt you or your skill, Kærasta. It's everyone else I don't trust."

She smiled at his grumpy admission. "I know, love. Is there anything I can do to help you feel better?"

Nord's eyes went molten.

Finley cleared his throat. "I believe there's still the matter of you making me feel better to settle first."

"Excuse me?" Nord snarled dangerously.

"The cars, mate. I was talking about the cars she promised me to make me feel better about sitting out today. Jesus, no need to throttle me." His eyes darted to Quinn.

"Don't look at me. You stepped right into that one," she said with a smirk.

Nord's amusement shot through Lina's chest, telling her he was just fucking with Finley. She bit down hard on the inside of her cheek so as not to give him away.

"Did you have that list for me?" she asked, holding out a hand.

Finley pulled it out of his pocket. "With my color selections, specifications, and pictures, as requested," he said, casting Nord a cautious look as he leaned over to hand it to her. "And they'd better work according to those specs too," he warned her. "I'm not looking for a couple of museum exhibits here. It doesn't count if they don't run."

Lina skimmed the list. "A Bugatti and a Lambo, huh?"

Finley made an offended sound. "You can't just speak about them like they're common street vehicles. That's a Bugatti La Voiture Noire and—"

"Here he goes," Quinn moaned, lifting her glass and draining it.

"—a Veneno. I could have chosen the Pagani Zonda Barchetta, but since there's only three in existence—"

"Is he still talking about cars?" Lina stage whispered to Nord.

He nodded. "'Fraid so."

"He's making me hungry with all those foreign words."

Nord's chest vibrated with laughter.

Finley threw his hands in the air. "The level of disrespect in this room is astounding."

"Now you sound like Kristoff," Quinn muttered. "They're just cars, Fin. Pretty and expensive ones, sure, but just cars. I promise your dick's not gonna grow, no matter how many of them you add to your stable."

Finley leveled her with a look so hot, Lina squirmed.

"You know, for someone who claims to have no interest in my dick, Satori, you sure love to talk about it."

Quinn scoffed, but there was no missing the color that crept into her cheeks. "Oh, please. As if the Vienna sausage between your legs is of any interest to me."

Finley tsked. His voice was low, his eyes never leaving Quinn's. "I think thou doth protest too much, sweetheart. You've just given yourself away. Now we're all in on your not-so-secret obsession with my cock. Or was it my balls?" He chuckled darkly. "I must admit, I'm having trouble keeping track with the way you keep carrying on. If you'd like, I can feed it to you, and you can tell me how small it is after you're finished choking on it . . ."

She made a strangled sound and stood abruptly with her empty glass in her hand. "Anyone need another drink?" Without waiting for anyone to respond, Quinn exited the room.

Lina made it approximately one second before she burst out laughing. "I don't think I've ever seen her run away like that before. Not that I blame her. Holy balls, Fin . . ." Lina fanned her face.

"She started it," Finley murmured, finishing his scotch.

"And you, what, set it on fire?"

Finley winked at her. "Just making an observation."

"Is that what that was?" Lina asked.

Finley shrugged. "I can only tolerate so many insults to my manhood in a single day. If she's going to insist on baiting the bear, she should be prepared for it to bite back."

"Fair enough," Lina said with a laugh. "I'm sure the message was received loud and clear."

Finley raised a brow. "Knowing her, I doubt it."

They shared a smile.

Nord bit down on her earlobe and growled. "Careful, Kærasta."

"Me? What did I do?"

"Have you already forgotten that I can feel what you're feeling?"

Lina shook her head, her breath hitching as he slid his hand under her shirt so that his fingers angled low on her stomach.

"Then unless you want me to knock his teeth out, I'd suggest you stop smiling at Fin while thinking about whatever it is that's got you so turned on."

"You're ridiculous," she protested, her laugh breathless as his fingers skimmed lower, dipping below the waist band of her pants.

"Be that as it may, I'm also a berserker. You should know by now how irrationally territorial we can be. Imagine how you'd react if our roles were reversed."

A growl slipped out as Lina did just that.

Nord chuckled in her ear. "Feeling possessive, little berserker?"

"Among other things."

"Want to do something about it?"

"Do you even need to ask?"

Nord stood and turned to lift her, hoisting her over his shoulder in one easy move.

"Oh, thank God. I was starting to worry you two were just going to go at it on the couch like a couple of feral bunnies," Finley said dryly.

"And you were just going to sit there and watch?" Nord shot back.

Lina craned her neck in time to see Finley toss Nord a cocksure grin. "I figured if you don't care, why should I?"

Nord summoned his magic so fast, Lina had only just made out the shape of a massive hand before it slammed into Finley's head.

Fin ducked forward, cupping the back of his skull protectively as he looked around for the source of the attack. His eyes widened comically when they landed on the giant replica of Nord's hand floating beside him. Lina had to give it to her Viking, for as fast as it happened, he still managed to get the details absolutely perfect, from his rings to the small scar on the side of his pinkie.

"What the bloody hell was that for?" Finley demanded.

"To help you remember that I *always* care," Nord answered as he turned away.

Finley scowled and called after him, "Lobcock."

Nord's steps didn't falter, but Lina snorted when the floating hand rearranged itself so that only the middle finger was raised.

"Love you too, mate!"

She was still laughing as Nord carried her to his bedroom, but they'd only made it a few steps when a knock on the door brought them up short.

Nord's body went rigid beneath her, and Lina's pulse spiked. No one should have been able to get up to the penthouse unannounced.

Finley was beside them in an instant. "Who the hell—"

"I'll get it," Quinn said, stepping out of the kitchen ahead of them.

"Wait, we don't know who it is," Finley protested.

She rolled her eyes at him. "Your fancy wards didn't go off. It's probably just the doorman with some misplaced mail or something."

Even Lina knew the odds of that were less than zero. Finley had a very strict protocol in place. No one was allowed upstairs without permission. Period.

Nord lowered Lina, moving to stand in front of her. She halted his movement with a hand on his ribs, leaning around him to call to her friend.

"Quinn, wait. Don't—"

It was too late.

Quinn opened the door with a flourish. "Can I help—" her words were consumed as they turned into one long ear-piercing wail.

CHAPTER 14

QUINN

No matter how many times she blinked, the bruised and bloody figure at her feet never changed.

Quinn's knees sagged, unable to support her trembling frame. "Mama?"

She heard the rush of footsteps behind her but couldn't seem to look away from her mother's disfigured form to acknowledge the others. Lifting her shaking hand, she reached out to check for a pulse but hesitated before making contact.

There wasn't a visible inch of Cora's skin that had been left unharmed. She would have been unrecognizable if not for the shredded shirt currently doing very little to cover her battered torso. Even soaked through with blood, Quinn recognized the floral pattern. It was the same one she'd worn to the meeting that afternoon.

Lina's shocked inhale told Quinn that the others were right behind her. She flinched as a warm palm came in contact with her shoulder.

"It's just me," Finley said, crouching down beside her.

"Is she . . ." Quinn's voice failed before she could ask the question.

"She's alive," Finley answered, his voice low. "Just unconscious."

"Oh, thank God," Lina said, her voice heavy with emotion.

Quinn's eyes fluttered closed. It was a small mercy, but she was thankful for it. At least if her mother was unconscious, she wasn't feeling any pain.

"Let's get her inside," Finley said.

Quinn's hand shot out reflexively to stop him from touching her.

His hazel eyes were gentler than she'd ever seen as he met her gaze. "It's okay. I'm not going to hurt her. I'm just going to carry her in so that we can take care of those injuries, all right?"

Quinn stared at him for several long beats.

"Let me do this for you, Quinn," Finley whispered. "Let me help you take care of your mum."

The tears she'd hereto managed to stave off slipped down her cheeks at his gentle request.

"Okay," she said, releasing his wrist.

Finley surprised her by reaching for her instead of Cora. He wiped away her tears and cradled her face between both of his palms. "She's going to be fine, love. She'll be back on her feet and bossing us around in no time, okay?"

Quinn let out a sound that was somewhere between a wet hiccup and a laugh before she nodded. "Just be careful with her."

"Of course," he promised, shifting his attention to Cora.

Somehow Quinn made it back to her feet, and Lina was right there, wrapping her in a tight hug. The three of them held a silent vigil as Finley lifted Cora in his arms. Quinn almost lost it at the sight of her mother hanging so limply in his hold. She was the strongest woman Quinn knew, seeing her like this . . . it was wrong on a fundamental level.

As if he could feel her unraveling beside him, Finley's eyes found hers. The determination and conviction she found there gave her strength, and she managed to breathe past the lump in her throat.

"You can use my room," Lina offered. "It's closest."

Finley gave a tight nod and moved past them, holding Cora as if she was both precious and fragile. Lina and Quinn followed, Lina's arm curled protectively over her shoulders, and their free hands grasped together in a white-knuckled hold. Nord trailed behind them, his expression grim.

Finley had already laid Cora down by the time they filed into the room. Bile clawed up her throat as Quinn cataloged the number of broken bones and other horrific injuries her mother sustained. It was so much worse than she'd thought at first glance. The sheer amount of hatred required to inflict this kind of damage was almost unfathomable. Quinn had seen professionals at work and knew firsthand that there were ways to inflict maximum pain with minimal damage. This was so far past that. It was overkill in every possible sense of the word. Which only made it more obvious that this attack was personal.

Whoever had done this to her mother wanted it to hurt. They wanted to break her, not just once, but repeatedly. They took their time. Drew it out. Enjoyed it.

Not killing her was almost worse. Cora would have to live with the memories of what had happened to her, never to feel wholly safe in her skin ever again. It was monstrous. Undeniably evil.

It was Mikel's MO.

"I'm so sorry, Quinn," Lina whispered brokenly. "This is all my fault."

"No," Quinn said, her voice wooden. "We all knew what we were getting into when we walked into that Council room. Mom more than anyone else."

"Yes, but if I hadn't taunted him—"

Quinn scoffed bitterly. "Mikel deserved everything we said and then some. It wouldn't have mattered anyway. The fact that we undermined him was more than he could stand. He was never just going to let that go. This is his way of telling us he's displeased."

"This is displeased?" Nord asked.

"Mikel doesn't do subtle," Quinn replied.

Finley was hard at work on Cora, his eyes glowing bright as he began the arduous process of repairing everything Mikel had broken.

"We should help him," Lina whispered to Nord. "It's"—her eyes darted to Quinn—"it'll go faster."

Quinn appreciated that her friend was trying to spare her feelings by being vague, but it was unnecessary. She could see for herself that the damage was too great for Finley to repair on his own. The Guardian was talented, but this level of healing required experts. Thankfully, Nord and Lina were more than qualified. Between the three of them, the task would be almost easy.

Nord and Lina joined Finley around the bed, each of them focusing on a different part of her mother's body. Wanting to feel like she was doing something useful, Quinn moved to stand near Cora's head, resting a hand on her forehead and brushing the blood-matted strands of her hair away.

When she'd been little and been plagued by nightmares, Cora would always snuggle up beside her and sing her a lullaby to help her fall back asleep. Quinn was a horrible singer, but perhaps there was something she could do to ensure that her mother's dreams were peaceful. It was the least she could do for the woman who'd given her so much.

Quinn drew on her power, slipping into the psychic stream that would lead her to her mother's mind. Some connections were easier to forge than others, depending on both the natural and magical defenses of the person in question. As her mother, Cora's mental plane had always been open to her, although there was still usually a bit of resistance.

Not this time.

She slid into the other woman's consciousness with no more effort than a blade of grass blowing in the breeze. The ease with which she made the transition left her completely unprepared for the carnage she discovered when she got there.

Quinn tried to exert her power, to modify the images playing out before her, but she couldn't. In a way, it felt as though her presence in her mother's mind had triggered some sort of spell. Helpless to do anything else, she watched the memory unfold, her anger mounting with each passing second.

She focused on Mikel rolling up his sleeves, revealing his tattooed forearms as he prowled lazily around her mother's ravaged form. He came to a stop at her side, sighing as he crouched down, bringing his blood-speckled body into Quinn's view.

That's when she realized the perspective was all wrong.

Cora was reliving her assault, but instead of experiencing the memory from the vantage point from which it happened, she was standing off to the side. No, that wasn't quite right. Cora was very much curled up in a ball on the floor, while whoever's recollection this was watched from the sidelines.

Regardless of where the images came from, the effect of seeing them play out was the same. Having already seen the results of Mikel's attack, Quinn thought she'd be more desensitized. But that wasn't remotely the case. Witnessing the brutality play out in front of her made her sick.

Mikel grabbed Cora by the hair, yanking her head back and causing her to let out a pitiful moan.

"Had enough?"

Cora's eye, the only one she could open, was a glittering lavender slit as she spat in Mikel's face.

He frowned, wiping away the spittle with the air of a disappointed parent dealing with a wayward child.

"Now, Cora. You know that's no way to behave. Things would go so much easier if you'd simply tell me what I wanted to know." He paused, almost tender as he ran the backs of his knuckles down her swollen cheek. "This all could have been avoided if you'd only learned to obey years ago. But it would seem I haven't quite beaten that independent streak out of you after all." He gave her cheek a sharp slap. "Perhaps today will finally be the day."

Cora croaked out a laugh. "That's unlikely. No matter what you do, I'll never be one of your dogs, Mikel."

Mikel leaned forward until his lips just about grazed her ear. "That's where you're wrong. Every animal can be broken. It just requires a patient and attentive master. Unfortunately for you, Satori. Breaking you will never lose its appeal." He punctuated the statement by snapping one of her fingers.

Cora cried out, tears leaking out of her eyes as she panted, "Then it seems we're at an impasse. You might as well kill me and save us both the time."

"Now, Cora, I don't want to kill you, but I do intend to make good use of you. If you won't help me willingly, then I'll see to it you send a memorable message to that impertinent daughter of yours." His cold, dead eyes lifted, staring Quinn—or whoever it was whose memory she was reliving—straight in the eye as he pulled out a lighter and started heating the signet ring on his pinkie. "Perhaps she'll see things more clearly than you."

With those haunting words, Mikel dropped the lighter and slammed the makeshift brand straight into her mother's eye.

Quinn was pulled out of the memory with a gasp. She dropped to her knees and heaved.

Finley was right behind her, not quite fast enough to catch her, but there in time to grab her hair and run a soothing hand down her back.

"You okay?" he asked.

She nodded, not quite able to look at him as she wiped her mouth with the back of her hand. "I'm sorry about your floor."

"Don't worry about it." He waved a hand, and the carpet was clean once more.

Her lips twitched. "Showoff." But then her stomach knotted as Mikel's savagery swam up in her mind. "Can I get some water?"

"Here you go, sweetie," Lina said, using her magic to conjure a full glass on the spot. She handed it to Finley, who offered it to her.

After Quinn drank almost the entire glass, she sat back against the wall, still breathing hard.

"Can you tell us what you saw?" Finley asked, still speaking to her in that soft, careful tone.

"What Mikel wanted me to," she said bitterly as the pieces of the puzzle she hadn't quite understood in the moment became clear. "My mom wasn't the only one he hurt. Mikel used Sheridan and Sylvia to ensure I saw exactly what he did to her. He made them watch and then place the memory in my mom's mind for me to find. He knew—" Quinn shook her head with a shudder.

Finley's hand was warm and sure on her shoulder. He gave her an encouraging squeeze. "He knew what?"

Quinn licked her lips, taking a deep breath before trying to answer. "He knew I'd find it. He wanted me to. That way, he could show me exactly what he'd do to me if I"—Quinn's eyes lifted to Lina's—"*we* continued to undermine him. This, all of this, is a warning about what's waiting for us if we don't back down."

Nord's nostrils flared, the blue of his eyes disappearing in a sea of black. Beside him, Lina's did the same. Her hands balled into tight fists on either side of her shaking body.

"You two, out," Finley demanded, his voice brooking no room for argument.

"You're kicking me out of my own room?" Lina asked, her voice more snarl than question.

"A sickroom is no place for two out-of-control berserkers. Sort your shit out before you set foot back in here. I mean it."

Lina bared her teeth at him, but Nord gave her arm a tug. "He's right, Kærasta. They don't need to deal with our rage on top of everything else. Let's go take it out on each other."

Quinn could see that Lina was torn.

"Go on, Lady B. We'll be all right."

After a second, Lina nodded and allowed Nord to lead her from the room.

Once they were alone, Quinn shifted her attention back to Finley. "Is she okay?"

He tucked a piece of her hair behind her ear as he nodded. "As good as new."

"Then why is she still unconscious?"

"She's just sleeping. Even though we've dealt with everything on a physical level, injuries like that take a toll. She'll wake when she's ready."

Quinn bit her lip as she stared at her mother's still form. Once she saw the slight rise of her chest and heard the soft sound of her breath, she relaxed.

"Thank you," she said, her voice unsteady.

Finley took her chin in his hand and turned her head so that she met his gaze. He studied her for a second and then shook his head. "Nope. Not happening."

Quinn blinked, completely confused. "What?"

"You're not going to keep all this in and let it eat away at you. It's poison, Satori. You need to purge it from your system."

"Uh, did you already forget me puking my guts out on your carpet? I think we've got the purging taken care of."

Finley twisted so he wasn't crouching in front of her, but sitting beside her. Without giving her any further explanation, he hauled her into his lap and cradled her against him. Quinn was too shocked to resist. Or to relax.

"Shh. Just accept the comfort, Quinn. Let me help you with this."

"Help me how?"

"By sharing the burden. Give it to me. Let me carry it for you."

She blinked at him. "Give it to you? It's not a suitcase, Fin. I can't just hand it over."

"Sure you can. You're the memory weaver. Just do what you usually do. Remove it from your mind and put it in mine or whatever. You don't need to remember your mum that way, or the vile things that man did to her. I can hold on to it so you don't have to."

"Fin," she whispered, something in her chest going loose and fluttery at the offer. "My gift doesn't work that way. I can't use it on myself."

He frowned. "Well, then I guess we have to do this the normal way."

"Normal way?" she asked, still feeling somewhat dazed by the rapid shift of events and her turbulent emotions.

"We're just going to have to talk it out. I'll sit here and listen while you tell me exactly what you saw. And if you need to cry, then I'll hold you until you're done. Or if you want to pummel something, you can use me for that instead. Whatever you prefer."

Quinn just stared at him, not sure what to say. "Finley—"

He pressed a finger against her lips, shaking his head. "This is what you need. Let me take care of you. Please."

It was the please that got her. She wasn't sure she'd heard Finley say please ever. Hearing it now, on her behalf . . . she had no defense against it.

"Fine," she sighed. "But I reserve the right to deny any of this ever happened at any point in the future."

"I'd expect nothing less," Finley said with a half-smile.

This time, she was the one that snuggled deeper into him, though she pointedly ignored the little voice that commented on how perfectly they fit together. Then, staring blindly at the wall, she began to haltingly recount every horrid thing Mikel had done to her mother.

And when she broke down in tears only a few minutes into her retelling, Finley only held her tighter, whispering so softly she could barely hear him, "I've got you, Satori. I'll never let you go."

CHAPTER 15
NORD

Lina shifted restlessly beside him, moaning and kicking her legs until the sheets were tangled around them like cotton shackles.

"Shh . . ." he murmured, leaning down to free her before reaching out to pull her body flush against his.

"Nord," she mumbled, her voice thick with sleep.

"I'm here," he breathed, placing a tender kiss on her temple. "You're safe."

She relaxed instantly, her limbs falling slack as she curled into him. They'd performed the same routine almost every hour on the hour all night long. It always started when she'd rolled too far away from him, and it wouldn't cease until he held her protectively in his arms once more.

As much as he took pleasure in being the source of her comfort, he couldn't help but frown at the proof of her continued distress. Her day's mission might have been accomplished, but her troubled sleep was telling. Mikel hadn't wasted any time striking back, and from the looks of things, Cora wasn't his only victim. Lina—and likely Quinn—were every bit as traumatized.

It was like their early days together all over again. While the sun was up, Lina would hide her fear behind a mask of competence and duty. But as soon as night fell and there was nothing left to distract her, those mental shields dropped and she'd toss and turn, no longer able to run from the truth.

Nord shifted Lina's sleeping form in his arms, turning her so that her head rested on his chest. Dropping his chin, he pressed another soft kiss to her forehead, fiercely wishing there was something he could do about her dreams. Hell, at this point, he'd dust off his mother's lullabies if he thought there was any chance the ancient Norse songs would bring her some sliver of peace. They'd worked for him . . . when he'd been four and afraid of the nameless, faceless things in the dark. Somehow he doubted they'd be as successful against real-life monsters.

Still, he was seriously considering giving them a go when she stirred again. This time, however, she sounded mostly lucid when she called his name.

"Nord?"

"Hmm?" he returned, brushing away the strands of hair that slipped onto her face.

"What's that you're singing?"

He froze, his hand suspended in midair. *Shit.* He must have unconsciously hummed the tune when trying to dredge up the long-forgotten lyrics.

"I wasn't."

She tilted her face up, blinking sleepy eyes at him. "Okay, so maybe there weren't any words, but I recognize a tune when it's rumbled in my ear."

He gave her a lopsided grin. "You must have been dreaming, Kærasta. I don't sing."

Lina huffed in exasperation, her expression so endearing and a far cry better than the distraught frown she'd worn most of the night. He decided to draw out this ridiculous conversation as long as possible. It wouldn't be the first time he'd made a fool of himself for her benefit.

"Is this like a stage fright thing? Because you have nothing to worry about. You sounded good enough to me. Okay, you were more than good."

Nord stared at her with a raised brow, amused by her flustered babbling.

"What? Are you expecting a glowing five-star review or something?" She glanced at the clock. "It's five in the morning; what do you expect? I was mostly asleep, and I only caught so much. If you want an actual, honest opinion, give me a real performance, and I'd be happy to provide it."

Nord bit back a laugh at her defensive backpedaling. "I didn't say I *can't* sing. I said I don't."

Which was true. Even though he'd been contemplating it, quietly singing for a fretful sleeper was hardly the same as performing for a captive audience. He hadn't done the latter since joining the Brotherhood, nor had he any inclination to . . . until tonight.

His clarification earned him a grumpy look. "Well, why not? Surely Vikings had war chants or, um, sea shanties or uh . . ." Lina snapped her fingers like it would help her recall the words. It must have worked because a second later, she pointed at him and added, "Battle hymns."

It was a struggle to keep his expression blank, especially when she looked so adorably rumpled and proud of herself. "What's your point?"

She poked him in the chest. "If singing is part of your heritage, surely even the badass berserkers joined in."

"They did," he agreed.

"So you do sing."

"I do not."

"But," she sputtered, sitting up, "you just said you did."

"Did I?"

"Nord," she groaned, slapping him lightly on the chest. "Stop being purposefully obtuse and sing me a damn song."

He chuckled and pulled her back down, snuggling her against him. "Forgive me, Kærasta. I'm just having a bit of fun. Did you know you're beautiful when you're flustered?"

She shot him a baleful glare. "Annoyed. The word you're looking for is annoyed. Or disgruntled, if you want to be fancy. Flustered is what happens when you get me all hot in public, and I can't act on it."

He kissed her nose. "Either way."

"Well, the way I see it, you owe me a song. It's the least you can do to make up for being a stubborn ass when I'm only half awake and unable to adequately defend myself."

He chuckled. "Would you accept a story instead?"

She gave him a suspicious look. "Would it happen to be about why you don't sing anymore?"

His lips lifted a little. "Well, that's not much of a story, to be honest."

"Oh?"

"My mom was the singer; she taught my brother and I all her favorites and would ask us to perform for her at night. After they died . . . well, there just didn't seem to be much point in it."

"Nord, I'm sorry," Lina said, looking stricken. "I wouldn't have pushed—"

"No," he said, shaking his head as he cupped her cheek. "There's no need to apologize. The memories don't cut as deep as they used to. I think it's because I have someone to share them with now." Nord paused and let out a soft laugh as a thought occurred to him. "Actually, I should probably thank you for that. Talking about them with you . . . remembering the happy times and those quiet, everyday moments, it's sort of like you've brought them back to me."

Lina's eyes went soft, and she pressed her lips gently against his before snuggling back down into his arms. "I love that I can do that for you."

"Me too," he murmured, running his fingers through the length of her hair.

Silence stretched comfortably between them as Lina traced the tattoo over his ribcage. He mentally tracked her progress, the lines of the ship's bow and the man standing at its helm taking shape in his mind. Lina had no way of knowing it, but he'd chosen that piece in honor of his mother and one of her favorite poems. What were the odds she'd pick that tattoo out of all the others, specifically after the topic of their conversation?

The coincidence was impossible to ignore. More so as the sensation of a hand brushing over his head sent warmth and contentment sweeping through him, bringing with them a sense of confidence and certainty.

If ever there was a sign . . .

Dipping his chin down so that his mouth was angled toward her ear, Nord whispered, his voice taking on a soft lilt as he translated the ancient words, "'*My mother told me, someday I would buy*' . . ."

Lina's breath caught and then washed across his chest in a warm gust as she melted into him. And as he continued to whisper-sing the rest of the song, her breathing turned slow and even. This time, when she drifted off, her sleep remained peaceful.

Nord stayed awake a while longer, just to be sure. But as his own eyelids grew heavy, he couldn't resist the impulse to thank the woman who, even from beyond the grave, helped him find a way to bring Lina some well-deserved peace.

"Þǫkk, Móðir."

And in those last seconds of consciousness, he would have sworn he heard her beloved voice reply, "Drøm søtt, minn son."

Nord stumbled into the kitchen a few hours later, his steps faltering at the sight of Cora perched against the bar blowing on a steaming cup of coffee. Sitting there in a pair of Lina's sweatpants and a faded black T-shirt, she looked like she could be Quinn's older sister.

"Pot's fresh," she said by way of greeting.

He wasn't quite awake enough to form actual words yet, so he let out a grunt of thanks as he grabbed the largest mug they had and proceeded to fill it to the brim. Unlike Cora, he didn't waste time attempting to cool the drink, not minding the slight scald as he downed half his cup in one go.

Cora watched all of this with a knowing smile playing about her mouth. "Better?" she asked when he set his mug down.

Nord grunted again.

"Well, you're a chatty fellow, aren't you?"

Realizing he wasn't getting off easy, he sighed and asked, "Should you even be up and about?"

"Ah-ha! He does speak. And I couldn't sleep . . . the dreams . . ." Cora shuddered, a dark look sweeping across her face, there and then gone.

It told him everything he needed to know. Her body might be healed, but it would take more than magic to wipe away the things Mikel had done.

Not giving him a chance to comment, she turned her shrewd gaze back his way.

Uh oh. He recognized that look. Nord braced himself for what was sure to be a patented Satori zinger.

"But what's your excuse? And why so surly? Do I need to have a talk with Lina? You should be walking around like a damn sunbeam with a woman like her warming your bed."

Nord glared at her. "You're just like your daughter."

Cora beamed at him. "High praise coming from you, I'm sure."

Nord huffed out a laugh and shook his head, reaching for his mug once more. "Well, I do like and respect her most of the time, so I guess that's something."

"And me. Don't forget, we're friends, too."

He raised both brows as he took a sip. "So you keep telling me."

She set her cup down and leaned forward in a conspiratorial fashion. "Admit it; you were worried about me."

Bracing his hands on either side of the island, Nord replied, "I would have to be one unfeeling bastard not to, given the state you were in."

Cora gave him one of her deceptively sweet smiles, her eyes gleaming with the same wicked amusement he found so often in Quinn's. "And I have a feeling you're the sort of man who feels things very deeply."

A little shiver worked its way down his spine at her signature saying, but he brushed it off with a shrug. "When something affects the woman I love or the people she cares about, yeah, that's probably a safe bet. That doesn't make us friends. Reluctant allies, maybe."

"Which, by default, means you *do* care about what happens to me. It's okay, I won't tell. Your secret's safe with me." She mimed zipping her lips and then settled back, reaching for her cup once more.

"What secret?" Finley asked, glancing between them curiously as he made his way into the kitchen. Spotting Cora, he changed direction, heading to her before the coffee pot. "Glad to see you're feeling better. Any lingering aches?"

If Nord hadn't been watching her closely, he would have missed the shadows that passed in her eyes before she flashed Finley a breezy smile. "Not a one, thanks to you."

"It was a group effort," he said, giving her knee a pat before stepping away to pour himself a cup.

"Yes, well, my girls were lucky to find themselves such a pair of strong, competent men."

"You forgot handsome," Finley said, tossing her a wink over his shoulder.

"And modest too," she added dryly.

"Now I see where Quinn gets it."

"I said the same thing," Nord replied. "She thinks it's a compliment."

Finley and Cora both chuckled.

"Isn't it? I have a feeling you wouldn't love her nearly as much if she didn't keep you on your toes."

Finley went rigid, his expression guarded as he lifted his mug. Cora met his gaze without flinching. It was the strangest battle of wills Nord could recall ever witnessing.

"You might be right," Finley eventually said.

"Darling, I'm always right."

There was no mistaking the plea for help as Finley's eyes found Nord.

Taking pity on his friend, Nord cleared his throat. "So, Cora, do you have any other feelings we should know about?"

"Good one."

Nord acknowledged Finley's telepathic comment with a slight dip of his chin. As much as he didn't like Cora using her gift to peer too closely in his direction, he couldn't miss out on an opportunity to learn what fate—or, more specifically, Mikel—had in store for them.

"Are you asking about you two in particular?"

"Does it make a difference?"

Cora considered the question, her eyes taking on the same liquid quality Quinn's did when she accessed her power. She was silent for a long, drawn-out moment before cryptically murmuring, "Photographs and phone calls . . . Misdirection and magic." Then she blinked and pointed to Nord's empty cup. "You may want some more of that. I have a feeling it's going to be a very long day."

Before Nord could even begin to formulate a response, Finley's phone rang. They exchanged a startled glance. Nord looked over at Cora, who wore a smug smile. 'I told you so' may as well have been written across her forehead, though she at least had the decency not to say it outright.

Finley pulled his cell phone out of his pocket, his brows knitting together as he read the display.

"Who is it?" Nord demanded.

"Nate," Finley said, hitting the answer button and lifting the phone to his ear.

Given the hour and the fact that Finley was still technically on leave, it was unlikely the Guardian was calling with good news.

Apparently, Finley thought so, too, because his greeting was a brusque, "What's wrong?"

Nord's unease grew as Finley's frown deepened.

"No . . . I haven't eaten yet. Why do you ask?" There was a beat of silence, Finley's expression sober and then confused. "No, he's standing right here. Why?" The hair on the back of Nord's neck stood on end as Finley breathed out a shocked, "Holy shit. Yeah, we'll be right there. Give us ten."

Hanging up the phone, Finley's troubled gaze found Nord's. "There's been a murder."

Something about the way he said it felt off, causing his berserker to stir. Like there was more to it than the untimely appearance of a dead body.

"So why's he calling you? Surely the Brotherhood's got it covered?" Nord asked.

"Well, that's the thing. He wasn't calling me in an official capacity, not at first, anyway. Nord, mate, I don't know how to say this exactly, but . . . up until about sixty seconds ago when I told Nate you were standing right next to me, he believed the corpse was yours."

Nord jerked back as if he'd been slapped, the sound of his blood rushing through his ears.

"In fact, every test they've run so far has only confirmed it. Nate was calling to let me know and ask me to come down and give a formal id."

"How is that even possible? Did they check for a glamour?"

Finley shrugged, looking every bit as concerned as Nord felt. "He didn't say. He just asked us to get down there as soon as possible."

"Right," Nord said, shock making his voice hollow. "I'll just wake up Lina and let her know we're heading out."

"You two should go," Cora interjected. "I'll tell the girls what happened." Nord was about to protest, but she stood and walked over, placing her hand on his arm. "Trust me. She needs her sleep. You're not the only ones in for a long day."

He frowned but eventually nodded his agreement. After the night she had, Lina deserved a few more hours of peace before having to dive back into the deep end. Not to mention the fact that Cora's track record for these things was unparalleled. If she thought Lina needed the rest in order to face what was to come . . . well, who was he to argue against anything that would help keep her safe?

"Have her call me when she wakes up."

"Of course."

Nord and Finley exchanged a look, both silently assessing the other and finding nothing but steely resolve staring back at them. As one, they turned to head for the door.

"Berserker—"

Nord glanced back over his shoulder, adrenaline already surging in preparation for whatever new bomb the Satori matriarch was about to drop.

"Don't forget to check the pockets."

CHAPTER 16

LINA

She woke with the disorientation of one who'd been asleep far longer than they should have. Rubbing her eyes, Lina sat up and eyed the sunlight streaming in the windows with suspicion.

Something was off. She couldn't put her finger on what exactly, but something was definitely different. Lifting the heavy mass of hair off her neck and tying it up in a bun, Lina took in the empty room and realized what it was.

This was the first time she'd woken up without Nord by her side since they'd started sleeping—and more than sleeping—together. Even when he'd wake up early to work out, he always made a point to invite her to join him or climb back into bed with her after his shower.

Lina frowned and ran her palm over his side of the bed, her unease ratcheting up when she found the sheets cool.

Why didn't he wake me?

Nervous flutters filled her stomach as she slid her legs out from under the blanket. As she pulled on a pair of discarded sweats and one of his shirts, a second source of her off-centered feelings registered.

The spot beside her heart felt hollow. Quiet.

She pressed a hand against her chest, the emptiness causing her to ache. Since the Transference, she'd felt Nord's presence there, a constant reminder of their soul-deep connection to one another. The unexpected loss of it robbed her of breath.

Before she gave in to the panic and did something stupid like slide into the bloodlust and run off on a full-blown rampage, Lina forced herself to stop and really focus. He couldn't just be gone.

Drawing in a deep lungful of air, she focused hard on the place he should have been, sending her consciousness down as deeply as she could.

Her knees just about gave out when she found the faint flutter. He was still there, but far away.

Lina's eyes snapped open, her anger surging now that she knew the worst hadn't come to pass.

"Where the fuck are you?" she snarled, her voice taking on the animalistic growl of her berserker. "And why did you sneak off without saying goodbye?"

Storming out of the room, Lina instinctively headed in the direction of what she assumed would be a source of answers: Finley. She slammed open the door of his office, ready to tear into him, but came up empty.

"They're not here, sweetie," Cora called unhelpfully from the living room.

"I can see that," Lina gritted out, anxiety sending her fury spiking. Since Cora obviously knew what was going on, she stomped down the last of the hallway to join her.

If she'd been more human and less seething war-beast, Lina might have appreciated how well Cora looked, curled up in one of Fin's armchairs with a book open in her lap.

"Morning, sunshine!" she chirped.

"What's going on?" Lina demanded. "Where are they?"

"They're fine," Cora insisted. "Now come sit down and relax. You look like you're about three seconds away from throwing furniture."

"That's funny; I feel about one second away."

Cora snickered. "Be that as it may. No need to start smashing things."

"Nord—"

"Is perfectly fine, I promise. Now *sit*. Breathe. Rein in the beast or whatever it is you need to do to get yourself together," she interjected with a dismissive wave of her hand.

After a beat, Lina begrudgingly sat. "You do know this isn't your house, right? And that you probably shouldn't make it a habit to boss around a berserker. I have it on good authority that rarely goes over well."

Cora lifted a mocking brow. "And yet you listened just fine."

"Yeah, well . . . I'm still learning how to embrace my inner alpha. You might not be as lucky next time."

"I have a feeling I'll be just fine."

Lina shook her head, not feeling remotely steady enough to perform the mental gymnastics required for a conversation with Cora right now. "Will you please just tell me what's going on?"

Quinn chose that moment to join them. "What's going on with what?" Then she glanced around. "Where are Tweedledee and Tweedledum?"

"I think you mean Tweedle B," Lina said with a snort, unable to help herself.

Quinn snickered as she crossed the room to sit beside her mother. "How are you feeling?"

Cora tipped her cheek up for a quick kiss and said, "I've survived worse."

"Mama—"

Cora shook her head, cutting off whatever Quinn was about to say. "Not now, mon coeur. Our dear Evalina has already made it clear that the furniture is on borrowed time."

"What the hell were you two talking about before I got here?" Quinn asked, sitting back with a puzzled frown.

Unsure how to explain what happened to someone unfamiliar with both the side effects of the Transference and a berserker's quicksilver temper, Lina gave them a helpless shrug. "I woke up alone and sort of . . ."

"Hulked out?" Quinn suggested.

Lina bobbed her head. "I wouldn't go that far, but it was a close call." She rubbed at her chest, still feeling the heavy ache that signaled Nord's absence.

The Satori women were too astute to miss the gesture and looked at her expectantly.

She blew out a breath and tried to give them the truth as best she could with her own limited understanding. "Nord and I haven't really been far apart since the Transference, so I hadn't noticed it before, but when I woke up this morning and he was gone . . . it felt like someone had scooped out a part of my heart and left my chest carved open and bleeding. It caught me off guard, and I guess the unexpected physical consequence of the separation triggered my berserker."

Frowning, Quinn asked, "What about when Crombie took you? You didn't notice it then."

Lina bit down on her bottom lip and shook her head. "No. But his stupid flowers were playing all sorts of tricks with my emotions, so I could have but just didn't realize it."

Quinn didn't look convinced. "Have you heard of anything like this before?" she asked her mom.

Cora was slow to respond. "No, but then, information pertaining to the ritual is scarce as it is. On top of that, our Lina is the first Animagi-turned-berserker in existence. That's bound to provide its own set of unique challenges." She peered intently at Lina. "How are you feeling now?"

Lina pressed her hand over her heart, noting its hollow throb beneath her palm. "Empty?" She shook her head. That wasn't quite right. "It just feels . . . wrong."

"I suppose that's to be expected," Cora said, releasing a heavy sigh. "Your very energies are linked and now draw from each other. It only seems fitting that one half would react to the absence of the other."

"Nord did lose his absolute shit when you were taken. Fin and I chalked it up to his rage at the time, but perhaps there was more at play than that," Quinn said, her voice considering. "Maybe after a while it will go away or at least tone down?"

"The Transference isn't like a bad dye job, Quinn," Cora said with a snort. "If anything, I expect the bond will only strengthen with time."

"Well, I'm working with limited information. Sue me."

Lina hoped Quinn was right. It was going to be damned inconvenient if every time one of them had to go somewhere without the other, it felt like her chest had been excavated by a rusty melon baller. Knowing the Codex was likely the only source of actual answers, Lina made a mental note to resume her studies of Alistair's translation. For now, she'd settle for the truth about where the hell Nord had run off to.

"We can figure all that out later," Lina said. "Tell me where he is, Cora. Please."

Whether it was in response to the thinly veiled desperation in her voice or her plea, Lina couldn't say, but Cora didn't hesitate to answer.

"A Guardian called earlier this morning to request their help with a murder investigation."

Lina's eyes narrowed. "But Nord isn't part of the Brotherhood anymore. Why would they ask for his help?"

Cora held Lina's gaze, almost as if bracing her for what she was about to say next. "The body was made to look like Nord's."

"Who would do such a—" Before the question was out, Lina already knew the answer.

Mikel. This had his name written all over it.

Icy fingers crawled down her spine, even as her blood began to boil. She jumped out of her seat. "That son of a bitch."

"Where do you think you're going?" Quinn asked, crossing her arms as she stared Lina down.

The berserker was demanding blood, but the still logical part of her brain knew she couldn't just walk up to Mikel and shank him. No matter how badly she wanted to.

Lina sighed and forced herself to sit back down. "We can't let him get away with this. First Alistair, then Cora, and now whatever twisted magic he used to make it look like he got Nord. He's a fucking psychopath, just like his son."

Cora nodded her agreement, though her voice was wooden as she said, "The apple never did fall far from the tree in that house."

"You both know he's just going to keep escalating things until he forces our hand. How long before he says, 'fuck the covenant,' and just comes after me directly?"

"He wouldn't do that," Cora said with a quick shake of her head. "He cares about the power the Council provides too much to risk blatantly disregarding its rules. When he strikes, it will be well-thought-out and completely underhanded, but technically aboveboard."

Lina swallowed a growl, hating that Cora was right. As per usual.

"Well, we have to do something," Lina insisted. "How many more people have to die before he's forced to answer for his sins?"

"I've been asking myself the same thing for years. You're not the only one who has to bide her time, Lina. We've all been forced to wait until all the pieces were in place. But, now that you've returned, I think we finally have the weapon we need to take him out for good."

The pain in Cora's eyes damn near broke Lina's heart. Alistair's death was far from Mikel's first. The pile of bodies that butcher was responsible for would easily span an entire continent. And among its countless victims would be Cora's husband James—executed for treason he didn't commit. All because he dared to stand up to the man who coveted his wife.

Quinn took her mother's hand, gripping it in her own.

The Satori women never spoke about James. Lina knew it wasn't lack of love that fueled their silence, but rather an abundance of it. Some losses you simply never recovered from.

"So where do we start?" Quinn asked.

"By ridding me of Crombie's stupid bond."

"When do you want to go to the vault?"

"Right now."

Quinn blinked. "Lina, Nico still has the Cuska key."

"Right, so give me yours," she said, standing once more and holding out her palm.

Quinn shot her mother a worried look. "I don't feel comfortable leaving her alone after last night."

"I'm not asking you to. You stay here with your mom while I go grab Crombie's heirloom. With only one key between us, it's not like we can both go anyway."

"But . . ."

"We already talked about this, Quinn. Alone or not, Mobius land is the safest place for me. Your mom just said Mikel won't break the rules to come after me directly. If I leave now, I may even get back before the others."

Indecision warred in Quinn's eyes, but eventually she nodded. "Fine. But when Nord finds out, I'm telling him you stole it from me. I want nothing to do with the temper tantrum that's sure to follow."

Lina laughed. "Fine. I'll make sure the blame lies solely at my feet."

"I hate this, and you for making me agree to it. You know that, right?"

Lina nodded, her smile soft and tinged with affection. "I know."

Sighing heavily, Quinn stood and pulled a long gold chain out from beneath her shirt, a crooked letter M dangling from the bottom. Pulling it up and over her neck, she slapped it into the center of

Lina's palm and then gripped her hand tight enough to bruise, forcing Lina's gaze to meet hers.

"Lina, I swear to God, if you do anything stupid, Nord and Mikel aren't the ones you're going to have to worry about. I've already stitched your soul back into your body once. Do. Not. Make me do it again." Quinn's voice was severe but thick with emotion.

Blinking back tears, Lina threw her free arm around Quinn, embracing her tightly. "I won't."

Cora caught Lina's eye from over her daughter's shoulder.

"Be careful," she mouthed, her expression grim and her eyes haunted.

It wasn't until later, when it was already far too late for her to ask, that Lina wondered why Cora felt the need to offer her final warning.

CHAPTER 17
LINA

There was one, or perhaps twenty, things wrong with this plan. Not the least of which was the part where Lina had never actually been to the vault. She knew where it was, but only in the vague, theoretical sense of someone who knew the North Pole was up. She had the name of a place and a general direction. Which is all to say, what she knew was not exactly helpful.

Thankfully, Mobius territory wasn't nearly as vast as the entirety of the Arctic Circle, so her chances of ending up at the vault were high. The real issue was whether or not she'd find what she was looking for before someone noticed her snooping around.

She wasn't a fan of her odds.

Then again, her odds had been pretty shit in general recently, but she'd made it this far *and* found her soulmate. As far as she was concerned, she wasn't just beating the odds, she was killing the game. So why stop now?

Lina laughed at her false bravado. The truth was, she was shaking in her goddamn murder boots.

When she'd left the penthouse earlier, insisting this was a task she could complete all by herself, she never imagined she'd end up *here.* How could she have known that Briar Hill was not the name of a park, like she'd so naively assumed, but a cemetery?

A. Fucking. Cemetery.

Who in their right mind hid the entrance to a super-secret collection of ancient magical relics in the middle of a graveyard?

Her demented ancestors, that's who.

She supposed it made a certain sort of sense in a macabre way. It's not like what was left of the decaying remains were going to rise up and rob them blind. Or spread their secrets. And most sane people tended to stay away from the resting place of the dead, either due to respect, superstition, or just a general sense of ick. Whatever the excuse, the living were no more likely to stumble across the entrance to the Council's vault than their dearly departed. The explanation did little to make Lina feel better in this moment, though.

Shudders of apprehension worked their way down her spine as she eyed the wrought-iron fence housing the countless tombs and mausoleums. Sending an ex-ghost who'd been buried alive to a graveyard had to rank high on the list of cruel and unusual punishments. Surely this was some kind of sick cosmic joke.

She hadn't given much thought to that part of her past life since Alistair and Quinn explained their motives, but it was pretty fucking hard to ignore it now. Just the possibility of falling into an open grave and ending up buried a second time had her feet rooted to the uneven sidewalk. Already she could taste the dirt in her mouth and feel the damp soil caking beneath her nails.

Rationally, Lina knew that wasn't likely to happen. It was the middle of the afternoon, and while overcast, there was more than enough light for her to watch where she was going. Plus, she'd see and hear anyone who tried to sneak up on her.

But trauma wasn't rational. You try explaining to someone who'd already survived the impossible that it wouldn't happen a second time. It should never have happened in the first place, so what was stopping it from happening again?

Lina squeezed her eyes shut and took deep, heaving breaths. Her berserker surged to the surface in response to her panic, infusing her with its strength.

You can do this.

You have *to do this.*

Feeling marginally better, she forced out an exhale and opened her eyes.

Right, Lina. Just get it over with. The faster you find the entrance and get what you came for, the sooner you can leave. In and out, just like you promised the others.

She slipped her hand into her pocket and gripped the chain with its embellished M. All she had to do was find the door to the vault. Easy. She didn't know what she was looking for specifically: a traditional lock, some sort of etching she'd fit the metal letter into, or something else entirely. But she was confident she'd recognize it once she saw it.

On the count of three.

As she counted down, she forced herself to relax, shaking out her tense limbs and willing her body to move. The first step was the hardest, but soon she was passing beneath the arched sign and walking across the pressed earth of the cemetery's main grounds.

It was quiet this far out of town. Tomb-like, even.

She snickered at her morbid joke, the laughter helping chase away more of her unease.

All right, genius. You got yourself into this mess. Which way now?

Casting her eyes around, Lina searched for an obvious answer. There were no paths or signs. Nothing to indicate Briar Hill was anything other than what it appeared. Row upon row of tombs stretched in every direction, with mausoleums peppered throughout. There was nothing for it; she was going to have to walk up and down each one until she found the unknown thing she was searching for.

Lina let out an aggrieved sigh.

In for a penny . . .

Turning right, she walked all the way down until she hit the last row and then began the tedious process of scanning each and every marker. It was fascinating in its own way, seeing what families chose to mark the lives of their loved ones. Some of the graves were all but forgotten, their tombstones crumbling and illegible. Others were well maintained with fresh flowers despite the passage of time.

To help pass time and force herself not to skip over anything, Lina made up a nonsensical chant in her head for each name she passed.

Ernest Kline was mighty fine.

Lisette Reeves hung out with thieves.

The rhymes had nothing to do with anything, but they kept her focused, which was what mattered. She had just started down row number five and was searching for a word to pair with Sinclair when one of the names carved into a marble façade made her do a double take.

Marcus Croft.

M. C.

Taking a few steps back, Lina turned and studied the crypt's edifice more carefully. There was nothing screaming 'Mobius Council' at her besides the initials, but she couldn't ignore the feeling in her gut telling her to look closer.

Glancing around to make sure she was still alone, Lina took a tentative step forward, inspecting what at first glance seemed to be random scrollwork around a banner containing the name Croft. Her second glance confirmed it really was just a bunch of random squiggles.

Lina blew out a frustrated breath, about to give up and carry on with her rhyming when something shimmered in the corner of her eye. Her head snapped up and to the left, homing in on the area.

There.

Concealed just under the slanted overhang was a crooked letter M, a perfect twin to the one in her pocket.

Yes. Yes. Yes! I knew it.

With nervous energy buzzing beneath her skin and her heartbeat racing in her ears, Lina pulled the Satori key out. Holding the necklace up, so the M swung with her movements, she moved closer to the mark, thinking to press the pendant against the marble. Before she could, there was a crack in the air, like something breaking free, and then the ground trembled beneath her feet.

She staggered, throwing an arm out to help steady herself when the shaking stopped just as suddenly as it had begun.

"What in the ever-loving-fuck . . ."

The space where there had just been a marble slab closing off the crypt was now wide open and pitch-black.

Lina nervously licked her lips. "You've got to be kidding me. I've got to go in there?"

There was no response. Thank God. She might have pissed herself if some phantom voice deigned to answer.

Still clutching the necklace, Lina took a bracing breath and made for the opening.

"Crombie, you better fucking hope I don't get my hands on you because I am so going to kill you for making me do this."

The anger helped. It burned away the nerves and gave her something else to focus on as she moved into the darkness. For a second, all that existed was the sound of her uneven breaths. Then a feeling like cobwebs brushing over every part of her body. Lina was torn between screaming, sobbing, and running the fuck away, but the sensation passed quickly. She was about to say screw it all when a torch blazed to life beside her, revealing a set of surprisingly clean stairs that led deeper down into the darkness.

She closed her eyes and swallowed, silently damning Crombie to hell with every heartbeat.

At least I have a light source.

Thinking it was probably best to keep the necklace out in the open, Lina tucked it over her head before reaching for the torch and starting her descent. She needn't have grabbed it. Every few stairs, a new one would blaze to life, lighting her way.

By the time she reached the bottom, her legs were shaky, her palms slick with sweat, and her throat raw from sucking down breath after breath in a desperate attempt to stay calm. Knowing she was inside a crypt and that the earth pressed in on all sides was really doing a number on her mind. It wasn't exactly being buried alive, but it was far too close for comfort.

Seeing the steel door just ahead and the tiled floor with its mosaic M and intersecting C helped. It reminded her of her purpose, and that on the other side of that door was the object that would free her from her bloodsworn vow.

Almost there. Not much farther until you're home free.

Unsure what to do with the torch she still held, Lina used her magic to extinguish it and tossed the unlit stave onto the ground for someone else to deal with. She crossed the floor, the steel door soundlessly sliding open as soon as she hit the center of the mosaic. It was only a matter of four steps after that until she was standing inside the vault.

Crossing the threshold was akin to entering a new world. The ceiling soared, the air within cool but sweet, and the light warm and welcoming. The main room was an octagon, five of the eight walls lined with shelves and display cases. Two branched off into new sections, and one was the exit behind her. It was not at all what she'd expected. It felt more like a fancy library than a storage facility.

With no real method to her madness, Lina picked a direction and tried to make sense of the organization. She'd skimmed two shelves, an egg-shaped crystal catching her attention when a darkly seductive voice crooned, "Well, well, well. Look at you."

Lina bit off a strangled scream, spinning around and sending the crystal clattering across the floor.

"You," she snarled, her anger rising hard and fast.

"Now don't go getting your panties in a twist," Crombie said with a sigh as he laid a hand over his heart and added, "I'm merely here to offer my assistance."

The move drew attention to the very un-Crombie outfit he was wearing. He looked every inch the broody, dangerous rock star in his black jeans and vintage tee. Lina couldn't help but roll her eyes when she noticed the all-too-familiar A and U scrawled across the front of it.

Cocky bastard. Who else would have the balls to parade the item they stole in front of its owner? Or alleged owner, in her case.

"How did you even get here, Crombie? You're not supposed to be in here. *No one* is supposed to be in here. Do you have any idea how many alarms you might have triggered?"

He gave her a smile that could have melted panties everywhere. Luckily for Lina, she was too busy dismembering him in her mind to pay much attention to it.

"Sweetheart, have you already forgotten? I can find and join you anywhere."

"Not for much longer."

"Yes, well, all good things must come to an end."

"You don't have your floral insurance policy to protect you this time, Crombie. As soon as this contract between us is complete, I'm coming for you."

Crombie's smile stretched, her threat not remotely fazing him. "I look forward to it."

"You wouldn't say that if you know what I have in mind."

He leaned forward and dropped his voice, dark hair slipping into his eyes as he peered at her. "Who says I don't?"

Lina growled, her nails cutting into her palms as she clenched her fists. The display of temper only caused Crombie to laugh like she was some adorably misbehaving puppy. She wanted to kill him. Rip his throat out with her teeth and see how cute he thought she was then.

"So much anger, Lina," Crombie breathed, his stormy eyes sparkling as he continued to taunt her. "You know what a great outlet for all that pent-up frustration is?"

"Crushing your dick in my hand?"

He winced and adjusted himself. "Well, that's not exactly what I was going to suggest, but you've got one of the appendages right."

It took everything in her to push the fury down. Raging out right now would only end up with her kicking her own ass. Stupid vow.

"You shouldn't be here, Crombie."

"I'm not leaving without what I was promised. So I guess you should stop flirting with me and find my treasure then, shouldn't you, sweetheart?"

"You're deluded," Lina said with an incredulous laugh. "I'm not *flirting* with you. It's taking everything in me not to kill you."

He waved a dismissive hand. "Call it what you want. I recognize foreplay when it's aimed in my direction."

"You're sick, you know that? Totally depraved."

Crombie's eyes were twinkling with laughter. He was having far too much fun baiting her. "Darling, that might be the sweetest thing you've ever said to me. It's like you truly see me. What a rare gift."

Lina shook her head, sending her hair flying as her fury spiked to dangerous levels. "Let's get one thing very clear, *darling*. You so much as breathe on me right now, and bloodsworn or not, I will unleash every ounce of this anger pumping through me on every single bone in your body. Do you hear me? I will *ruin* you."

"Lady above, it makes me hard when you talk like that. Can you say it again, but slower this time? Really enunciate it."

A scream ripped from her throat, and Lina lashed out, needing to find some sort of outlet for the molten fury surging through her veins. Her fist collided with one of the shelves and sent its various items flying. She was too far gone to care that she might have just destroyed centuries-old relics. That wasn't surprising, considering she was also too far gone to remember there was nothing stopping her from kicking his ass with her magic. But consumed as she was by her rage, the urge to tear him apart with her hands, to do it slowly, to make it *hurt*, was the only instinct driving her.

Her chest heaved as a trail of blood began to drip down the side of her palm. She eyed the sliver of glass poking out with a blessed numbness. She was still on the cusp of the bloodlust, but the small act of violence brought with it a momentary relief that allowed her to remain on this side of it.

For now, anyway.

She was hardly the poster child for control. If Crombie didn't shut his fucking mouth, there was no telling what would happen.

"Allow me," he murmured, his gaze zeroed in on the place where she was bleeding. He pulled the shard free before she even processed what he was doing. His mouth feathered over her injury a second before his tongue darted out and licked away the trickle of blood. "There. All better."

Just like the last time, the feel of his mouth on her skin sent unwanted tingles of pleasure zinging through her. Combined with his sensual croon, she was helpless again, the heat pooling low in her belly. She didn't want to feel these things, not from him. He wasn't the one her body belonged to.

Lina shoved him off with every bit of her strength. Crombie flew back into the nearest wall, sending even more of the irreplaceable items tumbling to the floor.

Completely unfazed, he brushed off his shirt and pushed himself away from the now broken shelves. "Is that all you've got?"

"Crombie," she growled through gritted teeth as her body shook with the need to tackle him and then repeatedly drive her fists into his perfect face.

A distant part of her brain, the only part not begging her to end him, reminded Lina that he was her friend. Kind of. Maybe. Actually, he'd been a pretty shit friend, come to think of it. But he had helped her when he had no reason to, and that should count for something.

Unfortunately for him, he'd screwed her over so many times, all her berserker could see when she looked at him was an enemy. The bloodthirsty beast wasn't feeling particularly inclined to forgive him. Especially after the way he'd silenced her last time. As far as she was concerned, Crombie might as well have been walking around with a flashing red sign over his head screaming, 'kill me now.'

He must have finally realized he'd pushed her too far, because his expression turned considering.

"You really are something, you know that?" He laughed. "I'm starting to believe that given the chance, you might actually be able to make good on your threats. Hell, I might even let you try just to see you in action."

"Compliments won't save you, Crombie."

"Oh? What about if I offer you the key to your freedom?"

"I'm listening." It was quite possibly the only thing he could have said that she'd actually be inclined to listen to.

"I can sense when I'm near fae objects of power. The item we seek is right through there." He pointed behind her to the space branching off from the main room.

"You couldn't have led with that?"

Crombie shrugged. "Got to get my kicks where I can, and I do love these chats of ours."

"I might actually hate you."

"Lie," he said with a smirk.

"Just lead the way, asshole."

He winked at her and made a point to brush her arm as he walked by. A snarl slipped free as she spun on her heel to follow him, her eyes landing on the autographed names on the back of his T-shirt.

"And I want my T-shirt back."

Crombie glanced at her over his shoulder. "Noticed that, did you?"

Lina's eyes narrowed. "Wasn't that the point of you wearing it?"

His shoulders shook with laughter.

"I mean it. That doesn't belong to you. I want it back."

As they moved into the next room, Crombie gave her a blatantly suggestive look. "What, now? Do you really want me to undress for you right here, Lina? Naughty girl." His hands moved to the hem of the shirt and lifted.

Her hand shot out and grasped his wrist, stopping him before he could reveal more than a sliver of skin. Surprisingly toned and tanned skin.

"Knock it off, Crombie."

He huffed. "Well, which is it? Do make up your mind and let me know. I'm only trying to be accommodating."

"Just show me where your trinkets are so we can end this," she groaned, pressing the heels of her hands into her eye sockets.

"As you wish."

When she dropped her arms, he was halfway across a room that was organized in the same fashion as the one they'd just left.

"It should be on one of these shelves," he said as she reached him, his eyes already scanning and discarding the items in front of him. "They're all faerie made."

Lina nodded to indicate she'd heard him and initiated her own search. Her fingers itched to stroke the beautiful objects. Tiaras, scepters, glittering jewels. They all called to her with their breathtaking beauty. But faerie things were notoriously dangerous. She didn't dare touch something when it could be a weapon in disguise, luring her into a false sense of security only to strike as soon as she made contact.

"Ahh, there you are," Crombie breathed beside her, his voice taking on a reverent note. "Come to daddy."

The whispered expression evoked all sorts of inappropriate images in her mind. Ones featuring a certain Viking and a nearly endless series of possibilities. None of which required clothing. Lina was making a mental note to test each one of them out as soon as she got home when a niggling in the back of her mind pulled her firmly back to the present.

She was thankful for her subconscious' sense of self-preservation a second later when Crombie's hovering hands made her recall lesson number one when dealing with the fae: when it comes to making deals, the details matter.

"Wait," Lina said, earning herself an arch look. "Don't *I* have to be the one to give them to you to complete our contract and nullify the vow?"

His grin was one hundred percent unrepentant sinner. "Aren't you a clever one? Most people fail to consider the loopholes."

The simmering anger, which had subsided in response to the promise of freedom, came surging back to the surface. "I can't believe you were going to trick me. Again."

He shrugged. "It's in my nature. A fae could no more resist the impulse to ensnare the unsuspecting than a berserker could their need for violence. Besides, this bond of ours is fun. Is it not?"

"Fun isn't exactly the word I would choose, no."

Crombie made a show of lifting his hands up and stepping away from the case. "Remember this moment when you try to hate me later. I could have taken it, but I didn't. I'm nothing if not a man of my word."

"You don't get to earn brownie points, Crombie. You lost that privilege."

He lifted his shoulders. "Can't blame me for trying."

"Yes, I can. I can blame you for lots of things."

He rolled his eyes. "For someone who wants her freedom so badly, you're taking an awfully long time to reclaim it."

Lina's jaw clenched, her teeth grinding together painfully as she turned her attention back to the shelf Crombie had been so interested in. She spotted the Night Court heirlooms instantly, the gems in the pendant and ring looking as if they'd been crafted from the very stars themselves.

Her breath caught; she'd never seen anything more achingly beautiful in her life. She hesitated only a second longer before scooping them both up in her hand. Power radiated out of them, practically burning her with the sheer amount of it. She had no idea what these items could do, but she was willing to bet it wasn't insignificant.

She could feel—and understand—the coiled need emanating from Crombie. He wanted these back. *Badly.* As much as he wanted them, she wanted to keep them, and that scared her. It was hard to force her hand open and offer the priceless treasures to him, but she managed.

Crombie's hand immediately sealed over them, his eyes squeezing shut as a shudder racked his entire body.

Lina didn't understand his reaction. She was expecting joy or triumph, vindication even, but not whatever this was. He looked tormented.

"Crombie?"

His eyes flew open, the silver depths unreadable.

"Are you okay?"

Before he could answer, a sound coming from the other room sent both their heads snapping back in that direction.

Shit, shit, shit. She'd known his presence here would set off some alarms. She just hadn't expected anybody to get here so fast to investigate. Briar Hill was at least thirty minutes out of town, and he'd been here what, ten, fifteen at most?

She was so focused on what was happening in the other room that she didn't notice Crombie had moved and slid something over her head until its cool weight settled beneath the hollow of her throat.

Brushing his lips against her cheek, he whispered a rushed, "Sorry about this, sweetheart."

"Wh—"

She didn't even get the word out before he vanished, leaving her all alone to face whoever waited for her out there.

Fucking prick.

Lina was so off-kilter by the unexpected series of events, she was still standing frozen in front of the case of faerie relics when a familiar blond head stepped into the room.

Nico's eyes widened with delight, making him look like a cat with a bird trapped beneath its paw. "Cousin, what an unexpected surprise."

His presence here sent her berserker shrieking with rage. "What are you doing, Nico? The vault is for Ascended Heirs only."

"You see, I should be asking you that." He held out the Cuska key with the tip of his finger, its dangling M glinting in the light. "Seeing as how I'm still in possession of the family key, that could only mean you've stolen one. It's you, cousin, who would seem to be here illegally."

Lina scoffed, but tiny sparks of unease were shooting off inside of her. As far as technicalities went, it was a pretty bullshit one, but it was exactly the sort of thing Mikel would build a case on.

Pocketing the key, Nico jerked his thumb back into the main room. "What happened in there, by the way?"

Fuck. She'd intended on fixing the mess before she left, but that was out of the question now.

He pulled a face, shaking his head and tutting softly. "Destroying Council property on your second day back. That's not a good look, cousin. In fact, I'd say it's downright suspicious."

Now Lina was truly panicking. Her heart raced in her chest, her pulse fluttering wildly in her throat. She was short on options here. She could try diplomacy, or she could fight. As Mikel's puppet, hurting Nico was going to come back to haunt her. And with the list of offenses both men already had against her right now, she couldn't afford to add any others. It was going to be hard enough to talk her way out of this as it was.

"Nico, listen—"

"No, cousin," he sneered, "you listen. I knew you were up to something, you fucking traitor."

Lina's eyes went wide as Nico stalked forward and slammed a pair of magic nullifying cuffs on her wrists.

His eyes darkened with hate as he leaned down to whisper, "I can't wait to watch you burn."

CHAPTER 18

FINLEY

Death was a cruel mistress. Appearing without warning. Sinking her poison-tipped claws into your chest and tearing out your heart. Haunting your dreams with memories of all those she'd lured into her eternal slumber.

Destroying your sanity over, and over, and over.

Despite his, dare he say, intimate relationship with the merciless lady, Finley was far from immune to her. He'd buried many friends over the centuries. It came with the territory when you were in his line of work. And yet, he couldn't recall any that cut quite like this one. Even if it was fake.

As horrific as it was, Finley forced himself not to look away. To memorize each and every terrifying detail. He needed to see this. To let the warning sink deep into his bones. Because if they failed, Nord wasn't the only one facing this eventuality. They all were. And he could not let those monsters get their hands on Quinn.

It was all too easy to picture her in Nord's place, especially after holding Cora's broken body in his arms. Cora, who looked so like her daughter that Finley had felt the world drop out from under him for one terrifying, unforgettable moment. He didn't think he'd survive the reality. Not whole, anyway. Not in the ways that mattered.

"I'm sure now you can appreciate our mistake," Nate said under his breath.

Finley gave a tight nod.

"Any explanation as to how this is possible?" Nate asked.

"Misdirection and magic," Nord replied tersely, his expression understandably grim as he stared at what could only be described as his corpse.

Finley didn't even want to begin to try to understand the level of mindfuckery he was dealing with. It was hard enough for him to see his friend's brutalized body. He couldn't imagine how he'd react if presented with his own.

Nate's brows furrowed. "We would have picked up magical traces."

Nord's gaze cut to the Guardian's, his eyes glacial. "Not this kind of magic."

"Impossible," he scoffed.

"And yet here we are."

Finley stepped in, already following Nord's train of thought. "There's a group of Animagi gifted in reality shaping. What they will, their power manifests into being. For all intents and purposes, this body *is* real, not magical."

To Nord, Finley asked, *"Do you really think Nico is capable of magic this advanced?"*

"Well, it sure as fuck wasn't Lina," he growled.

"No one is accusing Lina," Nate said with a confused laugh, glancing between them with a puzzled lift of his brow.

"Looks like the rumors regarding his lack of ability were purposely exaggerated."

Misdirection and magic. Just like Cora had said.

Nord grunted, which Nate took as taciturn acceptance of his comment.

A chill swept down Finley's spine as another thought occurred to him. *"Mikel's been playing the long game, hiding his secret weapon until the time was right. Fooling not just us, but the Council as well. The bastard's finally ready to make his move."*

Which meant this was just the opening salvo of whatever nefarious plan he was about to unveil. This wasn't about taking a pot shot at Nord. Or not *just* about that. He wanted them looking over here while he was busy elsewhere.

Misdirection and magic.

Fuck.

"So what does it mean? Why target you?" Nate asked.

"It's a warning," Nord replied, his jaw clenching as he battled back his rage.

Finley recognized the signs. The berserker was about to slip its leash.

"Care to elaborate?" Nate asked.

"No."

Nate crossed his arms. "Well, whatever you're involved in, it's spilling into the streets. Get it under control and soon. The Brotherhood isn't going to tolerate a spree of inexplicable murders, and I'm pretty sure the last thing you two want is a bunch of Guardians crawling up your asses." He gave Finley a pointed look. "Again."

"We're working on it," Finley assured him.

"Anyone check the pockets?" Nord asked.

"Yeah, they were empty. Why?"

Nord frowned. "Mind if I take a look?"

"By all means," Nate said, gesturing at the body. As Nord moved away, Nate lowered his voice, "Sure gives new meaning to the expression 'over my dead body,' eh, mate?"

Finley forced a smile he didn't feel. There was nothing amusing about what Nico—or more likely Mikel via Nico—had done to Nord's twin. It was a warning, all right. Not only about what they had planned for him, but about the sadistic pleasure they'd taken inflicting those wounds.

"Found something," Nord called, letting the corpse's jacket fall closed as he held up a bloodied slip of paper he'd fished out of its interior pocket.

"What is it?" Finley asked, as the other part of Cora's warning echoed in his mind.

By way of answer, Nord held out the picture of Lina. It was a close-up of her face. She was clearly frightened, with her head canted up and to the side as if searching for someone. There were two bloody Xs, one over each of her eyes.

Photographs and phone calls.

As if on cue, Finley's phone rang. Adrenaline shot through him, his heart pounding like it sought to escape the confines of his chest as he read the name on its display. He answered immediately, saying her name before the phone reached his ear.

"Quinn? What's wrong?"

"It's a testament to the sorry state of affairs our lives have become that you automatically assume the worst."

Finley's chest loosened. "Sorry, I—"

"Oh, no," she interrupted with a laugh that bordered on hysterical. "Don't get me wrong, you were absolutely right. Just making an observation."

Her forced casualness did nothing to mask the undercurrent of fear in her voice. The heavy weight in his chest returned with devastating intensity, turning his voice to steel as he bit out, "Start talking."

"Are you far enough away from the big guy to talk freely? It's about Lina."

Finley's gaze cut to where Nord crouched less than a foot away, close enough for him to notice only a sliver of icy blue ringed the Viking's pupils. He turned, giving Nord and the other Guardian his back. "Yes."

Nord's hand was wrapped around his forearm, pulling him back before Finley had a chance to step away. "Speaker. Now."

Finley read the barely restrained violence in the berserker's expression and complied.

"What happened?" Nord demanded.

Quinn's muttered curses filled the air. There was a sound in the background, and Quinn snapped, "Hey asshole, did I say you could come in?"

Nord took the phone from his hand and growled, "Who's there?"

"Nord . . . don't freak out . . ."

"It's a little fucking late for that."

Quinn blew out a heavy breath. "As you probably heard, we've got company. And, um, Lina's in trouble."

"We'll be right there," Finley said, already at work on summoning the portal that would bring them home.

"Hey! You can't just steal evidence," Nate shouted after Nord as he disappeared into the shimmering air. "Where are you two going?"

"To get things under control," Finley replied as he followed close behind, leaving Nate and the mystery of Nord's dead body behind them.

He was prepared for the worst when his feet hit the polished marble of the penthouse's entryway. What he hadn't expected to find was the prowling fae prince with a pissed-off Quinn glaring at him from the doorway. Though, with the way Crombie always seemed to squirm his way into the middle of things, maybe he shouldn't be so surprised.

"Crombie? What the hell are you doing here? Where's Lina?"

Crombie turned, and Finley spotted a familiar shirt. A *very* familiar shirt. One that had been strangely absent from its place in his closet.

"And what the fuck are you doing wearing my shirt?"

As if choreographed, both Crombie and Quinn's eyes flared wide.

"Your shirt?" Crombie hissed, plucking at the material as if it offended him.

"Oh," Quinn snickered. "Oh, this is *good*. I didn't realize you two were at the stage of your relationship where you were sharing clothes. Does this make him your Robin, Batman?"

Finley tossed her a quelling glare, not that she paid it any mind.

It didn't matter anyway. Nord had Crombie pressed up against the wall with a hand gripping his throat half a second later.

"What have you done?" he snarled, his face crowded close to Crombie's and flushed red with his fury.

Crombie gave Nord a long-suffering look and tapped him on the hand. Nord relaxed his grip the barest fraction of an inch, but it was enough for Crombie to draw in the breath required for his reply.

"*I* didn't do anything. I'm merely here out of the kindness of my heart—"

"Bullshit, you don't have a heart," Nord spat. "The only reason you're still breathing right now is because of the information you hold, so I suggest you get the fuck on with it before I reassess your value to me."

Crombie rolled his eyes. "Everything's all hellfire and brimstone with you, berserker. Can't you give me a little credit for coming here at all? I didn't have to, you know. Not like I'm getting anything out of it."

"No," Nord snarled, looking seconds away from ripping Crombie's throat out.

Crombie apparently thought the same because he finally offered a more straightforward answer. "Lina's little heist drew some unwanted attention."

"No thanks to you," Quinn pointed out.

"Her what?" Nord asked in a dangerously soft voice, his eyes cutting to Quinn. "You let her go to the vault by herself?"

Quinn held up a hand. "Yell at me later, or preferably not at all. It's a little beside the point now anyway, don't you think?"

Nord's glare said he didn't. Finley couldn't blame him. It was the second time in as many days his woman had gone missing. They were lucky he hadn't gone on a full apocalyptic rampage, all things considered.

"How do you even know all this?" Finley asked, sensing there was more to the story than what Crombie was telling them.

When Crombie didn't immediately reply, Nord slammed him into the wall. "Answer. The. Fucking. Question."

The fae prince gave him a look filled with loathing as he replied, "Seeing as how I had a vested interest in her success, I was there for moral support."

"Sure you were," Finley said.

"It was your fucking presence there that got her caught, you festering herpe," Quinn said. "If you hadn't felt so damn helpful all of a sudden, no one would have been any the wiser. But no, you just had to go pop in where you aren't wanted. Like you always do. No wonder you don't have anyone in your life who gives a shit about you. All you seem to be capable of is ruining lives."

Finley bit back an inappropriate laugh, loving how Quinn could eviscerate someone with a mere tongue-lashing. Especially when that someone wasn't him.

That's it, princess. Tear him apart and expose him as the pathetic worm he truly is.

The woman was a master at ferreting out a person's weakness and then wielding it like a finely crafted weapon. No wonder she'd never spent any time learning how to physically defend herself. She could destroy a man with words alone.

Quinn Satori wasn't a princess. She was a fucking queen.

It took Finley a second to recognize the warm glow in his chest as pride. An emotion Crombie did not share.

The fae's eyes flashed, his face going disturbingly blank. "Thank you so much for the reminder, Weaver. I don't know what I was thinking, coming here and assuming Lina's friends might appreciate knowing she was in danger so that they could flock to her rescue."

Quinn took a threatening step forward, her upper lip pulling back in distaste. "If you cared so much, why didn't you stay and help her yourself, you self-absorbed cum-dumpster?"

"Because I couldn't risk getting caught," Crombie snapped, seeming surprised by his own answer.

"So now that you've gotten what you want from Lina, she's disposable?" Nord asked, his voice dripping with icy anger.

"That's not what I said," Crombie protested. "I'm here, aren't I?"

"But you left her there. Alone. At the mercy of men you know will show her *none*," Nord growled, the promise of death shining in his eyes as the hand around Crombie's throat tightened. "She's the only one who's ever spoken on your behalf, and this is how you repay her? How little you value the life of one who has done nothing but offer you kindness and loyalty. You are not fit to lick her boots, let alone breathe the same air as her." Nord's voice dropped until it was little more than a guttural whisper, "*You* are not deserving of breath at all."

His fist tightened until a strangled gasp was torn from Crombie's throat. Despite the pain he surely felt, Crombie jerked his chin up and sneered at Nord, his voice barely more than a labored rasp as he gritted out, "You don't know a fucking thing."

Nord's hand folded closed on empty air as Crombie vanished.

"No!" he roared, his fist punching through the wall and causing the entire thing to shake from the onslaught.

"Save your rage, berserker," Cora said, surprising all of them by stepping around her daughter and joining them in the entryway. "You're going to need it."

CHAPTER 19
NORD

"Mama, I told you to stay inside and let us handle it."

"And so I did," Cora said as she offered her daughter an unrepentant smile and turned her attention back to Nord. "If Mikel or one of his goon squad caught Lina, I know where they will have taken her. I'm assuming you intend to free her?"

Chest still heaving, Nord managed a nod. The single, controlled movement was a feat of massive proportions, considering every cell in his body was screaming at him to start ripping heads from bodies.

"Very well. Listen closely. I have a feeling what I'm about to tell you might just be the difference in whether you're successful tonight."

His heart stuttered as his rage battled momentary panic. "I'm listening."

"Should we take this conversation in—"

A low, primal growl slipped free, a reminder for the others that while he might look human, and as such rational, the predator had broken out of its chains and was now in control.

Finley held up his hands. "Never mind, carry on."

"Mikel will want to do everything by the book. He's likely planning to bring Lina before the Council in the morning to formally petition for her removal, if not outright exile. He'll use her trip to the vault as some sort of proof of her ulterior motives, though I wouldn't put it past him to present additional evidence against her as well. He won't risk a trial he's not sure he'll win."

"Where will he keep her until then?" Nord asked, impressed with how steady his voice sounded despite his tempestuous state.

"Is it safe to even assume it's Mikel who caught her? We weren't there; it could have been anyone," Finley pointed out.

"All roads lead to Mikel," Cora said emphatically. "Whether he personally found her or not, you can bet your ass he's the one calling the shots right now."

Quinn frowned, her teeth biting into her bottom lip. "What other evidence could he possibly have?"

Cora shook her head. "I don't know. We'll have to assume it's significant."

The answer came to him, and Nord ground his teeth together with enough force to crack them. "Mataius."

"Shit," Quinn breathed. "You're right. I thought it odd he wasn't trying to shout that transgression from the rooftops, but it makes sense. He was saving it for when it would have the most impact."

"Lina won't stand a chance if he can prove she was directly involved in the death of another heir," Cora said, her expression tight with worry.

"She wasn't," Nord said. "Mataius' blood is on my hands."

Cora's eyes softened. "It doesn't matter. You are irrevocably tied to her. Guilty or not, Lina may as well have held the blade in the eyes of the Council. Loyalty has always been paramount to the Animagi. To turn against one of our own is the highest offense."

Quinn laughed bitterly while Finley shook his head.

Nord forced out a breath as his vision tinged red at the edges. While he hadn't been foolish enough to believe that the distinction would actually matter to Mikel, he'd hoped the rest of the Council might be swayed by it. But Cora's quiet insistence snuffed that tiny spark right out.

"How twisted is that?" Quinn asked, disgust etched in every line of her face. "Mikel and his merry band of asshats can literally get away with murder because they hide behind the law, and yet in the same breath, he's actively hunting and plotting against the people he's supposed to protect. How the hell are we supposed to win when he's untouchable?"

"We don't give him the opportunity to call the shots," Finley stated firmly. "We find Lina tonight and get her out of there before he can hold his sham trial. Then we work on exposing his crimes and use the laws he loves so much against him."

Quinn tipped her head to the side and pursed her lips. "I can't decide if it's sweet or tragic you actually believe that will work."

Finley's brows dipped low. "If he's going to preach about the importance of upholding your justice system, then he's as beholden to it as anyone else."

She rolled her eyes and leaned back against the wall. "Because history has proven that's exactly what happens when the misdeeds of powerful men are brought to light. Do I need to remind you how things went down with the Director?"

Nord heard the conversation happening around him, but the words and their meaning were drowned out by the endless roar of agonized denial sounding in his mind. Each second that ticked by was like a dagger being driven straight into his heart. If someone didn't tell him where Lina was being held right fucking now, he wouldn't be responsible for the slaughter that would follow.

These might be the closest thing to family he had, but right now, they were also the people standing between him and his woman. If they had any idea just how far past the edge he'd slipped, they might have taken more care with their lives.

His eyes cut to where Cora stood, still hovering near the door, her steady gaze trained on him.

"Where is she?"

It was the last time he'd ask. After this, location or not, he was going to raze this city to the fucking ground.

"He'll have taken her to one of his safe houses, knowing anything controlled by the Council will be too easy for us to access."

"That could be literally anywhere," Quinn said.

Cora shook her head. "No. I have a feeling she's nearby. He wouldn't waste time taking her somewhere when he needs her close for tomorrow."

Nord started a mental countdown.

"Do you know of a safe house around here?" Finley asked.

"He owns a building in the city—several actually—but the one I'm thinking of acts as a front for some of his more unsavory business dealings: 907 Dumont. It's the only one of his properties where he used an alias when he purchased it."

"If he's trying to bury his association with it, it's the first place we should look," Finley said.

"Not we," Nord corrected. "Me. I'm going alone."

Quinn and Finley appeared to be outraged by his declaration. Cora merely looked as though she'd expected as much.

"People running off on their own is what got us into this mess in the first place," Quinn pointed out.

"And whose fault is that?" Nord growled.

The normally unflappable Quinn flinched at the sheer violence threaded through his voice.

"Who's going to watch your back?" Finley asked.

"Me. You'll only slow me down. And if I fail, Lina's going to need allies in the trial tomorrow."

Neither looked happy with him, but he was well past caring.

"Anything else?" he asked Cora.

"Don't kill anyone once you're inside."

Nord barked out a laugh. *Yeah. Right.*

"Heed my warning, berserker," she said, as serious as he'd ever seen her.

He dipped his chin to acknowledge he'd heard her but knew

anyone stupid enough to stand between him and Lina tonight wasn't going to live long enough to speak about the experience. Nord turned to Finley, who was muttering under his breath about turning into a taxi service while summoning a portal without having to be asked.

"Happy hunting, brother," Finley said as Nord stalked toward him.

They shared a look filled with meaning. Without another word, Nord stepped through the portal, leaving the others behind.

Along with the last shred of his humanity.

Nord knew Cora's instincts had been right about the Dumont property when he spotted two guards at the door and the four men patrolling its perimeter.

Regardless of their presence, the raw ache in his chest eased with each step he took toward the steel and glass monstrosity, telling him everything he needed to know. He wasn't close enough to pick up on what she was feeling yet, but he had zero doubt Lina was inside. Instead of soothing the bloodlust, the knowledge only stoked his frenzy.

His gaze dropped to his forearm and the familiar lines of the Viking tattoo he and Lina now shared. He allowed himself a second to run his fingers over it.

I'm coming for you, Kærasta.

He watched the patrol only long enough to time and track their route and then broke off, stalking two of the four from the shadows.

It didn't take him long to discover these men weren't close to professionals. They spoke freely, their voices echoing down the dark alleyway. Nord didn't bother masking the sound of his footsteps as he approached, and even then, they didn't realize death was coming for them until his breath washed over the back of one of their necks.

By then, it was too late.

Nord snapped the first man's neck in less time than it took to draw in a breath.

His partner had already taken several steps forward before he noticed the other man was no longer beside him. He turned and spotted Nord, his confused expression shifting to violent intent as he drew his gun.

Nord grinned, his dark roll of laughter sounding sinister as it bounced off the walls on either side of them. He drew on his magic, and the sorry excuse of a sentinel looked down in surprise as the weapon vanished in his hands. Nord used the distraction to close the distance between them. Before the guy had a chance to react, Nord already had his skull gripped between his palms and his drawn knee up. In one lightning-fast move, he snapped the guard's head down and drove his knee into his nose with enough force to shatter his eye sockets and send bone and cartilage splintering into his brain.

He was dead before he hit the ground.

A quick check confirmed Nord was alone. He'd dispatched two of the six lookouts in less than sixty seconds, and no one even knew he was here. He contemplated hiding the bodies but decided against it. If the others discovered the corpses before he got to them, their defenses would be up. And frankly, it'd be more fun for him if they put up at least a little resistance.

Spotting a fire escape, Nord scaled it quickly and used the metal platform as a perch while he waited for the other two patrolmen to pass down the alley.

He didn't have to wait long. As suspected, as soon as the guards set foot down the alley and spotted their fallen comrades, they were on high alert. There was a shout of surprise, and then they were running over to investigate, all the while having absolutely no clue they were heading straight into harm's reach instead of away from it.

One of the guards crouched down, checking for pulses, while the other craned his neck side to side, searching for a trace of their murderer. Too bad he didn't think to look up, but then Nord had banked on the fact that no one ever looks up.

He waited until the idiot was right beneath him and dropped down, wind ripping at his shirt and roaring in his ears as he free-fell. Nord's elbow crashed into, and then through, the man's cranium with a resounding crack that radiated up his own arm. He rode the body to the ground, noticing as he freed his arm that the momentum of his attack forced the man's skull down into his body. The unexpected brutality of the attack caused the creature within to roar with savage approval.

This. This is what his blackened soul craved. What it had been denied for far too long. *More,* the creature begged. *Don't stop until the streets run red with their blood.*

Nord looked up with a ferocious smile, catching the ripe scent of fear and urine as his gaze landed on his next victim.

"Wait—no, please—ahhh!"

The man's pleas turned to a wet gurgle as Nord conjured two daggers and leaned over, thrusting one into each of his ears.

He didn't bother pulling the weapons free. There were more where they came from. Instead, he stood and turned, whistling an old Viking war song as he left the alley and turned to the last of his targets.

The men on either side of the door spotted him, looking at each other with amused smirks, and then back at Nord.

"Hey buddy, you lost?" the one nearest to him called.

Nord ignored the question, his steps unhurried as he continued with his song.

The guards shared another look.

"You deaf, asshole? My friend asked you a question."

Nord was about twelve feet away when the closer of the two turned to face him, legs spread wide, hands on his hips. Nord broke into a sprint and dropped into a slide, two conjured hand-axes in his grasp as he passed through the man's legs.

"Wha—" the man asked, his eyes wide with shock as Nord severed the arteries on either side of his groin.

He could taste the guard's blood, knowing he was likely covered in it, as he cocked his right arm back and sent the ax flying at his friend. It struck true, sinking right between the man's eyes.

Nord was up and on his feet, the two men forgotten as he pulled open the door and walked through without a backward glance.

The berserker was high with the kill, the sweet thrill of victory singing in his veins. Six dead in under five minutes. Not a personal best, but he'd take it.

He glanced around the building's lobby, wondering where Mikel would hold a prisoner when his eyes landed on a directory. He didn't expect there to be anything obvious, but perhaps the map beside it might be of some use. If not, he could always search floor by floor, using his and Lina's bond like a pseudo-tracker to determine if he was getting close.

Nord blamed the bloodlust for what happened next.

A door opened on his left, sounding like a gunshot to his hyper-alert senses. Nord spun, the weapon flying before he realized he even conjured it, let alone threw it. The guard's eyes widened, blood burbling out of his mouth as his hands went up to touch the dagger sticking out of his throat.

He dropped to his knees, revealing a second man behind him.

The sight of Nico's smirking face caused Nord to bare his teeth in a snarl, another weapon taking shape in his hands.

"Ah-ah-ah, not so fast, berserker," Nico called as something cool formed around his wrists.

Nord glanced at the nullifying shackles with a growl of denial. Cora's warning chose that moment to come back and haunt him. He hung his head as shame warred with the need to wipe the smug smile off Nico's face.

Godsdamnit.

Nico's hands were in his pockets as he calmly crossed the lobby, coming to a stop a few feet away.

"I don't need my magic or even my hands to end you. Come a little closer, puppy, and I'll show you."

Nico tilted his head. "Am I supposed to be scared?"

"Only if you value your life."

"Do you really think you've proven anything, coming here? We knew you'd come for her. Why do you think we used those hired thugs outside?" Nico's smile grew at Nord's murderous expression. "What? Did you think we'd waste our best men? You've proven nothing, except that you're a pussy-whipped fool."

Two hands grabbed Nord's upper arms, and he snapped his head back, breaking the nose of whoever had been stupid enough to try to restrain him.

Nico's smile fell. "Do that again. It's of no consequence to me. Each wound you inflict will be repeated on my darling cousin."

Nord's blood boiled, but he resisted the urge to give in to the fury, managing to stand completely still.

"Not in the mood to fight anymore? Pity. I was looking forward to slapping that uppity bitch around a little more. Maybe I'll do it anyway, just for fun, eh?"

It took everything in Nord not to charge forward. It would be nothing to jump up and crush Nico's throat between his thighs, but he was smart enough to recognize when he'd lost the upper hand. The men with their weapons trained on him from every corner of the room proved it well enough.

"Now be a good boy and come with me. Your room is ready for you."

Nord swallowed back a bellow of rage as he took a begrudging step forward.

"That's it, what a well-trained beast you are. My bitch cousin certainly brought you to heel, hasn't she?"

"Keep talking, puppy. All you're doing is determining how quickly I kill you."

Nico threw back his head and laughed. "You still think you can win. Don't worry. That assumption will be rectified soon enough." He tipped his head toward the open elevator. "After you."

Nord ground his teeth together as he stepped inside.

All right, Finley. It's up to you. Don't let me down, brother.

CHAPTER 20
LINA

S he wasn't sure what hurt more, her pride or her body. The answer came to her as she eyed the supply closet Nico had stuffed her in last night with deep-seated anger.

Her pride. Definitely her pride.

I can't believe I let myself get caught by that douche bucket.

Lina pushed herself up off the abrasive industrial carpet and back into a seated position. With no direct light source or windows of any kind, she could only guess as to how long she'd been trapped in here. She assumed overnight, at the very least. The sharp twinge in her neck from being kept at an odd angle for too long, along with the heavy ache in her shoulder and hips from where they'd been pressed into the floor, told her she'd slept for hours.

Her head smacked against the wall behind her with a dull thud as she let out a soft groan. *Fucking Crombie. After everything we've been through, why did you ditch me? And why give me this?*

Lifting her shackled hands, Lina cupped the sparkling moon pendant hanging around her neck. She brushed her thumb over its glittering surface as she tried for the hundredth time to figure out what possible significance there could be in his leaving it with her.

With her hands bound, she hadn't been able to slide the necklace off to inspect it more thoroughly, and there didn't seem to be a clasp she could unhook either. The only way she could study it at all was if she awkwardly tucked her chin in and held it up with her hands. Even then, she could only just make out the bottom half of the crescent.

Lina let the necklace fall back down, cool tingles shooting out from where the pendant made contact with her skin. That was a mystery for another day. For now, she needed to focus on how she was going to get out of here.

Without her magic, her options were limited. And without a cell phone, she couldn't exactly call for reinforcements. The only comfort she could take in her current predicament was that Nord would have returned home and gone after her as soon as he realized she wasn't there.

Nord.

She pressed a hand over her heart. The raw, hollow feeling had eased somewhat, making her wonder whether she'd simply grown accustomed to it or if it was possible she was actually closer to him. Lina smiled softly at the thought, picturing Nord prowling restlessly through hallways and throwing open doors in his search to find her.

For a second, Lina contemplated shouting, on the off chance he might hear her if he was actually nearby, but ultimately decided against it. Until she found some way to defend herself, she really didn't want to give Nico or one of his thugs a reason to come in here and make her shut up. They'd found enough reasons for that the night before.

Turns out her instinct to behave was a sound one. Not even a minute later, there was a scratch at the door, and then it was flung open, momentarily blinding her with the flood of fluorescent light.

Lina threw her hands up, trying in vain to protect her eyes, but it was several long moments before she blinked away the last of the black spots.

Nico stood in the doorway, a shit-eating grin on his face and two beefy bodyguards on either side of him. Not recognizing the men, Lina mentally dubbed them Thing 1 and Thing 2.

"Morning, cousin. Sleep well?"

She pursed her lips and tilted her head to the side, giving him a scathing once-over. "Tell me, Nico, how's it feel being relegated to Mikel's errand boy? What did he promise you to make you agree to be his little bitch?"

The Things snickered, making Lina's own lips twitch with amusement, but they quickly schooled their expressions into impassive masks before Nico could catch on.

Nico glared at her. "I'm no one's bitch."

"Spoiler, if you take it up the ass without getting anything out of it, you're a bitch."

Anger sparked in Nico's gaze as he stepped forward and cracked her across the face.

Pain blossomed behind her eyes, but Lina merely tipped her face up and spat out a mouthful of blood on his pristine white shirt.

Nico looked down, his face twisting with disgust.

"Oops," Lina gave him an insincere pout.

"Call me a bitch again."

She shifted her legs beneath her and awkwardly scrambled to her feet. "Looks like I touched a nerve. It's okay to enjoy being taken advantage of, Nic. Lots of people get off on being degraded and treated like worthless sacks of shit. I'm not one to yuck your yum, so long as it's consensual. But I've got to say, cousin to cousin, your choice of master is a little concerning."

This time she was ready when his hand snapped out. She ducked out of the way with a laugh. "Ooh, so close." The bloodlust was calling to her, filling her with euphoric anticipation as undercurrents of violence simmered in the air. "Want to see what happens if you try that a third time?"

Nico's jaw tightened, but he must have sensed the manic rage swirling up inside her because he took a step back. "We don't have time for this."

"Too bad. I was just starting to have fun. How about you take these sexy cuffs off me, and we make it a real party?"

"How about you shut the fuck up?"

"Good one, cuz. You really nailed the whole mafioso vibe you've been going for with that one."

Lina didn't bother to hide her smirk as Nico ground his teeth together.

"I said. Shut. The. Fuck. Up."

"Or what? You gonna come over here and make me? I'd love to see you try."

Anger turned Nico's face a mottled red as a vein pulsed wildly in his forehead. She knew it wouldn't take much more to push him over the edge. If she could get that last thread of control to snap, she might be able to turn the tables here and get some leverage.

"That smart mouth of yours is going to get you in a whole world of trouble one day."

"Been there. Done that. Sold the T-shirt."

"Don't believe me? Keep going. You'll find out soon enough what Mikel does to bitches with smart mouths."

"Know from firsthand experience, do you? Cause I'm pretty sure we've already established you're the bitch in this family."

Nico stepped forward, his arm raised and ready to clock her, but Thing 1 placed a meaty hand on his shoulder and pulled him back. Her cousin closed his eyes, a shudder working its way down his body as he brought himself back under control.

"Grab her, and let's get out of here. We're going to be late."

Lina blew out her own breath. *Shit.* She almost had him.

Thing 2 stepped into the supply closet; a black silk hood clutched in his hands.

"What's that for?" Lina asked, leaning back as he went to slip it over her head.

Thing 1 gripped the chain between her cuffs and tugged. Lina surged forward as she was pulled off-balance. Thing 2 used her lack of coordination to cover her head and send her world back into darkness.

"Is this really necessary?"

She wasn't sure which one of the men shoved her, but she wouldn't put the petty move past her shit-for-brains cousin. Lina stumbled but managed to keep her footing as the men led her bound and blindfolded through the building, down several sets of stairs, and into what Lina guessed was a tunnel based on the damp air and unmistakable smell of mold and rot.

"Hurry up," Nico growled, giving Lina another shove.

Lifting her elbow, she jerked it back until it connected with something soft. It was impossible to know where she hit him, but her cousin's grunt of pain told her wherever it was, she'd made it hurt.

"I'd move a lot faster if I could see where I was going."

"That would ruin the surprise."

Lina was too familiar with Mobius protocols not to have an idea of what Mikel had planned for her. Still, it would be nice to confirm whether or not she was about to face trial so she could mentally prepare herself.

It could have been five minutes or twenty until the path they took led back up. Lina's heart sped up, knowing they must be getting close to their final destination. Her suspicion was confirmed when the sound of their footfalls was joined by excited whispers.

"Ah, the guest of dishonor has arrived."

Kristoff?

Lina was thankful for her hood in that moment, if only because it hid her look of uncertainty at hearing someone other than Mikel running the show. Of course, that was when Nico grasped the top of it and shoved her for a third time, robbing her of its small protection.

The hood was whipped from her head as she fell to her knees. She winced as her kneecaps smacked into the hard floor and blinked furiously as she readjusted to the light. Gasps rang out as the crowd realized just who was on trial.

Lina knew she looked ridiculous, with her hair flying up in every direction, sleep-smeared makeup, and yesterday's clothes. It was a far cry from the image she'd presented the last time she stood before the Council.

Actually, speaking of the Council, only three of the five family thrones were filled. Natalia, Kristoff, and Quinn were seated, but Mikel was suspiciously absent. The Cuska seat was obviously empty, as both she and her cousin were in the center of the room. But aside from those two vacant seats, the rest of the Animagi community appeared to be in attendance to bear witness to her shame.

Lina glanced around, trying to get a feel for the tone of the room and see if she could spot any familiar faces. Her eyes found Quinn first. Her friend didn't dare smile as their eyes met, but she gave Lina a tiny nod, as if urging her not to lose heart. From there she looked to her right, immediately spotting Cora in the crowd. She'd thought Nord might be seated with her, but her Viking was nowhere to be found. It didn't appear that Finley was present either, not that she'd really expected him to be, but a part of her had hoped he might have snuck in.

Cora must have realized who she was searching for because she gave Lina a slight shake of her head.

Lina frowned, but she only had enough time to hope there was some sort of rescue plan in place before Kristoff cleared his throat and called the room to order.

As he cast his eyes over the crowd, Lina was struck once again by the absence of the Drake patriarch. Surely he'd want to be present for this? Her stomach twisted with unease. She knew better than to assume his not being here was going to work in her favor. The dick was up to something.

"Thank you all for gathering on such short notice," Kristoff began.

She barely resisted the urge to roll her eyes at his inflated sense of self-importance. The Alinari never got to lead these sorts of things. They were almost always in the background, their gifts making them ideal candidates for matters such as security and crowd control. She wouldn't be surprised if he was sporting a serious power boner behind that podium.

"Two days ago, Evalina Cuska returned to us. After claiming her seat on the Council, she was found the next day destroying irreplaceable artifacts in the vault after stealing another member's key— likely to frame them for the senseless destruction."

Lina fought off a yawn as Kristoff continued listing off her crimes. What a load of crap. As if she'd ever set up one of the Satori. Everyone knew she and Quinn were closer than most sisters. There's no way she'd engage in any activity that would implicate Quinn or her family of wrongdoing.

He was going to have to do better than this if he actually expected to cut her off at the knees.

"Well, do you have anything to say for yourself?" Kristoff asked, his expression severe.

Lina blinked at him. "Only that you're full of shit."

There were a few shocked snickers and gasps from the crowd. Quinn bit her bottom lip, fighting against her own laughter.

Kristoff looked like he was in the midst of an apoplectic fit. His mouth snapped open and closed like a fish, and his olive skin was flushed with rage.

"That's not what happened, Kristoff. And you know it. In fact, I'm certain Quinn and her mother have already tried to disabuse you of your misinformation. I'm not even sure why you felt it necessary to proceed with this bullshit trial."

Lina clasped her hands together, hoping to disguise her nervous tremors with the casual stance. Her blatant disrespect for the other Council member was a risky move. She'd either alienate the other Animagi or endear herself to them. It was impossible to know how many allies she was gaining—or losing—with her choice. All she could do was trust the instinct telling her that these people were sick of being under Mikel's thumb, and they'd rally behind whoever was brave enough to take him and his followers on.

A door opened behind her, and dread pooled in her stomach. Her eyes fell closed for a brief second, the hair on the back of her neck standing on end as that ice-cold voice rang out.

"Sorry I'm late."

Lina refused to turn around, not wanting to give Mikel the impression that she cared about his appearance one way or the other, but then an insistent fluttering filled the hollow ache in her chest. It was so unexpected; it took her a second to realize what it meant. Her breath caught.

Nord. He's here.

"I had to pick something up on my way over."

Lina barely heard the words as heat exploded in her chest. Her knees almost gave out at the intensity of Nord's rage pulsing inside of her. Her emotions careened wildly in the space of a single heartbeat as she started to turn.

Weightless hope. Giddy relief. And then bone-numbing dread as she realized she could make out two distinct sets of footsteps as Mikel strolled into the center of the room.

No. Nonononononono.

But even as the denial shot through her mind, she knew it was true. The something Mikel had stopped to pick up was really a someone: Nord.

Lina didn't know how Mikel had managed it unless something went terribly wrong during Nord's rescue attempt the night before. But as her eyes landed on her lover covered in dried blood, bound in chains, and wearing a set of cuffs that matched her own, she knew she was well and truly fucked.

Her heart fell, hope snuffing out completely as his blue eyes found and held hers.

Her Viking wasn't here to save her.

Mikel was going to use him as the weapon of her destruction.

CHAPTER 21
LINA

Mikel's cold, dead eyes flashed with triumph. Watching him already mentally celebrating a victory he'd yet to earn made Lina's jaw clench and her hands tingle with the need to coat them in his blood. One side of his mouth curled up in a slow, taunting smile.

He knew. He fucking knew what she wanted to do to him, and he was *laughing* at her.

A primal growl slipped from her lips as her berserker thrashed within, desperate to wipe that smug grin off his face, ideally by ripping his actual face off and beating him with it.

Fucking Drakes with their fucking mind games and goddamn unnatural luck.

The slight flexing of Nord's arms pulled her attention back to him. Despite the tidal wave of their combined fury crashing through her, the sight of him steadied her. He stared at her without blinking, promising her something with his gaze. They might be bound and without their magic for the time being, but that hardly meant they were defenseless. Two berserkers against about two hundred

Animagi wasn't what Lina would call a fair fight, but they'd go down swinging until the bitter, bloody end.

And it would be bloody.

If she had anything to say about it, by the time she and Nord were through, they'd be swimming in it.

Lina bared her teeth, silently promising herself that Mikel would not walk out of this room intact. If she had to tear him apart limb from limb herself, she would see to it he was punished. Not just for capturing Nord, but for orchestrating Alistair's death. For raising the Spawn of Satan who had tortured and murdered her and grooming her cousin into a soulless husk instead of the man he could have been. He needed to pay for every corrupt and horrific thing he'd ever done in his godforsaken life.

She lifted her chin and met Mikel's gaze once more, pouring every drop of her contempt and loathing for him into the look.

Judgment Day is here, motherfucker. And you've earned yourself a one-way ticket straight to hell.

The skin around Mikel's eyes tightened slightly, and Lina grinned.

That's right, asshole. Who's laughing now?

The crowd's anxious whispering had amplified since Mikel and Nord's dramatic entrance. Likely due to the Animagi's attempts to figure out who the mysterious blood-coated prisoner was.

Kristoff whistled sharply to reestablish order. "All right, all right. Settle down. Mikel, what's this about?"

As if you aren't a part of this charade, dickweed.

Quinn rolled her eyes, clearly conveying her own thoughts about the Alinari leader to the rest of the Animagi in the room. It may have seemed like a small thing, but publicly standing against any of the other Council members was a massive statement. Mikel and Kristoff might be trying to make a spectacle out of Lina, but Quinn was putting on a performance of her own.

As for the crowd, if the whistle wasn't enough to get their attention, Kristoff's question certainly was. Lina could practically hear the sound of a couple hundred people leaning forward in their seats so as not to miss a single word.

Mikel dropped his eyes as he lifted his hands and adjusted the cuffs on his expensive black shirt. Lina studied the tattoos inked on the backs of his hands and fingers and wondered what secret meaning the symbols contained. From her position, she could make out a blackened skull on his index finger, a single die with three dots on his middle finger, and a burning rose on his hand. They were too intentional to be random, and everything about Mikel was precise and methodical. Though she supposed the skull was easy enough to decipher.

Once his little show was finished, Mikel glanced back up, the tension in the room at an all-time high—just as he'd intended.

"Well, you see, it's quite simple. This is the man Evalina Cuska hired to murder my son."

The Council chamber exploded in shouts of shock and accusation.

Even though she'd been expecting him to do something like that, Lina found she wasn't quite prepared for the backlash. The mood shifted instantly as the crowd turned against her, their curiosity replaced with outrage. The feel of so many angry and bloodthirsty eyes on her made her skin crawl, and Lina had to fight the urge to duck her head.

Time to do some damage control . . . if that was even possible at this point.

"First of all," she drawled, feigning a bored, unaffected air to match Mikel's, "I did not *hire* him. Nord is my true mate. Second of all, your heir kidnapped, tortured, and attempted to murder me— likely under your instruction."

No need to complicate things further and explain that Mataius had actually succeeded in his attempt, and she was only standing here because of her best friend's foresight and her uncle's thieving ways.

"And third, you're responsible for the death of both my father and my uncle. So, tell me, Mikel, which one of us deserves to be on trial right now?"

If Mikel's proclamation sent the room into chaos, Lina's robbed it of air. No one dared to breathe as they waited for his reaction to her words, herself included.

She knew she'd shocked the Animagi in a number of ways, not the least of which was declaring Nord as her true mate. There hadn't been such a pairing in their community for centuries. For her to return after decades with one in tow was the stuff of legends. Then on top of that, for her to come out and accuse the man who'd black-mailed almost all of them of treason . . . well, she may as well have pantsed him and then run around him in circles singing 'Ring Around the Rosie' at the top of her lungs while pelting him with a bunch of flaccid dicks.

Hell, if she'd been in the crowd, Lina might have conjured herself some popcorn. This was the show of a lifetime, and they had front-row seats.

"I can't help but notice you're not denying it," Mikel replied coolly.

Lina arched a brow. "That Nord slit Mataius' throat to protect me from the homicidal psychopath? No. I'm not denying it. It was self-defense."

More like revenge, but, again, leaving out details seemed prudent right now. The crowd was already against her, no need to throw more gasoline on this dumpster fire by telling them how Nord had tortured the scumbag for hours before ever picking up a dagger.

"Self-defense hardly applies here," Mikel scoffed. "An heir—my heir—is dead because of you. Anything that occurred after that is justifiable retaliation."

The crowd's murmurs swelled, and there were shouts of agreement ringing out all around her.

Lina battled to keep hold of her calm.

"What about my father?"

"What about him? Do you have any proof that Anatoly died by my hand?"

She bit down hard on her cheek, barely managing to keep her berserker in check.

"No?" Mikel asked, taking her silence as an opportunity to build his case. "I didn't think so. All that falls from your lips are lies and baseless accusations." He turned back to Kristoff and the other Council members. "In light of Ms. Cuska's grievous actions, including last night's destruction of our priceless property, I move to have her stripped of her title, banned from the Council, and exiled from the Animagi community, just like her traitor of an uncle."

Lina's mouth dropped open, and her eyes flew to Quinn, who was sporting a matching expression of disbelief.

Exile?

It sounded like the lesser punishment, but Mikel was nothing if not meticulous and supremely intelligent. Before he took her off the board entirely, he was trying to cut her off from any potential allies. If the motion passed, Quinn and her mother would be barred from having any continued relationship with her. Not that Quinn would actually obey such a ruling, a fact which would see her severely punished as well.

This was bad. Very, very bad.

Quinn and Lina shared a look before Quinn's mask snapped back in place. She leaned back in her pseudo-throne, seeming for all the world like she was bored by the proceedings. Lina wasn't as skilled at hiding her reaction. Her nails cut bloody crescents into her palms as she fought against the urge to tear Mikel's throat out.

"As for the matter of Ms. Cuska's mate, there's no proof such a bond is legitimate or, in fact, real. I move for his immediate execution."

Lina's head snapped to Mikel, the black chamber taking on a reddish cast as wrath unlike anything she'd ever experienced crashed into her. She shook with barely suppressed violence as she glared at him. Mikel could threaten her all he wanted, but Nord? If the fucker so much as pointed a finger in his direction, she would flay the flesh from his body and then craft herself a crown made from what was left of his bones.

No one threatened her mate and lived.

Nord's eyes shone with a fierce tenderness as they swept over her face. As if her malevolent vow had echoed in his mind like a declaration of her undying love and he whole-heartedly approved. Then his attention shifted to Mikel and all trace of warmth guttered out of his eyes.

He smiled, the expression so devoid of anything remotely human, shivers of fear cascaded down her spine. He was the stuff of nightmares standing there, decorated in the blood of the men he'd killed, with murderous intent pouring out of him.

"I'd love to watch you try."

Mikel didn't spare Nord a glance. "I do not *try*. I succeed. Every time."

Lina blinked, shoving her fury down as far as she could so that she could appeal to reason one last time. Whether they liked her right now or not, the Animagi were still her people. If she and Nord gave in to their bloodlust, innocents would die. She owed it to them to at least try to avoid that outcome.

"What about Mikel's crimes?" she demanded. "Doesn't he have to answer for them as well? Or does your hypocrisy truly know no bounds?"

Kristoff sneered at her, looking like he was ready to jump down and take her on himself. The two Alinari guards behind him drew their weapons and aimed them at Lina's chest. As if that would possibly stop her.

Nord let out a warning growl. The Alinari were too stupid to recognize the threat. They'd never seen a berserker in action. But if one of them dared to pull the trigger, they wouldn't live to repeat the mistake.

Natalia stood and joined Kristoff in the center of the stage, her voice soft as she said, "You have no evidence of such crimes."

So much for appealing to reason.

"You're cowards," Lina spat. "All of you. Cowards for letting him get away with this and for letting him rule your lives. Mikel Drake is nothing but a money-hungry, power-obsessed dickhead with a god complex. And what's worse, you created this monster. You let him get away with it. All the lives he's taken, the people he's hurt, their blood is on your hands every bit as much as his."

Natalia flinched as if struck, but she was the only one who looked moved by Lina's impassioned speech. The Drakes and most of the other Animagi didn't like it at all. They began hissing at her from throughout the room. Well, fuck them. She didn't think a whole lot of them either.

"I second the motion," Kristoff announced, his eyes flashing with vindictive glee.

"Well, I sure as fuck don't," Quinn said, inspecting her nails as she reclined in her seat. She glanced up. "Oh, are we standing now?" She sighed heavily, uncrossed her legs, and pushed to her feet. "These heels are a killer; I wish you would have gone over today's choreography before I chose my outfit."

There were a few appreciative snickers from the crowd, likely other Satori. Lina couldn't help but notice there were hardly any Cuskas in attendance. Not that that was surprising. There were very few of them left compared to the other Animagi families, maybe ten in total, if that. She'd never given it much thought growing up, but now she couldn't help but wonder if Mikel's plan to overthrow the Council had been brewing for far longer than anyone suspected, and he'd been systematically taking out her family line in preparation for this exact moment.

"That's one against one. Natalia, what say you?" Mikel asked.

As the two accusers, Mikel and Lina couldn't cast a vote. That left Natalia's as the deciding factor. The Thorton matriarch visibly cowered under Mikel's regard, and Lina knew what her answer was going to be before she even opened her mouth.

"Wait," Lina said, surprising everyone in the room. "Two parties have been harmed here today, and both have a right to justice. Since we're both members of the Council, it's only fair we handle this in the old way. I'm invoking the Rite of Requital."

Gasps rang out throughout the chamber.

"Lina, no," Quinn whispered, her carefully constructed façade falling away to reveal genuine fear.

Lina could feel Nord's eyes on her and the turbulent wave of his confusion pressing against her chest. He wanted to know what she was up to. Frankly, so did she.

This was either the bravest thing she'd ever done or the absolute dumbest. Maybe both. Time would tell. The Rite of Requital stated that in the case of an extreme situation where two Animagi both claimed to be irrevocably harmed by one another, they could leave the verdict in the hands of fate. The victor would be declared innocent, absolved of their sins. And the loser, well, they'd be dead, so it didn't really matter.

Mikel's head swiveled to her, his eyes flashing with interest. "Are you sure that's what you want, Evalina? There's no going back once I accept."

She licked her lips, her berserker practically vibrating with delight at the prospect of facing off with him at last. Holding up her hands, she shook her wrists. "Just so long as these little bracelets are removed so it's a fair fight."

"I hardly doubt it's going to be a fair fight, little girl."

Lina smiled. He had no idea just how true his words were. Although, he was the one about to be severely out of his league. While she'd never seen Mikel in action, she knew full well what she was capable of. Her fully unlocked powers, combined with the strength of the berserker? He didn't stand a chance.

Or so she hoped.

"Very well. Just remember, you asked for this."

Mikel nodded at Nico, who had been watching everything play out like a child on Christmas morning. Lina glared at her cousin as he rushed forward and used his magic to remove the shackles.

You're next, you sniveling pissant.

Nico's stupid smirk wavered, and he quickly stepped back while Lina rubbed her chafed wrists and waited for the tingle of healing warmth to surge up now that her magic was unbound.

Mikel removed his jacket, passing it off to one of his many butt-lickers as he rolled up his sleeves. His voice rang out loud and clear in the stunned silence that filled the chamber. "I accept."

Kristoff beamed like he couldn't believe his good fortune. "Very well. Let the Rite begin."

Lina was still waiting for that telltale tingle when four men stepped forward and surrounded Nord to bodily move him out of the center of the room. He fought them the entire way, managing to break one guy's nose and throw an elbow in another's eye before the other two wised up and stood out of range.

And she was still waiting for it when Mikel turned to face her.

She would have sworn his pupils were two vertical slits as he lazily called a ball of fire into his palm. Her eyes narrowed in confusion as she stared at the flickering flames.

Fire? She'd only ever seen the Drakes manipulate weather, the strongest of them able to call up wild tempests and summon lightning. She just assumed Mikel would use more of the same. Lesson learned.

Lina's heart drummed a frantic tattoo as she reached for her magic, preparing to snuff out the flames—only to come up empty. She dove deeper, but her healing magic's silence made a sudden, terrifying sort of sense. There was nothing within her but a yawning chasm where her power was supposed to be.

Her magic was gone.

The pendant around her neck slid across her skin, sending icy prickles in its wake as Lina dove out of the way of Mikel's fireball. Horror shot through her as Crombie's parting words echoed in her mind.

'Sorry about this, sweetheart.'

Lina clutched the chain and yanked, but all she managed to do was cut through her skin. Her fingers were coated with blood, and she was pretty sure more trickles dripped down the back of her neck, but the necklace didn't budge. If anything, it seemed to tighten, feeling more like a choker than a necklace.

Her head shot up, her eyes finding Nord as her fear collided with his.

Crombie, what have you done?

CHAPTER 22
NORD

A hand shoved Nord roughly from behind. "Keep moving."

He glanced over his shoulder with a deep growl, memorizing the younger man's rodent-like features.

Ratboy laughed, looked pointedly at the shackles on Nord's wrists and ankles and mistakenly assuming that meant he'd been tamed. "You're not so tough without your woman to protect you, are you?"

Nord chuckled, his dark laughter rolling through the hallway like the first rumbles of thunder heralding a storm.

Ratboy's smile fell and he paled, gulping as he gestured with his chin for Nord to keep walking.

Mikel led the way down the hall, having met up with them in the same lobby where Nord had been captured the night before. Other than a disgusted sneer, Mikel had mostly ignored him up until now.

"Bring him to me," Mikel demanded without turning around.

Ratboy gave Nord a wary once-over before gripping him by the elbow and pulling him to Mikel's side. "Here you are, sir."

Nord fought against another laugh. Mikel's lackey was transparent in his search for praise. As if he'd actually forced Nord to move against his will. As if he even could. The only reason Nord was here at all was because he wanted to be. In fact, his compliance since his capture was all part of the contingency plan he and Finley had put in place as soon as it had become clear they'd be infiltrating the Mobius Council.

Capture had always been a possibility. Staying captured, however, was never part of the plan.

He'd been biding his time ever since Nico left him in an empty office with nothing more than the blood-soaked clothes on his back and magic-suppressing shackles on his wrists. There wasn't much he could do about the metal cuffs, which bit into his skin, leaving little room for him to maneuver, but a quick test of the thick chain connecting them had confirmed Nord could easily snap it in two. A surprise he'd save for when the time was right.

As they neared the end of the hall connected to the Council's formal meeting chamber, Nord knew he was about to find out what Mikel had in store for him. He just hoped Finley had had enough time to prepare, because his gut told him he and Lina were going to need all the help they could get.

Mikel stopped just short of the door, taking a moment to straighten his tie and adjust his suit jacket. Nord used the reprieve to close his eyes and focus on Lina. She was close. He could feel her presence settling back into his chest, her return a balm to his soul as she refilled the aching void that had slowly been driving him mad.

It was nearly impossible to resist the call of the berserker and deny that primal part of himself. But with every step, Lina's essence twined more firmly with his own, calming the churning anger begging him to wrap this chain around Mikel's throat and pull tight until his strangled gasps ceased and his legs gave out.

Nord pushed out a breath and clung onto his self-control despite his near-euphoric reaction to the mere thought of taking Mikel's life. Because no matter how badly Nord wanted to end the man, a quick death now would only lead to more death and uncertainty in the future. Lina may not have vocalized the desire, but he knew she wanted a place among the Animagi. In order for that to become a reality, they had to play this right, which meant no killing.

At least, not yet.

Resigned to wait, Nord sighed and opened his eyes in time to see Mikel push through the chamber doors with a flourish.

"Sorry I'm late."

As the interior of the chamber revealed itself, Nord distantly noted the crowded seats, the number of people on the stage, and the startled gasps of the audience. But at that moment, he only had eyes for the woman in the center of the room, her spine ramrod straight and her chin tipped up defiantly as she faced off with a smug-looking Kristoff.

Lina.

His relief at seeing her was so potent his knees buckled, and his steps faltered, causing Ratboy to reach out and give him another shove. Nord snarled in warning but ultimately obeyed, his footsteps matching Mikel's as they made their grand entrance.

Lina twisted their way, her frustration and fury coiling with his own, setting him on high alert. It was an all-out internal war not to go to her, but they both had parts to play. The most he could do right now was allow himself a single second to drink in the sight of her and to check for any sign of mistreatment. Other than the purple smudges of exhaustion beneath her crystalline eyes and the chains at her wrists, he didn't find anything to suggest she'd been treated badly.

The slight hitch of her breath was her only outward reaction to seeing him beside Mikel, but there was no hiding the electric jolts of panic exploding in his chest like tiny fireworks. Nord did his best to reassure her with a look, to offer her his strength and remind her who they were and what they were capable of. It must have worked because the phantom sparklers stopped, and the conversation picked back up.

Nord listened to the proceedings with half an ear as he scanned the crowd, taking in every detail and mapping out several possible escape routes if things went badly. He had every reason to believe they would.

The seats which had been empty the last time he'd been in the Council chambers were now occupied, the room filled wall to wall with people, their necks craned in his direction. The expressions on the Animagi's faces were a combination of fear, excitement, and shock.

As Nord searched the crowd, sussing out potential enemies and counting the number of armed guards posted throughout the room, his gaze collided with Cora's lavender-eyed stare. She tipped her eyes discreetly up and to the left. He followed the motion, catching a glimpse of a familiar dark brown head ducking back behind a vent he hadn't noticed the day before.

Finley.

Nord took a deep breath, his shoulders relaxing at the confirmation that his partner hadn't failed. He'd managed to sneak in and evade detection thus far, which meant they still had options. Fin wouldn't act unless necessary, but there was comfort in knowing that no matter what happened to Nord, his friend would make sure Lina got out. It went without saying he'd also ensure Quinn and Cora were taken care of.

He was so focused on his reconnaissance, Nord almost missed it when Mikel charged him with Mataius' murder. He opened his mouth, fully prepared to accept the blame for the heir's death, and more than ready to admit he wished it was possible to kill the whoreson more than the one time. But Lina beat him to it.

"First of all," she drawled, filling him with absolute pride as she came to his defense. And when she called him her true mate, Nord's berserker roared with bestial approval, drowning out the rest of what she said as his inner monster reveled in the public claiming. Not that there'd been any doubt, but still.

Things happened quickly after that, Mikel and Lina ping-ponging accusations back and forth as the crowd watched on with rapt fascination. Most of what Mikel said was expected as he called for Lina's removal and banishment, but it wasn't until the molten tendrils of her rage shot through him that Nord gave the proceedings his undivided attention.

"I move for his immediate execution."

Nord looked first to Lina, reading the righteous fury and desire for violence in her eyes as if they were a love poem she'd written just for him. Then his gaze cut to Mikel, and he smiled, welcoming any opportunity that would let him shake off the vestiges of humanity and embrace his true nature.

"I'd love to watch you try."

Nord ignored Mikel's scathing reply, already bracing himself for the fight to come. It didn't matter what the man said; Nord's record spoke for itself. Of the countless one-on-one battles he'd fought, there were very few he'd lost. He didn't intend to start today.

The bloodlust rose up, filling him with its divine strength and hunger for bloodshed. His eyes sought out the hidden vent near the far side of the room and found Finley hovering behind the grate.

The Guardian gave him a tight nod as his determined whisper sounded in Nord's mind, *"Ready when you are, brother."*

Nord's biceps flexed, his muscles tensing in preparation to break through his chains. If not for the confusing tangle of Lina's emotions pressing into his own, he would have.

"I invoke the Rite of Requital."

His head snapped toward her.

What are you doing, Kærasta?

Her eyes slid to his, begging him for something. Forgiveness maybe? It was hard to sort through what she was feeling to know for sure. But Quinn's panicked objection told him he wasn't going to like whatever she'd just set in motion.

The predatory gleam in Mikel's eyes confirmed it.

Nord may not understand the nuances of this Rite, but it didn't take a genius to figure out a fight was imminent as Nico stepped forward to remove Lina's cuffs, and Mikel began to roll up the sleeves of his shirt.

Finally.

He would never be a fan of Lina putting herself in danger, but he fully supported any Rite that allowed him to start bashing some heads.

The sound of rushing footsteps met his ears.

Ah, right on cue.

Nord glanced over in time to find Ratboy and three of his friends running straight at him.

Smart of him to recognize he needs the backup. Too bad it still won't be enough.

He bit back a smile and cracked his neck in preparation, letting the bloodlust take over as the first man moved into range. A well-timed headbutt knocked him out as a second thug moved into position behind Nord. He drove his elbow back without looking, the satisfying crunch and resulting groan telling him he'd broken the guy's nose. The third man grabbed Nord by both his elbows and pulled him to the side of the room, just beneath the stage. Nord waited for him to stop moving and then broke his shin with a sharp kick. Those three dealt with, he looked up and grinned at Ratboy, beckoning him forward.

The man looked ready to piss himself as he nervously licked his lips and cast his eyes side to side, seeking backup.

"Not so tough without your buddies protecting you, are you?"

"I-I-I'm just doing my job," he stuttered.

"So am I."

Lina's overwhelming panic interrupted Nord before he could take Ratboy out, the oily feel of it nearly suffocating him and pulling his attention back to the couple in the center of the room. Fire danced in Mikel's outstretched palm while Lina struggled with an unfamiliar piece of jewelry. Blood dripped down her hands and neck as she tugged, trying to free herself from the silver chain.

Nord's eyes narrowed as he tried to figure out why she'd bother fiddling with a necklace instead of summoning her own magic. He got his answer when Mikel launched the ball of fire, and Lina threw her body to the side, tucking into a roll and springing back to her feet a few yards away.

His eyes flew wide with understanding. She wasn't using her magic because she *couldn't*. Something was still cutting her off from it. The showdown, which had seemed evenly matched, if not outright in her favor only seconds prior, now seemed like a suicide mission.

"Lina," he roared, her name turning into a battle cry as the berserker took over. He surged forward, intent on reaching her, only to be pulled back by several hands.

He fought like a man possessed as he grasped the wrists of one man, lifted him up over his head, and threw him to the ground. Then he twisted, wrapping the chain binding his wrists around another man's neck and pulling taut, managing to snap both the man's neck and his chain.

On and on it went, men coming at him from every direction, most with weapons, some armed only with their enhanced strength and agility. Nord wasn't sure which Animagi family they belonged to, but he was guessing Alinari if Kristoff's horrified expression was anything to go off of. Nord wasn't overly impressed with their training. They fought like men who'd never participated in an actual battle, their strikes tentative and aimed with the intention of taking down rather than killing. It made them easy targets because Nord held nothing back while they fought with only half their strength. If that.

None were a match for him. He disarmed two men with guns by grasping the barrel of one and using it to pistol whip the other before turning back and unloading the clip into the first man's chest. No one else attempted guns after that.

Eventually, there were only two men left still actively trying to restrain him. Both were sweating profusely, neither looking particularly happy about their assignment. Nord punched one of the two men in the throat while a bullet between the eyes took care of the last of them. He sent Finley a mental thank-you as he turned and started sprinting to the center of the room.

More men flocked toward him, cutting him off from Lina. Nord roared, his chest heaving as he mowed them down, leaving their mostly broken bodies in his wake.

"Mikel, end this!" Kristoff cried out.

"Gladly," Mikel replied.

Nord had been busy fighting off what had felt like never-ending swarms of men, but even so, the battle could have only been going on for a handful of minutes at most. It was clear Mikel had been toying with Lina in that time, using his fire to herd her and keep her from being able to land a hit on him. Nord could tell from here that she was in a full-blown rage but unable to do anything with it. Her clothes were charred, bits of them still smoking from the times she hadn't quite managed to dodge Mikel's fiery attacks.

Without magic, there wasn't much Nord could do against Mikel either, save perhaps tackle him. And the wall of men that had already reformed between Nord and the center of the room was making that currently impossible.

"Now, Mikel!" Kristoff insisted.

Nord glanced up at Kristoff, only a few feet away.

He might not be able to reach Mikel, but Kristoff was another story. Nord turned, taking a running leap up onto the stage. Kristoff was too surprised by the change in his direction to react. Bullets tore into Nord's back as the guards throughout the room tried to stop him. He barely even registered the pain as he slid into position behind Kristoff, cupping the back of his head with one hand and his chin with the other.

"Ah-ah-ah, I wouldn't do that if I were you. There are rules to be followed after all."

Nord bared his teeth as his gaze lifted to Mikel's. "I don't care about your rules."

"Oh? You should. They're the only thing keeping your mate

alive." Mikel tilted his head. "Well, actually, *I'm* the only thing keeping her alive."

Nord's eyes shifted to Lina, who had ropes of fire winding their way up her body. She cried out as the flames seared into her flesh, though thankfully, the fire snuffed out as soon as she was well and truly tied up.

He shook with anger. "Let her go."

"You first."

Nord held Mikel's stare, not trusting him to keep his word, but too afraid of what he'd do to Lina if Nord refused. Huffing in frustration, Nord released Kristoff and held his hands up as he stepped away.

"Good boy," Mikel taunted, leaning down to pull a dagger free from an ankle holster. He moved slowly, putting on a show as he ran one hand over the blade, setting it alight.

Then he held his arm out, pointing the tip of the dagger at Lina's throat. Nord tensed, his entire body primed to jump down and protect her. The slight shake of Lina's head was all that kept him in place.

"Now, here's what's going to happen. Evalina is going to forfeit, or else I am going to use this blade of mine to slit her lovely throat. By Rite, that's what I *should* do. That's what she agreed to. But I am a generous man, and my original mission was to see her exiled. So, instead of seeking her death, I will accept her exile."

Lina's eyes were wide as she watched the hand that held the blade. "Why would you do that?"

"There has been enough bloodshed amongst our people. They deserve peace, don't you think?"

Lina could hardly deny it. Mikel had laid his trap perfectly. Either way, he got what he wanted, but by not killing her, he came out a hero.

The room descended into absolute silence as Quinn stepped forward. She couldn't quite manage to hide her trembling limbs as she stood at Nord's side. "If you seek her exile, the Satori will defect and stand with her and any Cuskas who choose to follow."

"Do not presume to speak for my family," Nico shouted from the back of the room.

Mikel kept his gaze on Quinn, his pale green eyes sharpening with interest. "You would divide our people for her?"

"I would," she said, holding his stare and practically daring him to call her bluff.

"Have you forgotten what your family owes me? What would happen if you walked away before those debts are repaid? Do you value your family's life so little?"

Pain lanced through Quinn's eyes as she shook her head.

"Perhaps you would like to rethink your little declaration, Satori."

Nord thought he might be the only one in the room who heard the hammer of a gun being cocked back. If Mikel's threats turned physical, Finley would pump the man full of lead, politics and strategy be damned.

"I'm sorry," Quinn whispered to Nord beneath her breath.

Lina's eyes fell closed, a single tear trickling down her cheek as she exhaled. But her blue eyes blazed with anger, not sadness, when they reopened and landed on Mikel. "If you let Nord go free and promise not to seek retaliation against my family, then I will agree to a forfeit and to my exile."

Mikel's smile was slow, but no less cruel because of it. When he spoke, his voice was so low it only just reached Nord from his position on the stage. "What do you take me for? A monster? I've never harmed an innocent person in my life. I don't intend to start now."

Lina stiffened, but Mikel didn't give her a chance to speak further before his voice boomed out once more.

"Nico, would you like to do the honors?"

Lina's cousin came forward, his eyes shining with malicious glee as he accepted the dagger from Mikel's hand. The flames went out as soon as Nico's fingers closed around the hilt, but that didn't seem to bother him.

Without a second's hesitation, Nico cut into each of Lina's cheeks, leaving thin rivulets of blood trickling down her face. Lina snarled at him but didn't so much as flinch when the dagger kissed her cheeks.

Nord made to jump down, but Quinn's hand slid into his.

"You'll only make it worse for her if you interfere," she warned him softly, her eyes urging him to stay put.

Holding up the dagger dripping with crimson drops of Lina's blood, Nico turned to face the crowd.

"As of this moment, Evalina Cuska no longer exists. The Mobius Council does not recognize her as Animagi, nor will the Cuskas claim her as theirs. She is a blood-traitor and has forfeited any and all right to walk among us. She is banished, now and forever more. Let this be a warning to the rest of you. The Council will not tolerate traitors. Nor will we be so lenient in the future."

Nord had been so focused on Nico, he didn't realize Kristoff had moved until a sharp prick jabbed him in the neck. Fire licked at his veins as pain lanced through his body. The last thing Nord heard before the room went black was Lina's desperate cry and Mikel's cruel laugh.

"I said he'd live, but I never agreed he'd leave unharmed."

CHAPTER 23
LINA

Lina sat up, clutching her head with a groan, the rancid stench of rotting garbage assaulting her nose and causing tears to well in her eyes. She tried to open them, but the light cut through her head like a knife, forcing her to squeeze them shut again.

"Easy now."

"Fin?"

"That's right, love."

"Wh-where are we?"

"Well, you're in a wheelie bin, and I'm standing in the middle of an alleyway."

"Wheelie bin?"

"A dumpster."

Ugh. That explained the smell.

Lina rubbed her throbbing head, trying to make sense of how she ended up here. Everything after Nico finding her in the vault was fuzzy. The harder she tried to chase her memories, the foggier they grew.

"What happened?" she croaked. "How did you find me?"

"Let's just worry about getting you two out of there for now. We can talk once I get you home."

"Two?" There was one terrifying moment of blankness, and then her heart spasmed painfully in her chest. "Nord. Oh my God, Nord!"

"Shh, he'll be fine. Nothing I can't handle. Come on, up you go."

Strong arms curved under her, lifting her easily. Even through her eyelids, Lina flinched against the light, feeling like thousands of tiny needles simultaneously stabbed her eyes. She ducked her head and pressed into the warm expanse of Finley's chest to escape it, only to whimper and flinch away as his shirt rubbed her cheek, sending searing bolts of pain shooting through her.

"Here, let's do something about those cuts and burns."

"Burns?"

The question broke through her body's numb shock as her mind flooded with images of balls of flame and fiery rope, but she couldn't quite understand them. Everything hurt. Her skin felt raw. She couldn't tell if she was hot or cold, and her head seemed to weigh a thousand pounds. All she could manage at the moment was curling into Finley as he set about taking care of her.

"There, that's better."

Lina finally managed to open her eyes, her body blissfully free of pain once more, though her head was still oddly heavy. She stared up at a rumpled and dirty-looking Finley, lines of tension crinkling his eyes and bracketing his mouth.

"Thanks, Fin."

"Don't mention it," he murmured, setting her on her feet.

There was a wave of dizziness at the shift in position, but it passed quickly.

"All good?" Finley asked, his hands grasping her forearms.

Lina nodded. "Yeah. I'm fine."

He released her and moved back to the dumpster, casting a considering look her way before reaching in. He must have decided Nord looked pretty rough because his eyes glowed a brilliant silver for several long moments, only to fade just as Nord let out a deep groan.

"Careful, mate."

Lina bit her lip, anxious energy making her fidget restlessly as she waited. She knew Nord was all right, but she couldn't shake the feeling something had gone terribly wrong. Why else would they both have ended up unconscious in a dumpster? It made her twitchy with the need to hold him.

Rather than pick Nord up, as he'd done with her, Finley grasped him by the forearm and pulled, helping him to climb up and out. Nord landed on the ground in a half-crouch. He grimaced, pulling something wet and rank off the side of his face and tossing it back into the bin as he righted himself.

"I'm going to guess we didn't win that one," Nord said, giving Finley a wry glance as he moved to Lina.

"No, I don't think we can call what happened back there winning."

Their words should have set off all kinds of alarms, but Lina was too relieved to care as Nord wrapped his arm around her waist and pulled her into his side. She leaned into him, the warmth of his body and steady beat of his heart doing a lot to alleviate her concern.

She still couldn't quite shake off the grogginess, though. Her mind was muddled, like someone had reached in and scrambled everything up. She'd only felt like this once before . . . the morning after her eighteenth birthday when she and Quinn had 'gotten tattooed.' Knowing now that the memory had been a false one, she couldn't help but wonder if someone really had been playing around in her mind.

"Where's Quinn?" she asked with a frown.

Finley's expression shuttered. "She couldn't leave with us, but I'm sure she'll meet us back at the penthouse as soon as she can."

"Oookay," Lina replied, worry rearing its head once more. If Quinn wasn't here, it was only because forces outside of her control kept her away. As tough as she was, Lina hated that Quinn might have to face anything alone, especially since it was probably Lina's fault she was in that position in the first place.

"Come on, let's get out of here. I'm sure you two have questions you want answered, and I don't mind saying you both could use a shower or five."

Nord raised a brow. "I could say the same to you, brother."

Finley ran a hand through his already mussed hair, looking pained as he replied, "Yeah, well. That tends to happen when you go wading in rubbish."

Nord reached out, his expression grave as he placed his hand on his friend's shoulder. "Seriously. I owe you. Thank you for keeping your word."

Finley shrugged him off as Lina's eyes bounced between the two men, wondering what they were talking about.

"I'm serious about the showers. Don't you dare sit on anything in the penthouse until you get yourselves cleaned up," Finley said, his eyes glowing with power once more as he summoned them a portal home.

Lina smirked. "Don't be so uptight, Fin. I promise to replace anything we accidentally contaminate. We can redo the entire penthouse if you'd like."

As the words left her lips, a pit formed deep in her stomach, filling her with dread. There was a flicker of a memory, but it was gone before she could focus on it. Her heart beat faster as she realized whatever she was forgetting was a whole lot worse than losing a fight.

Finley's wince and Nord's somber expression confirmed it.

Heart in her throat, Lina reached for her magic, her mind already screaming a denial seconds before she discovered the void where her power should have been.

"My magic—" she started.

"Not here," Finley insisted, glancing around them nervously before gesturing to the portal. "Come on."

Lina obeyed, her steps wooden as she followed him through the displaced air. He'd made it about three steps from the door when she spun him around and demanded, "What happened after Nico found me at the vault, Fin? Where's my magic? Why can't I remember anything?"

She lifted a hand to her head, wincing as the throbbing returned with a vengeance. The harder she tried to remember, the worse the pain grew.

"I don't know what happened to your magic, love," Finley said, his eyes filled with apology. "But the reason you can't remember anything is that Mikel forced Quinn to wipe your memories."

"No," Lina said, shaking her head in denial. "Quinn would never do that to me."

"It wouldn't be the first time," Nord pointed out, his voice soft.

Lina frowned. "That's different. She was only trying to protect me."

"Maybe this time she did it to protect herself."

As much as she wanted to refute Nord's words, Lina couldn't disagree. Had their positions been reversed and it had been her back against the wall, she would have done the same. Quinn would have insisted on it.

"For what it's worth," Finley said, "I don't think Quinn obeyed him. Not to the letter. His instructions were for her to perform a complete wipe of anything relating to the Animagi, which clearly she didn't do."

Lina bit her lip, nodding a little. "That sounds like Quinn. She must have just done enough to make it look like she was following orders."

"That probably means any modification she made is temporary, or something she can undo at the very least."

"Yeah. You're probably right." Lina sighed. "That explains my memories, but what led up to that point? What happened to my magic?"

"I can't help you there," Finley said.

"Do you know?" Lina asked, peering hopefully up at Nord.

"Not much. We were apart for most of it. There was this one point, though, after Nico removed your cuffs where you were trying to pull off your necklace," Nord said, his eyes narrowed on a spot at the base of her throat.

"Necklace?" Lina patted at the spot, her hand closing around a cool pendant. A memory surged forth, this one wholly intact. "Crombie," she whispered, recalling the feel of his lips brushing across her cheek as he slid the necklace over her head as well as his apology right before he vanished.

"Crombie?" Nord repeated, his voice a dangerous rasp.

Lina's brow furrowed as she nodded, her words coming out slow as she tried to assign meaning to what she was remembering. "He put it on me before ghosting me in the vault. I'd thought he was apologizing for ditching me, but now I think he might have been apologizing for this." She lifted the pendant with trembling fingers.

"What is it?" Finley asked, stepping closer to investigate the bejeweled crescent.

"Part of the set he wanted from the vault."

Nord's eyebrows dipped low. "That's the reason he bloodswore you?"

Lina nodded. "He told me it was an heirloom for his court."

"If he wanted it back so badly, why did he leave it with you?"

"Well, he took the ring that goes with it," she said, as if that explained anything.

"They must be connected somehow," Finley murmured, letting the pendant fall back into her outstretched hand. "Do you mind taking it off so we can examine it more thoroughly?"

"No, of course not."

Lina reached around, feeling for a clasp and finding none. Frowning, she tried to lift the chain over her head, but it wouldn't move up past her chin.

"Here, let me help," Nord said, his thick fingers grasping the delicate chain and giving it a sharp tug.

Instead of breaking, the chain slid across his skin, cutting open his fingers while also slicing into the side of her neck.

"Ow!" Lina cried.

Nord dropped the chain with a hiss. "Son of a bitch."

Finley held up a hand to each of their injuries, healing them with a faraway look in his silver eyes.

"The necklace is clearly enchanted to stay put, and likely only able to be removed by whoever placed it on you. As to what else it does, that's harder to say for sure. Since it's part of a set, I'd hazard a guess that it's parasitic in nature."

"Parasitic? You mean Crombie *stole* my power? He's using it for himself?"

Finley nodded slowly. "That would be my guess. I don't see how else it benefits him otherwise. And everything that fae prick does is for his benefit."

A harsh ringing sounded in her ears, and she reached out for the wall as her knees buckled.

Nord's hands shot out, grasping her waist and helping her remain upright.

"Why would he do that to me? Why would he leave me alone in the vault without any way to defend myself? I thought . . ." she trailed off, unable to continue.

She'd thought they were friends. That no matter his bluster and posturing, he'd never actually do anything to harm her. But what he'd done . . . she could have been killed, and it would have been his fault. Worse, he hadn't even thought twice before doing it.

The betrayal cut deep, her bright surge of anger eclipsed by her pain.

"It'll be all right, Kærasta. We'll find him and make him remove the necklace. You'll get your power back."

Lina nodded absently. She knew Nord would see to that, but the damage had already been done. She didn't think she'd ever be able to trust Crombie again. The realization made her sadder than it probably should have. Like she'd lost something special she could never get back. Lina was used to betrayal—her father practically raised her on it—but this was the first time she'd ever been blindsided by a person she'd considered her friend. The circle of people she trusted was small; to find out she'd made such a grievous misjudgment in who she'd allowed in had her seriously questioning herself.

"I guess that also explains what happened when you faced off with Mikel," Finley mused.

Lina's gaze snapped back to Finley. "When I *what*?"

"The Rite?" he asked, as if it might trigger something.

She shook her head, still having no clue what he was referring to.

He let out a heavy exhale. "Come on, let's go inside. I'll pour us some drinks and do my best to relay what I know. I won't be able to fill in all the blanks, I only witnessed so much firsthand, but it will at least explain how you two ended up in the alley. Maybe it will be enough for you to connect the dots as to the rest."

She rubbed her aching temples, instinct warning her that Crombie's treachery, while soul-crushing, was about to be the least of her worries. Perhaps it was a mercy she couldn't recall what had happened. Hadn't her last bout of amnesia taught her that?

As Lina trailed into the penthouse behind Finley, she couldn't help but wonder how far he'd get into his recounting before she ached to forget once more.

The answer, as it turned out, wasn't long at all.

CHAPTER 24
LINA

Lina sat in the oversized armchair, staring at the fireplace without really seeing its flickering flames. Nor did she notice how the city outside was blanketed in white and tiny ice ferns climbed up the penthouse's wall of windows thanks to the swirling snow. She might have appreciated her cozy surroundings more if she wasn't so wracked with guilt. But her thoughts were wholly turned inward, too busy reliving the absolute disaster she'd made of everything.

She sighed, curling her legs beneath her and resting her cheek on her fist. Her hair was still wet from her shower, little splashes of water dripping down her neck every now and then as a cocktail sat forgotten by her elbow. Her breath hitched as she silently berated herself for her countless failings, burrowing deeper into Nord's massive sweatshirt, which she'd paired with some leggings, needing the comfort of being surrounded by something that belonged to—and smelled like—him.

Quinn still wasn't back, and Cora hadn't checked in either, their movements likely being tracked by Mikel and the Council. The lack of contact left Lina with nothing to do but picture scenario after horrific scenario. If anything happened to them, she'd never forgive herself. She was having a hard enough time wrapping her head around just how spectacularly she'd fucked up already.

The Rite of Requital . . . what had she been thinking?

"Stop beating yourself up, Kærasta."

Lina glanced up, tracking Nord's progress through the living room until he stood just in front of her. She was too upset to appreciate how good he looked fresh from the shower wearing low-slung sweats and nothing else.

He crooked a finger beneath her chin and tilted her head back until her eyes met his. "I mean it."

"Easier said than done, Viking. I can't just snap my fingers and make myself stop feeling like a bag of shit."

"Try."

She rolled her eyes and twisted her head to the side, but Nord grasped her chin with his thumb and index finger and turned her face back to his.

"You did the best you could with the knowledge you had. That's all any leader can ever hope for. No one gets it right one hundred percent of the time. What matters is what happens after. Are you just going to wallow and give up? Or are you going to regroup and keep going?"

"Wallowing sounds pretty nice."

Nord's mouth curled up on one side, and he ran his thumb over her bottom lip. "You'd never forgive yourself if you quit now."

A tendril of warmth unfurled in her chest, breaking through her pity party long enough for her to admit he was right.

Lina sighed and shook her head. "Promoted and exiled in less than forty-eight hours, I think that must be some kind of record."

"To be fair, it was more hostile takeover than promotion. Those rarely end well."

She snorted. "And you didn't think to mention that before I ran off and did it?"

Nord's smile was warm as he took a seat on the arm of her chair and crossed his feet at the ankles. "Would you have listened?"

"No."

He laughed. "There's your answer."

Shifting her weight, Lina rested her head against his hip. "I don't know what to do now," she admitted softly.

"We'll figure it out."

"Where do we even start?"

"With the next logical step. Then the one after that. And so forth, until we've accomplished what we set out to do. It's never truly over unless you stop trying, Kærasta." He reached out and brushed his knuckles down her cheek. "And I don't believe you have it in your heart to ever stop."

Tears pricked her eyes and her inhale was shaky, but her voice remained steady as she replied, "So the next step is finding Crombie."

"It would seem so."

"He's not going to make it easy for us. If his endgame has been stealing my power all along, he won't just hand it back over now."

"We won't give him a choice."

The simmering violence in his voice made her smile. It was hard to doubt anything when he said it with that much dark conviction.

"I wonder why the necklace only affects my Animagi abilities and not the berserker," she wondered aloud, a crease forming between her brows.

Nord brushed the hair off her forehead, running his index over the furrow and smoothing it out. "Maybe it only steals arcane abilities? Or maybe it can only take what's inherently yours, and the berserker is tied to me?"

She chewed on her bottom lip as she thought it over. "I guess that makes sense. But your powers aren't affected, right?"

"Not so far as I can tell."

"That's something, I guess," she said with a gusty exhale.

Finley joined them then, smiling as he padded over. "You're

looking better," he commented, dropping a kiss to the top of her head before taking a seat on the sofa across from them.

"Looks can be deceiving."

"How well I know it," he said, picking up her cocktail and taking a sip.

She didn't even have the energy for a feigned protest. A fact he noticed with a slight frown before his eyes brightened, and he looked up at Nord.

"So, is this her first official meeting of the Exiles Club? Have you already taught her the secret handshake?"

"What?" she asked with a little laugh.

"Not yet," Nord said, the smile evident in his voice.

Finley mimed wiping sweat off his brow. "Phew. I thought I might have missed something important. Well," he said, lifting her glass in the air, "welcome to the club, darling."

"You're an exile too?"

He drained her glass and then winked. "All the best of us are."

Lina sat up straight, suddenly curious. "What did you do to get exiled?"

"That's a story for another day."

"You mean this isn't one of those meetings where all of us have to go around introducing ourselves and sharing our tragic stories?"

"God no," Finley said with a horrified laugh. "That would be entirely too depressing. This is more of a drinking club for people with authority issues."

"Sounds like my kind of club."

"See, it's only your first meeting, and you're already right at home."

Lina laughed, a true belly laugh that made her cheeks hurt and did wonders for her lingering sense of guilt and heartache. Then she groaned as reality came crashing back in.

"How are we supposed to face off against Mikel when I'm not even going to be able to get near him?"

"We'll worry about that when the time comes," Nord assured her.

"I know it may not feel like it yet but being kicked off the Council really isn't the worst thing that could have happened," Finley added. "Now you don't have to worry about following anyone's rules but your own."

"True, but my people all hate me and think I'm a traitor."

Finley shrugged. "They'll come around."

"How can you be so sure?"

"I've lived a long time, love. One thing I've found to be true across countless realms and lifetimes is that people do what they need to do to survive. Right now, for the Animagi, that's following Mikel's lead. If they're presented with a viable alternative, I can't imagine they wouldn't leap at it."

"So we need to give them that alternative."

"Exactly so," Finley said with a smile. "And if anyone can figure out how, I'm sure it's you."

"Well, I'm glad one of us—"

Nord cleared his throat.

"Two of us," she corrected, "feel confident. But it seems like any plan for dealing with Mikel is going to start with getting my power back. And that's not much of a plan. Mikel isn't going to sit around and do nothing while we try to convince Crombie to hand it over. Today was just the tip of the iceberg when it comes to what he's got in store for me. He'll be coming at all of us with guns blazing now."

"Maybe you can explain something to me," Finley said, leaning forward and bracing his elbows on his knees, "not that I'm complaining, mind you, but why go through all the trouble of exiling you and wiping your memory when he could have killed you outright?"

Lina sighed. "That does seem like the easier option, doesn't it? Which is actually the exact reason he didn't do it."

Nord's hand shifted so it curled around the back of her neck. He pressed into the knotted muscles there, helping soothe her with his touch.

"Unraveling Mikel's intentions is sort of like thinking you're playing checkers only to find out it's really seven chess games at once. He operates on a whole different level. He's not just interested in killing me, he wants to make a point because his goal isn't my death, it's to supersede the Council. To do that, he needs to act above reproach."

"So he let you dig your own grave to discredit you," Finley said, starting to understand what she was trying to say.

"If he can discredit me, then I can't be a martyr. Martyrs have loyal followers. Traitors don't."

"Which leaves the path clear for him," Finley said, still following along.

"Exactly. He wants the Animagi to believe he has their best interest at heart when the truth is, he couldn't give a shit about them. All he wants is power." Lina scoffed. "I mean, anyone who would save the announcement of their son's death for when it would have the highest political payoff is not exactly an upstanding guy."

"Okay, so I'm understanding the thought process behind your banishment. He turned the Animagi against you so no one will care and there won't be any personal repercussions when he comes after you. But why the memory wipe?"

"Because I'm a liability. As an heir, I possess information he doesn't want me to share. Combine that with the fact that I pretty much confirmed I have access to a Codex by showing up with Nord, and it's too dangerous for him to allow me to retain any knowledge I might have discovered in its pages."

Finley gave her a thoughtful look. "So why not take Nord's memories?"

Lina shrugged, having wondered the same. "Mikel probably just assumed he didn't know anything."

"Seems like a stupid assumption to make. He's your true mate; surely they'd suspect he knows everything you do."

"Your assuming Mikel places any value in those sorts of bonds."

"Which just proves how little he understands about them," Nord rumbled from behind her.

She twisted around to smile up at him. "And makes it the perfect weapon to use against him."

"My thoughts exactly," he replied, returning her smile.

Lina turned back toward Finley, using Nord as her headrest as she leaned back into him. "So, anybody got any bright ideas about what to do about Crombie?"

"You mean you're not going to just show up on his front door and demand he return your magic?" Finley asked with a lift of his brow.

She gave him a sideways smile. "While that is my trademark, I'm not sure it's going to work this time."

"We need to surprise him. Catch him off guard somewhere he can't easily escape," Nord said. "Do you think Zilla would help us?"

"Zilla?" Lina repeated, the suggestion a surprise but not an unwelcome one. "I mean, he did help us last time, so maybe?"

"It couldn't hurt to ask, at the very least," Finley said.

"Um, does anybody have his number? Or a phone?" she added, wrinkling her nose.

Nord grasped her hair and slowly pulled it back, tilting her face up to his. "Where's yours?"

Lina shrugged. "Beats me. Haven't seen it in weeks."

He shook his head, muttering under his breath as he pulled his cell out of his pocket. "Use mine."

She blew him a cheeky kiss and immediately started scrolling through his contacts until she reached the Zs, pleased to see Nord had him listed there, unlike Quinn, who still had him saved as Linc.

Lina's smile slipped at the reminder that her friend wasn't with them. She wanted to call or text her, but if Quinn got caught communicating with them right now, there'd be hell to pay. She settled for sending her thoughts out to the universe, hoping wherever Quinn was, she'd somehow sense they were thinking about her.

Stay safe. Don't do anything stupid. Come home when you can.

Lina hit the call button with a soft sigh.

Zilla answered before the first ring ended. "Hello?"

"Zilla? It's—"

"Lina," he said, drawing her name out, "to what do I owe the pleasure?"

"You may not think it's such a pleasure when I tell you why I called," she warned him with a nervous chuckle.

"Hearing from you is always a pleasure, regardless of the circumstance. How can I be of service?"

"I promise one day I'm going to call just to say hi and see how you're doing, and not to ask you for a favor."

Zilla's chuckle flowed through the phone, the warmth of it curling around her and making her smile. "I'm not sure I'll know what to do with myself when the day comes."

"Usually, my friendships aren't so one-sided. Why don't you call and ask me for help sometime? You know, settle the score a little." Then Lina remembered why she'd called, and her nervous babbling turned into a heavy sigh. "Although, I'd probably be pretty useless to you right now unless you just needed help beating the crap out of someone. But I feel like you probably have that covered."

"I doubt you could ever be useless, milady. Now, why don't you tell me why that beautiful smile of yours is missing from your voice."

Lina thought it inordinately sweet of him not only to notice, but to care enough to ask. She wasn't sure she deserved Zilla's loyalty, but she was grateful for it all the same.

"It's Crombie."

"Of course it is. What's he done this time?"

"He stole my power. I need to find him so I can make him give it back."

There was a beat of silence and then an explosive, "That ripe bastard. I should have known he was up to something when he took off without so much as a 'how's your mother'."

She gripped the phone tighter in her hand. "Took off? What do you mean? Where is he?"

Nord's hands squeezed her shoulders, and Finley shot her a worried look.

Zilla blew out a breath. "I'm sorry to have to tell you this, but Crombie went back to Faerie."

"He what?" she shrieked, her heart dropping to her feet. "Did he leave you with any way to reach him? You know, in case of an emergency or something at the club?"

"'Fraid not."

"So there's no way to get ahold of him?"

"None I have access to. You can't exactly make a call across dimensions. That kind of message would have to be delivered in person, and I don't know anyone who can make the trip. 'Cept him, of course."

"Of course," she repeated, her voice hollow, a high-pitched ringing in her ears. "I don't suppose you have any idea when he's coming back?"

Or if.

Lina shoved the thought away, too afraid of the possibility to even consider, let alone give voice to it.

"I don't, but I'll give you a ring as soon as I catch a whiff of him."

"Thanks, Zilla. I appreciate it."

"I'm sorry there's not more I can do for you. If there's anything else you need, don't hesitate to give me a call, all right?"

"Okay."

"Chin up, love. You'll get this sorted."

"Yeah," she said, though her heart wasn't in it. "Bye, Zilla."

She pressed the end button, the phone sliding out of her limp hand.

"What happened?" Finley asked, at the same time Nord demanded, "Where is he?"

Lina looked up with a humorless laugh. "I don't suppose you've ever been to Faerie, have you? Or that you have any contacts there?"

Finley shook his head. "No, can't say that I do. Why?"

"Crombie went home. I don't—" Lina struggled to draw in a

breath, her chest feeling like it was caving in on itself. "I don't know what we do from here. If we can't get ahold of him, my magic—"

Nord wrapped his arms around her, hauling her up until she was cradled in his lap.

"Shhh. We'll figure it out."

She was hyperventilating, her vision going hazy at the edges as her body struggled to draw in air.

"But," she gasped.

His arms tightened around her, though instead of making it harder to breathe, it seemed to help.

"There's always another way, Lina. We'll figure it out. We always do."

Lina wasn't sure how. Crombie was in the one place they couldn't seem to follow. And even if they could, where would they even begin to search? For now, she was just going to have to make peace with the fact that her magic was gone, and Crombie along with it.

It might have been easier to do if it didn't feel like a death sentence.

CHAPTER 25
NORD

"How's Lina doing?"

Nord glanced at Finley's reflection in the window, answering him without turning around. "She's still locked in her room, pouring over Alistair's notes and trying to decipher the rest of the Codex."

"Did she really lock the door?" Finley asked with a hint of a laugh.

"No," Nord said with a sigh, trying not to sound as aggrieved as he felt, "but I figure the fact that she shut it in the first place was her way of asking for some space. I'm trying to respect it."

Finley remained silent for a beat before asking, "So how much longer are you going to give her before you storm in anyway?"

Nord glanced over his shoulder with a self-deprecating grin. "Am I that transparent?"

"You've nearly worn a hole in my carpet with all your pacing."

"You try to ignore the need to take care of your woman and see how well you do."

Finley crossed the room, holding out one of the two highball glasses he'd filled with amber liquid. "I'm more familiar with that particular battle than you might think. Cheers," he said, clinking Nord's glass with his and taking a healthy swig of the forty-year-old single malt.

"Skål," Nord replied, following suit. Heady warmth expanded in his chest, and he gave the glass an appreciative look as he asked, "Still haven't heard from Quinn?"

Finley groaned and scrubbed a hand over his face. "It's been radio silence since she refused to leave with me."

"So you did manage to catch up with her and talk after the trial?"

"If you can call it that. She wasn't exactly happy to see me."

"I wouldn't take it personally; she was probably just worried about getting caught with you."

Finley nodded, though his expression was drawn. "She said as much."

"Did she give you any idea of when she'd be back?"

"No."

Nord winced in sympathy, the agony of Lina going missing still fresh in his mind. He clapped a hand on Finley's shoulder. "Sorry, brother."

"It's fine. Comes with the territory when you're dealing with women like ours. Though it might be easier if mine wasn't so damn prickly. At least Lina allows you to care for her. Trying to take care of Quinn is like convincing a feral cat to have a cuddle. Hell," he said with a snort, "the cat might be easier to convince, come to think of it."

"I find it helps when the woman in question actually agrees to be yours," Nord said, biting back a laugh.

Finley punched him in the arm.

Nord raised a brow, giving him a pointed look. "I'm going to let that one go because you're clearly not in your right mind. Do it again, and I'll turn every bone in your hand to dust."

Finley gave him a sulky stare. "Why are you the only one allowed to go around punching things?"

"Because I have the superior facial hair."

Finley gaped at him and then threw his head back and roared with laughter. Once he'd caught his breath, he asked, "Is that some sort of Viking thing?"

Nord smirked. "It is, actually."

"Figures."

They fell quiet, both of them sipping their drinks and staring out at the snow-filled night sky.

After a few minutes, Finley broke the silence and said, "We may not have many quiet nights left, at least not in the near future. You shouldn't waste it."

"I already told you I'm—"

"Wasting it," Finley cut in. "I know because you're out here with me instead of spending it with her."

Nord hated it when Finley was right, not that he'd give him the satisfaction of admitting it aloud. He killed his drink, handing his friend the empty glass.

Finley gave him a knowing smile. "You should show her the spa. I bet she'd enjoy a nice soak after everything she's been through."

Nord froze, his eyes narrowing with suspicion. "Have you contracted a deadly virus or something? Are you dying?" he asked, holding up his hand to Finley's forehead as if checking for a temperature.

Finley slapped his hand away. "Why do you automatically assume I'm dying because I'm being nice?"

Nord gave his friend a pointed look. "Because you never share your toys."

"I let you live here rent free, don't I? And I literally just shared some of my best scotch. Doesn't that count?"

"Let me rephrase, you never share anything you actually care about. I'm pretty sure you threatened to geld me the last time I asked to borrow one of your cars."

He grinned. "I did, didn't I? You should probably take advantage of my generosity before I change my mind."

Nord lifted both his brows. "Seeing as how the only time

you've even let me set foot in your sacred spa was during my tour of the house the night I moved in, I think I will. If you'll excuse me."

Finley's laughter chased him out of the room, but Nord's focus had already shifted back to Lina. He knew she was spiraling; he'd felt her emotions bubbling over since he and Finley had filled her in on what Mikel tried to make her forget. Knowing the only way to help her work through her guilt and fear was to force her to face it head-on, Nord strode into her bedroom without knocking.

She was right where he'd left her, huddled up on the bed with the Codex and Alistair's notes spread out in front of her. Lina spared him a brief glance before returning her attention to the page she clutched in her hands. "If you've come to check on my progress, there hasn't been any."

"Put that down and come with me."

"Nord, I'm right in the middle of—"

"I wasn't asking, Kærasta."

She set the page on top of her notebook and really looked at him. "You're going to come over here and make me if I don't, aren't you?"

He gave her a slow smile.

Lina sighed and swung her legs over the side of the bed. "Let's get this over with then so I can get back to my research."

"Get this over with? Is spending time with me suddenly a chore you need to cross off your to-do list before you can get back to more fulfilling things?"

She froze, likely replaying her words back in her mind before giving him an apologetic smile. "I didn't mean it like that."

"I know. But trust me, you'll like what I have planned."

"I'm sure I will," she said, padding over to him and lifting on her toes to brush her lips against his. "You just caught me at a bad time."

"Which could arguably be the perfect time."

She studied him, one of her eyebrows lifting. "What are you up to?"

He held out a hand. "Come on, I'll show you."

Lina didn't hesitate before placing her hand in his. "Is it really the best idea for us to be going on field trips right now?"

"We aren't leaving the penthouse," he said, leading her out of the room and down the hallway.

"What could you possibly want to show me in the penthouse? Unless you're finally going to admit to your musical talents and put on a proper concert for me."

"Ha, not quite."

When he pulled her behind him into the gym, she stopped walking and tugged on the hand holding hers. "Nuh-uh. I'm drawing the line at working out. I know you think training is the answer for everything, but I promise you, in this case, it's definitely not."

"Training is an excellent way to work through most emotional and mental blocks, but I swear to you that's not what I have in mind. Trust me."

Her gaze turned suspicious, but she finally consented.

He smiled as he led her to the back corner of the room and the secret door Finley had hidden behind a wall of shelving and random equipment. Once there, he lifted the latch, sending the door sliding away to reveal the luxurious room behind it.

Lina gaped. "How did I not know about this?" she asked, her eyes wide as they took in the sauna, salt water infinity pool, and hot tub.

"Finley is particular about what he considers his."

"Is this like his car thing?"

Nord chuckled, hooking an arm around her neck and reeling her in so he could press a kiss to her head. "Exactly like his car thing."

"I guess I can understand that. Everyone needs a place to escape and relax."

"I see you're finally starting to understand my purpose."

"Is this something Finley is going to try to murder me for later, or do we have his permission?"

"It was his idea," Nord confirmed.

Lina let out a little squeal and ran into the room, kneeling beside the pool to dip her hand in and test the water. She made a face and pulled her hand back out. "Too cold." Then she looked at the sauna and scrunched her nose. "Too hot."

"Are you Goldilocks now?"

Lina stood and moved to the hot tub, pausing to dip in her toes and let out a satisfied moan. "Juuuuust right. Guess that makes you the bear."

His grin took on a predatory edge. "You do know what happened when the bears caught her, don't you?"

Lina blinked at him. "They all snuggled up in one big cuddle pile?"

"They ate her."

She sent him a coy look from beneath her lashes. "I love it when you eat me, so if you're trying to dissuade me, you're doing a terrible job."

"As long as we're on the same page."

Lina blushed, but her lips were tipped up in a smile he had no trouble interpreting. "Why didn't you tell me to grab a swimsuit? Or was that all part of your master plan as well?"

He raked his gaze over her body, calling on his magic as he replaced her borrowed hoodie and tight black pants with a skimpy black bathing suit.

Lina glanced down, her expression a mix of surprise and appreciation. "A one-piece, huh? I would have had you pegged for a string bikini kind of guy. Not that this leaves a whole lot to the imagination," she said, twisting around and giving him an eyeful of her delectable body.

"That was the point."

Her eyes caught his. "Why bother with it at all then?"

Nord lifted a shoulder. "Gives me something to peel off."

"So I'm like a present?"

"The best one I've ever had," he agreed, his eyes tracking her with undisguised hunger as she lowered herself into the steamy water.

"Guess you should come over here and unwrap me then."

"You never need to ask me twice, Kærasta."

"Uhhhh, I'm pretty sure you've made me beg a time or two, Viking."

His steps were slow and measured as he moved over to the side of the hot tub. "And I'm sure I'll have you begging again in no time."

She watched him with unabashed desire as he hooked his thumbs in his sweats and let them drop to the floor.

"What, no banana hammock for you?"

He winked as he slid into the water on the other side of the tub. "Too much slippage."

Lina's peals of laughter echoed around the room. She tilted her head to the side, eyeing him carefully. "You know, I've got to say, you're handling things really well. A lot better than I am, truth be told."

"What do you mean?"

She bit her lip as she tried to figure out how to explain herself. Gesturing to the crescent moon hanging around her neck, she said, "Well, you know . . . After everything Crombie has done, I sort of expected you to be more"—she balled her hands into fists and slammed them into the surface of the water, sending waves rippling out and water surging up out of the pool—"Nord smash."

He laughed. "Nord smash?"

"Well . . . yeah."

Nord grasped one of her balled-up hands and tugged her through the water until she straddled his hips. "Perhaps I'm just better at hiding it."

"No," she said, her eyes solemn as they searched his, "I know what you're feeling, remember?"

He lifted her hand and pressed a kiss to each of her fingertips before turning her hand up and pressing one into the center of her palm. "Well, maybe having you safely in my arms does a lot to abate the worst of my destructive urges."

"And if I wasn't? Safe in your arms . . ."

Nord pushed the wet strands of her hair off her shoulder, so they floated behind her on the water. "Do you even need to ask?"

"Boom?" she asked, her hands mimicking an explosion.

"Big badda boom," he confirmed, his expression serious despite his teasing words.

She rested her palms lightly on his shoulders, her face grave. "I still don't remember a whole lot about what happened today with Mikel. But there's this moment I feel so vividly it must have imprinted itself on my soul. All I know is I thought you were in danger, and it was like—" She looked off to the side and shook her head. "I don't know how else to explain it except to say absolutely nothing could stop me from protecting you."

"I'm familiar with that feeling," he said, curling his arms tightly around her waist so her body was flush against his.

"I've lost a lot of things, but I don't think I'd survive losing you."

Her words carved into him, flaying him open and laying him bare.

"Lina," he said, cradling her face in his palm, "there's not a person on this earth that would survive if I lost you."

Even though she looked down, her hands fiddling with the ring he wore around his neck, he could feel her reaction to his confession. Her sense of wonder and unbridled joy followed by something else. A wistful sort of longing he didn't quite understand. He dropped his gaze, watching Lina slowly slide the tip of her finger through the ring.

As a possible answer took shape, hope detonated in his chest, causing his heart to race with a fierce longing of his own. If he was wrong about this, he was about to make things incredibly awkward.

"Would you like to wear my ring, Kærasta?"

It was obvious to Nord when her eyes snapped up and her mouth rounded in a small O, she knew he wasn't casually asking about a random piece of his berserker jewelry, but something far more specific.

Just to make sure his intentions were perfectly clear, he continued, "To have something that proclaims to the rest of the world you belong to me, and I to you?"

She opened and closed her mouth, looking at him with so much love and hope shining in her eyes it took him a second to remember how to breathe. It was impossible to know who was responsible for the bubble of happiness swooping around in his chest with thousands of tiny wings, but he liked to think it was both of them.

Grasping the chain that he'd never, not once since donning it, taken off, he snapped it easily, letting the ivory-colored ring fall into his palm. Then he lifted it between his fingers, holding it up to her.

"I do not have the words to describe what it did to me when you stood before your people and publicly claimed me as yours. And while you might not currently remember it, I don't think I'll ever forget. I want the opportunity to do the same. You know I'm already yours in every way that matters. Every way, except for one." His lips hooked up as she sucked in a watery breath. "I'm a selfish man, Kærasta. I crave claiming you in that final, most public manner. I want us to be bound together every possible way, so mortal and god alike know they cannot ever come between us. I need everyone to know what my heart recognized the first time I ever laid eyes on you. You're mine, Lina. Will you make it official and be my wife?"

He took her hand in his and slid the ring onto her finger, where it fit like it had been made for her. Nord knew the odds of that had to be astronomical, but he'd already discovered in matters of fate, rules rarely applied.

Lina angled her face down, her lips claiming his in a kiss that started off sweet but turned into an act of pure possession.

One of his hands slid into her hair, gripping tight as he ravished her mouth. The other smoothed down her spine to tilt her hips down and press her core into his swelling length.

She moaned against his mouth, her tongue tangling with his as she mimicked what her body so desperately desired.

Nord wanted to draw the moment out, to make love to her slowly and prove that hers was the only altar at which he worshipped. But the second her hips ground wantonly against him, he lost any grasp he had on his self-control.

"Lina," he groaned, his teeth grazing her bottom lip as she dragged the tips of her nails down his back.

"No one has ever owned me so completely. My body, my heart, my soul, all of them are yours for as long as you want them."

"Forever, Kærasta. There will never come a day where I stop loving you."

"Show me," she begged. "Show me who I belong to."

"Fuck, Lina."

She leaned forward, the warmth of her breath fanning over his lips as she whispered, "All I want is to feel you moving inside me, claiming me with your body."

The battle for slow and sweet had already been lost, but that was when he surrendered to her completely. From that moment forward, her will would be his own. Her every wish, his personal mission. Until the day the gods called them from this world into the next, but probably even long after. He never had been very good at denying her anything anyway.

The hand he'd rested on her back slid lower, curling down between her legs to pull the wet fabric to the side.

"Yes," she hissed, pressing down against his fingers as he ran them over her bared center. "More, Nord. Please."

She worked her hand between them, grasping him at the base and lining him up with her entrance. She leaned back, just far enough that her gaze could hold his as she bit her lip and slid down his length. Her eyelids fluttered as she stretched around him, fighting hard to stay open.

"That's right. You know how I love to watch you come undone. Show me how much you love taking my cock, sweet Lina. Show me how much you love being mine."

She whimpered, easily finding her rhythm as she started to ride him, setting a relentless pace that had his hips driving up to meet her downward thrusts.

"You know what happens when you close your eyes," he whispered, one thumb feathering over her clit while the other circled her nipple.

Lina gasped and pressed into him, chasing the pressure she needed. Her fingers spasmed on his shoulders, alternating between digging into his skin and smoothing over the crescents she left behind.

He could feel how close she was, her inner muscles fluttering along his throbbing length, milking him as she spiraled closer to her climax. He adjusted their angle, taking control of the tempo so that he was hitting the spot she loved.

Lina let out a low, desperate moan. "Oh, God, Nord, yes." Her voice was little more than a breathy whisper as she added, "Just like that."

He was a slave to her pleasure, following the commands of her body, leaning forward to claim her mouth as his thumb worked tight circles over her sensitive nub.

She slammed herself down, sending the water around them sloshing in every direction.

"I'm so close," she panted.

"Come for me, Lina."

Her eyes were the same deep sapphire as the water around them as she clenched down hard on his cock, riding him faster, his name leaving her lips in a desperate mewl as she plummeted headlong toward her climax, but not quite reaching it.

"There's nothing but us, Lina. Just us and the life we'll build together. Now come for me."

He pinched the swollen bundle of nerves at the apex of her thighs, causing her to cry out as sensation overrode all reason.

She gasped, her forehead pressing against his as she lost herself to her pleasure. Nord watched her fall apart, groaning his own climax against her lips as he spilled inside of her. Pulling her close and holding her until the pounding of their hearts merged into one perfect symphony.

"In case it wasn't obvious," she panted, "that was me saying yes."

CHAPTER 26
LINA

Lina stared at the ring on her left hand, a smile which had become nearly permanent since last night fixed on her lips as she thought about the man who'd lived countless years and never offered any woman what he'd so freely given her the night before. Her heart lifted in her chest, and she wiggled her fingers, unable to stop her smile from stretching wider.

"You don't have to keep staring at it," Nord said, laying his hand on top of hers. "It's not going anywhere."

"I know; I just still can't believe it. I've got bruises on my leg because I keep pinching myself to make sure this is really happening."

He leaned over and placed a lingering kiss on her lips. "It's as real as my love for you."

"Gah, stop it, or I'm going to make you bone me on every surface in this kitchen, and Finley will never speak to us again."

Nord's eyes twinkled. "You say that like it's a bad thing."

They shared a heated look that was interrupted by the sound of the front door.

"Do you think it's—"

"Honeys, I'm ho-ome," Quinn singsonged as she breezed into the kitchen like she hadn't disappeared off the face of the earth for the last thirty-plus hours.

She moved to Nord first, pressing a kiss to his cheek and snatching a piece of fruit off his plate. Taking a bite, she smiled and ruffled Lina's hair before dropping into the chair next to her.

"Uh, are you forgetting something?" Lina asked.

"Good morning?" Quinn asked after she swallowed the last of her fruit. At Lina's pointed look, she said, "What? Not good enough? Oh! You probably want your memories back, don't you?"

"I was thinking more along the lines of, where the hell have you been? Is it even safe for you to be here? Are you okay? Should we be worried? But yeah, I wouldn't say no to that either."

Quinn grinned. "I missed you, too, Lady B. Don't worry, I wouldn't be here if Mom hadn't assured me we'd have a safe window this morning. That reminds me, she wanted me to pass on her congratulations. Something about having a feeling they were in order?" Quinn raised a brow curiously. "Did I miss something?"

It shouldn't have been a surprise that Cora's intuition tipped her off to their news. But considering it'd only just happened the night before, and they hadn't had a chance to tell anybody yet, it still came as a shock.

"Oh, well, um." Lina glanced at Nord, looking for help.

Quinn grabbed half of Lina's bagel and took a bite, still staring expectantly at Lina. Not sure what to say, Lina held up her hand. Quinn's eyes shot from Lina's finger to Nord's neck, clearly recognizing the ring. She gasped and began choking on her bagel, smacking her chest a few times as her eyes watered.

Once she recovered, she pulled out her phone and started furiously typing. "I am going to hire you the hottest strippers. Do you think those Magic Mike guys do private shows? No matter, we'll just pay for the entire venue. Or would you rather bribe Søren and some other hunky Novasgardians to strip down, lube up, and beat the crap out of each other? Though I bet they'd probably do it for free. Gotta love Vikings." Quinn finally stopped chattering and looked up at Lina. "Well?"

Lina's stomach cramped from the laughter she was struggling to contain. Nord, however, merely shook his head and uttered one very firm word.

"No."

Quinn was completely undeterred. "You don't get a say, big guy. You might be her husband-to-be, but I'm her reigning best friend. Bestie beats out fiancé all day long. Besides, bachelorette parties are a single gal's most sacred ritual. You don't want to deprive Lina of this once-in-a-lifetime experience, do you?"

Nord gave her a long-suffering look and turned to Lina. "Is this something you want?"

"I hadn't really given it much thought, to be honest. A night out with the girls sounds fun, but I'm not sure about the half-naked dancing men part."

Quinn gave her an obnoxiously fake wink. "Riiight. No strippers. Got it."

"What's all this about strippers?" Finley asked, looking like he'd just rolled out of bed. He stopped dead at the sight of Quinn sitting at the table like she'd been at the penthouse all along.

The tension in the room cranked up as Quinn and Finley stared at each other.

"Does this mean you're back?" he finally asked, turning away from them and walking over to a cabinet filled with mugs.

If Lina hadn't been watching him so closely, she might not have noticed the slight tremor in his hands as he selected one at random and then reached for the kettle.

"Just a drive-by, I'm afraid," Quinn said.

Finley nodded to acknowledge he'd heard her but didn't comment further. It was obvious something was going on between them, but Lina knew better than to ask. Neither of them would admit to anything in front of the other. Stubborn jackasses.

"So, about those memories," Lina said, hoping to dispel some of the awkwardness.

"Oh, right," Quinn said, straightening up in her chair. "It's just a matter of removing a small block. This will only take a second." She brushed crumbs off her hands and reached out for Lina, her eyes swirling pools of deep purple as she called on her power.

Lina braced herself, anticipating the worst. And while the feel of Quinn rooting around in her mind was an odd one, this wasn't like last time, when the onslaught of information hit Lina like a jackhammer. It was more akin to the rush of a rollercoaster, though it was her mind and not her stomach dipping and diving as the memories that had been just out of reach became accessible once more. It took her a second to organize the abundance of pictures, emotions, and sensations that had been blocked, but just like with a rollercoaster, her mind quickly righted itself and every-thing fell back into place as quickly as it had been turned upside down.

"Thanks," she said, feeling a bit shaky and grateful for the fact she was seated. Had she tried to walk right now, Lina was pretty sure her legs would give out on her.

"Don't mention it. I'm just sorry I had to do it in the first place."

"I know. No hard feelings."

They shared a smile that spoke to the years of friendship and sisterhood between them.

"So," Lina said, as Finley finally joined them around the breakfast bar, "what happened after we, uh, left the meeting?"

Quinn's lips quirked up at Lina's euphemism. "Things wrapped up pretty quickly. Although, Mikel cornered me and provided me with a list of chores he's expecting me to complete by the end of the day." She rolled her eyes, letting out an annoyed sigh. "He's trying to keep me on a very short leash. Too bad for him I'm excellent at slip-ping out of them."

"Quinn, I'm so sorry," Lina said. "I never wanted to put you in this position. I know how hard you've been trying to stay away from him since inheriting your gifts. The last thing I ever wanted was to send you straight into the dragon's den."

"It's not your fault, Lady B. This was unavoidable. We always knew going up against him would be a gamble. We'd have to be some real lucky fuckers to knock him off his throne on our first go, and that's never been the case for us. You and I learned long ago how to fight tooth and nail for the things we want in life. So I don't mind playing my part, as long as I know it's temporary and that you're safe. Besides, if anyone should apologize, it should be me. I'm the one who just stood there and watched while Mikel played with you and then listened to Nico make that god-awful speech."

"There was nothing you could do."

Quinn shrugged. "Maybe not, but it would have felt incredible to claw that little shit's eyes out. I can't believe he let Mikel groom him into the perfect little soldier." She shook her head, looking disgusted. "The nerve of him calling you a blood-traitor when he's the one who completely turned his back on his family."

Lina had given the topic of Nico's allegiance quite a bit of thought during the night she spent locked in the storage closet. "Maybe he's the one who feels abandoned by his family," she said.

Quinn's brows flew up. "You can't really be defending him right now."

"No, absolutely not. I'm just saying he didn't have very many options in the role-model department, did he? With so many of us gone, he was ripe for the picking."

"You weren't gone, you were dead," Quinn said. "And Nico wasn't completely abandoned. There are still other Cuskas around, not to mention other Animagi. Mikel wasn't his only choice."

"I know, I know. I'm just trying to make sense of how it happened. People don't wake up one day and turn into heartless bastards for no reason."

"For the love of God, please stop defending him." Quinn looked to Finley and Nord for backup. "He does not deserve your forgiveness or understanding. He chose Mikel over you and the rest of his family.

There's nothing he could do or say, no reason he could come up with, that will make that okay."

"She's right," Finley said, looking up from his tea. "Whatever the reason, he's a grown man who made his choice. You'll be hard-pressed to convince me it was the right one."

"Thank you," Quinn said, sitting back in her chair and throwing her hands up.

"I'm not saying it was okay or that it was the right choice," Lina said, appreciating their outrage on her behalf. "I was only trying to point out that something led him down that path."

Lina could feel Nord's anger coiling in her chest like a snake ready to strike. All this talk of Nico and Mikel was stoking his rage. She needed to hurry up and make her point so she could pull the ripcord on this topic before things got out of control.

"Listen, regardless of what Nico's done, we can't afford to forget who's behind everything. Nico may be the weapon, but Mikel's the one holding the gun. And no matter how powerful the gun might be, it takes someone to pull the trigger."

The room fell quiet. The silence turning oppressive as the weight of everything and everyone they were dealing with hung between them.

Lina sighed, already missing the happy bubble she'd been lost in not even half an hour earlier. Hoping a topic change might help restore the mood, she asked, "Did Cora have any other feelings she wanted you to pass on?"

That seemed to be the distraction the others needed, because instead of nursing their anger, they turned expectant eyes on Quinn.

"Actually, she did," she said, folding her hands in front of her. "Mom said she had a feeling you'd find what you were looking for if 'you stepped through the doorway of light and shadow'."

"Uh, I'll get right on that," Lina said, prickles racing along the back of her neck as Cora's cryptic message ran through her mind. She hadn't really expected Quinn to have more to share, otherwise she would have probably asked to hear it sooner. After a few seconds, Lina shook her head with a frustrated sigh. "I can't shake the feeling I've heard that phrase somewhere before. I just can't seem to remember where."

"Don't worry, you'll figure it out," Quinn said, taking another bite out of her stolen bagel.

Nord brushed his knuckles against hers. "I've found that Cora's warnings don't always make sense right away. Maybe it's just me, but usually I have to sit with them for a minute before they'll make themselves clear."

"It's good you're learning how to decipher my mom's messages because she wanted me to pass on something to you as well."

Nord tensed, his hand flexing over Lina's before he nodded for Quinn to continue.

"Lina is the key that will unlock the door, but you are the carpenter who will build the frame."

Nord and Lina shared a look as they turned her words over in their minds. Meanwhile, Finley stole less-than-covert glances at Quinn, like he still couldn't quite wrap his head around the fact that she was there acting for all the world like it was just a regular morning for them.

Lina didn't blame him. Very little about their current circumstances were normal. Or good, for that matter. Things tended to blow up in their face with incredible frequency, just when they least expected it. Maybe the only thing that was truly ever normal for them was how they faced the upheaval together.

"Was there anything else?" Nord asked.

"No, that's everything."

Lina chewed on the inside of her cheek, still trying to make sense of Cora's message. *Shadow. Light. Doorway. Key.* The words danced around each other in her mind, rearranging themselves as she tried over and over to decipher their meaning. Unfortunately, they made no more sense now than they did the first time.

Quinn glanced down at her watch, a small frown furrowing her brows. "I should probably get going. But I'll be back tonight in time to help with whatever it is you're planning."

"Assuming we have it figured out by then," Lina said.

"You will," Quinn said with a confidence Lina envied. She stood, leaning over to give Lina a hug. "Just keep your head down and stay safe until then, okay?"

"What about you?" Lina asked, hugging her tighter when Quinn went to straighten.

"What about me?" Quinn asked.

"You're out there facing all of this alone. Don't take any unnecessary risks, okay?"

Quinn winked. "I've been taking care of myself for a long time. I know how to deal with men like Mikel. I mean, I had Crombie wrapped around my little finger, didn't I? And the entire time he believed it was the other way around. This is just more of the same."

"True, but Mikel and Crombie are nothing alike—although I'd love nothing more than to use both men's ball sacs as punching bags."

Finley grimaced and made a soft sound of discomfort while Nord gave Lina an approving smile. The more creatively violent her acts of revenge, the prouder he tended to be. Though for a berserker whose personal motto seemed to be 'the bloodier, the better,' it was hardly a surprise.

Shaking off the observation, Lina added aloud, "Just be careful. You never know what he's planning to do or who he'll use to hurt you if he finds out you've been disobeying him."

"I always am," Quinn insisted. Her words were for Lina, but her eyes were trained on a very tense-looking Finley. Those two shared another long, unreadable look before Quinn turned and made her way out of the room. Without looking back, she raised a hand and wiggled her fingers, calling, "See you tonight."

Finley, Nord, and Lina sat at the table in a sort of mutual stunned silence.

"Hurricane Satori strikes again," Finley mumbled, his eyes still trained on the empty space Quinn had just occupied.

"Like mother like daughter," Nord agreed.

Lina rubbed at her temples, feeling like she'd sustained emotional whiplash after the twists and turns of that unexpected visit.

"What's that?" Finley asked, his voice low and mildly accusing.

Lina raised her head, finding Finley staring at her hand with narrowed eyes. She followed his gaze, a soft smile lifting her lips when she spotted Nord's ring.

Finley had no trouble interpreting her expression because he sat back in his chair with a wide grin. "I guess that explains the stripper talk." His attention shifted to Nord. "I'll have to make you an appointment with my tailor. What are you thinking? Something classic?" Finley's eyes blazed silver.

Nord and Lina exchanged amused glances.

"Here we go again," she mouthed as Nord rolled his eyes.

One second, Nord was seated at the table in his workout shirt and shorts, and the next, he was decked out in a black tuxedo.

"Wow," Lina breathed.

He looked absolutely edible. Well, so long as you ignored the grumpy cast of his face. But even that sort of worked in his favor.

"Finley," he growled.

"Too formal? Something more traditional, perhaps?" Finley asked, his lips already twitching mischievously as Nord's clothes changed again.

Lina didn't immediately notice the change, except the jacket seemed to be cut differently.

It wasn't until Nord's eyes dropped to his lap and he huffed in exasperation that Lina caught on to Finley's joke.

"A kilt? Really? Since when is a kilt the traditional garb of a Norseman?" Nord stood, his empty mug in hand.

He may not be Scottish, but Lina secretly wished he was as she eyed the way he filled out his plaid and the accompanying knee-high socks.

"I'll be honest, I haven't the foggiest what counts as traditional for you. Animal pelts and war paint, maybe?"

Lina snickered.

"How is it possible you've known me this long and still know nothing of my people?"

"Bit before my time, mate," Finley said with an unrepentant grin. "How about something like this?"

Nord's scowl deepened as Finley changed his clothes once more. This time, Finley had opted for a loincloth, a necklace made of fangs, and had even taken it a step further, adding a bone through Nord's septum.

Lina nearly doubled over in laughter, her stomach cramping as she tried to catch her breath. His expression was fierce, which only made his ridiculous getup even more authentic-looking, but she could feel his amusement lacing with her own.

"Consider yourself uninvited," Nord said, already walking away from the table.

"Who else are you going to get to be your best man? In case you've forgotten, I'm your only friend."

Nord flipped him off as he left the kitchen.

She was still laughing when Finley turned to her, his expression soft, his eyes warm. "Glad to see he took my advice to heart."

"What advice?" she asked, tilting her head to the side as she studied him.

Finley shook his head, standing and then leaning down to press a soft kiss to her cheek. "You're going to make a beautiful bride, Lina. Isn't it funny how even in the midst of our darkest days, we still find things to celebrate?"

"I think we call that hope," Lina murmured.

He ran his hand over the top of her hair. "Whatever you call it, I can think of no two people more deserving of a happy ever after."

With that, he gave her another smile and then followed in the direction Nord had taken.

"Hey, Fin?"

He paused and half-turned back to her.

"I'm not sure what you said to him, but maybe it's time for you to take your own advice? You deserve to be happy too."

His expression shifted from curious to moved and then back to the loveable rogue she knew so well. "Don't worry about me, love. I have every intention of it."

He left her with a wink, and in the silence that followed, her smile slowly fell. Was it foolish of them to make plans for a future they may not have? Or was the fact that tomorrow wasn't guaranteed the exact reason they should?

A steely resolve filled her then, replacing her fear with a single-minded determination. She knew Mikel was coming for her. It was simply a matter of when, but she'd be damned if she let him rob her of her hope. She may not have her magic, or a prayer in hell of beating him, but that didn't mean she wouldn't try.

Or that she wouldn't live in the time she had left.

CHAPTER 27
NORD

The sun had just begun to set when Lina's shouts sounded down the hall. Nord and Finley were both on their feet, instinctively responding to the sound of her door crashing into the wall and her running down the hall like a bat out of hell. Nord's heart still hadn't quite returned to a normal tempo by the time she came flying into the room.

"I found it! I found it! Look," she said, waving a piece of paper around and giving him absolutely no opportunity to read what was written on it. "I knew I'd recognized the phrase from Cora's message. See, it's right here."

"Lina," Nord said, drawing her attention and giving her a meaningful look.

She blushed. "Sorry. Got a bit carried away there for a second." She handed him the paper covered in Alistair's scholarly scrawl.

Finley peered over his shoulder, reading it along with him. "What is this? A summoning spell?"

Lina nodded excitedly. "I think so, at least so far as I can tell. But look, that's not all. Do you see about halfway down, Alistair's notes in the margin?"

Nord's brows furrowed as he read the notation out loud, "'Only once the summoner is ready to release the bindings should they make use of the final phrase.'" He looked up. "So the spell also acts as a cage?"

"That's how I interpreted it as well," Lina said, clapping her hands and bouncing up and down on her toes. "Do you know what this means? Not only can we summon Crombie back here, he won't be able to just pop off again until we're done with him!"

"How do you know it will work across realms?" Finley asked, not seeming skeptical, merely curious.

Lina moved to stand beside Nord, pressing into his side as she pointed to a line in the middle of the page. "'If successful, the doorway between worlds will open, allowing the summoner to cross, or if the appropriate anchor is used, draw forth the desired object.' It's the doorway Cora was referring to."

"How can you be sure?" Nord asked. "Didn't she mention something about shadow and light?"

"I thought about that too, but I'm pretty sure she meant it metaphorically. Like the doorway would be made out of magic rather than a real door. Or, perhaps shadow refers to the Fae realm since Crombie is likely back in the Night Court, and our side is the light?" Lina shrugged. "I don't think it matters, to be honest, because this spell is obviously what she was trying to point me to. It's the only reference to a doorway anywhere in the Codex."

"And if we assume the rest of her message was metaphorical, Nord being the carpenter means he has to be the one to perform the spell, or in other words, create the doorway."

"Well, he's the only Animagi in the room with access to his magic, so I feel like that's a safe assumption," Lina replied dryly.

Nord wrapped an arm around her waist and squeezed. "Not for long."

She offered him a grateful smile. "If all goes well." She touched the pendant at the base of her throat. "I guess we should be happy he gave me this little present. Since it's part of a set and he's holding onto the other, I think it can act as the anchor the spell refers to."

"Which is why Cora referred to you as the key, since it's currently attached to you," Finley said.

Lina nodded. "That was my takeaway." She let out a disbelieving laugh. "God, can you picture the look on Crombie's face when he realizes we finally have the upper hand for once? It's almost too good to be true."

Her excitement buzzed through Nord, though it was closely chased by her doubt. He had no trouble deciphering her conflicting emotions. After everything she'd been through, she was afraid to believe this might actually work.

"If this is what Cora meant for you to find, then there's no reason to doubt we'll be successful," he said softly. "She wouldn't send you down a dead end with everything that's at stake."

Lina shot him a startled glance. "Can you hear my thoughts now?"

"No need. I just know how your mind works."

She gave a little shudder. "Well, that's terrifying."

Nord chuckled. "I'll prove to you later it's not as bad as you might think."

"I do like the sound of that," she murmured before her eyes fell back to the spell he still held in his hand. "So should we wait for Quinn to try it out, or do we go for it right now?"

"Do we need to gather any components?" Finley asked.

"This spell seems to rely purely on the caster's magic," Lina replied. "Other than chalk to draw a circle, all it calls for is an object attuned to the realm in question, which in this case is doubling as our anchor since it's also linked to Crombie."

"Then I don't see any reason to wait. Do you?"

Nord and Lina shook their heads.

"All right then, let's clear out some space so he doesn't go around breaking things if he throws a temper tantrum."

Lina laughed and reached down to grab Nord's hand, giving it a tight squeeze. "You going to be okay with seeing him?" she asked quietly as Finley set about moving furniture.

He knew what she was really asking was whether he'd be able to keep the berserker in check long enough for them to get what they needed.

"Will you?" he countered, since he really didn't have an answer to her question.

"Oh, Crombie already knows exactly what I have planned for him. I was quite vocal about my intentions. He even promised me a free shot."

"And you think he'll keep his word?"

She considered it a while before nodding. "Oddly enough, I do. He's taken great pleasure in misleading me, but he's never lied. If he says he's going to do something, he's always followed through."

"Well then," he said, lifting their joined hands and brushing a kiss to her knuckles, "I look forward to seeing what you have in store for him."

Her smile took on a dangerous edge. "You and me both."

"There," Finley said, standing back and wiping chalk off his hands as he eyed the six-foot circle he'd traced on the floor. "We should be all set."

"Where should I stand?" Lina asked.

Nord reread Alistair's translation and immediately frowned. "The anchor needs to be placed in the center of the circle."

"Of course it does," she groaned.

"So she'll be trapped in there with him?" Finley asked.

Nord gave a tight nod, not remotely happy about the realization. "Lina can't remove the necklace, so we don't have a choice."

"For fuck's sake, I knew things sounded too good to be true." Lina sighed and moved into place. "At least I can beat the crap out of him without injuring myself now."

Knowing she was equipped with her own inner monster was the only thing keeping Nord from calling the whole thing off. It went against his nature to knowingly put her at risk, but without Crombie to remove the necklace, they had no way to get her magic back. And berserker or not, without her power, she'd be helpless against an enemy such as Mikel.

Not that Nord had any intention of letting him get her alone, but the Animagi leader had already proven himself to be a wily foe. They were going to need every weapon in their collective arsenals if they had any chance of beating him.

"You ready?" he asked her once she was in place.

Lina nodded.

"You rip his fucking heart out at the first sign of danger, do you hear me?"

She smiled. "I promise."

He exhaled heavily, muttering curses under his breath as he lifted the paper.

Finley came to stand beside him. "We'll be right here. She's going to be fine," he promised.

Right. Because things are always that simple.

Nord grunted and fought to reclaim a sense of calm. He knew better than attempting any sort of magic with a scattered mind. The last thing he wanted to do was mispronounce a word and accidentally send Lina to Faerie because he was distracted.

"Here goes nothing," he said, taking a deep breath before reciting the ancient spell.

As soon as the first word left his lips, a small shock wave went through the air, filling the room with a current of electricity that only grew in intensity with each progressive word Nord spoke.

Lina's hair lifted, floating on an invisible wind, while the pendant around her neck began to glow and pulse with a brilliant amber light. Her eyes found his, and she nodded, urging him to keep going.

The buzzing energy soon grew painful, feeling like a continuous series of electric shocks racing along his skin, but Nord knew he couldn't stop. When the last word of the spell left his lips, there was a sound like a branch breaking off of a tree, and the space before Lina tore open, allowing more of that amber light to spill through.

Nord threw up his arm, trying to protect his eyes from the burn of the light, but it wasn't enough. The beam swelled until it swallowed the entire room.

"Lina!" he shouted, his heart galloping in his chest as he struggled to find her through the blinding light.

"I'm here!"

Just when he was about to go tearing forward to grab her, the light dimmed, revealing Lina and a figure huddled at her feet.

Lina gasped, her attention trained on the ground before her.

Nord's eyes dropped, his body growing still as he spotted the prone form. It was Crombie, but not as Nord had ever seen him. He was naked, covered in blood and wounds even Nord's violent mind couldn't conjure explanations for. Perhaps oddest of all, his matted hair was significantly longer, falling down the length of his back when only a few days prior it hadn't reached his shoulders.

"C-Crombie?" Lina ventured.

At the sound of his name, Crombie looked up, his eyes wide with terror, his mouth opening on a terrible wail.

"No! No more! Please, no more," he begged, visibly shaking as he tried to scramble away from her.

"Crombie. Crombie, it's me. It's Lina," she said, employing her most soothing tone as she crouched down.

He continued to crawl backward, whimpering pathetically as his body slammed into an invisible barrier. He flinched when Lina reached out, but she immediately held her hands up to signify she had no intention of harming him.

When she didn't try to touch him further, Crombie shuddered and finally seemed to take notice of his surroundings. He sucked in breath after breath, his pale chest rising and falling as his eyes shot wildly around the room, finally coming to rest back on Lina.

"Is it really you?"

He looked so pathetic, so afraid to hope, that Nord almost pitied him. But then he remembered every vile thing the bastard fae had done, and any potential sympathy he might have felt died a swift death.

"What the hell happened to him?" Finley asked.

Nord shook his head, his eyes still trained on the scene playing out in front of them.

"Yes, Crombie," Lina said slowly. "It's really me."

Tears streaked down his dirty face as Crombie stared at Lina. He fought to speak through his tears, his voice a broken rasp. "I'm sorry. I'm so fucking sorry." The fae curled in on himself then, his body sliding down the circle's barrier until he was lying on the floor. Stretching his arm out to her, he whispered an exhausted, "Th-thank you for—"

Crombie never finished his sentence. Instead, his eyes rolled back in his head, and his ravaged body fell completely still.

"Crombie?" she whispered, leaning closer, her hand hovering just above his. And then again, her voice cracking with panic, "Crombie?"

The fae didn't move, not so much as the twitch of an eye or the slight rise of his chest. He was utterly and frightfully still.

Lina's fear shot through Nord like ice pouring through his veins as she glanced back at him, her face leeched of color, her hands trembling.

"Is he . . . dead?"

The series continues in Call of Danger, out now!
But before you go, keep reading for a special bonus scene.

BONUS SCENE
QUINN

The penthouse door fell shut behind her with a soft click, and that's when her carefully constructed mask dropped away. Quinn shut her eyes and leaned back against the cool wood. Her palms pressed against the barrier as if she could reach beyond it to touch the people she'd left within.

If anyone came upon her now, they'd see her for the fraud she was. The truth she'd worked so desperately to hide. The secrets. The shame. The lies. It was all written there in the quiet anguish of her expression.

Quinn's breath flowed out of her in a jagged exhale while tears pricked the backs of her eyes.

You can do this, Satori. You have to do this. It's the only way to keep them safe. So keep your shit together, or all this deception and heartache will be for nothing.

Everything she'd left unsaid, the chaotic, distorted mess her life had become over the last two days, crashed through her. It felt a bit like she'd walked into a funhouse but couldn't find her way back out. These images, these memories, they couldn't possibly be real.

And yet the sick, twisted feeling slithering around in her gut said otherwise.

After everything she'd worked so hard for, the fact that this is where she'd ended up was the cruelest twist of all.

Quinn swallowed back a wave of nausea as her mind conjured up images of the Alinari cutting their pound of flesh out of Nord's unconscious body—repayment for what he'd done to their brethren. Of Lina's grief as she'd been forced to watch, and then the look of understanding and forgiveness shining in her eyes as Quinn had been coerced into playing with her mind once again.

She could still hear Mikel's cruel whisper in her ear, forcing her to do things she would never willingly do. There was no escaping the memory as his voice echoed in her mind, as horrific now as when it'd happened.

"Cut it out. All of it. I want no trace left behind, do you understand?"

She gave him a jerky nod, unable to speak around her anger.

"And I want her secrets. The things she stole from the vault. The name of who she was working with. The location of the Codex. The Prism—"

Quinn couldn't quite hide her flinch at the word.

"Oh, yes, I know all about Alistair's scheming. Evalina is no longer one of us; she has no right to such heirlooms. You will give me all of it."

"No," she gritted out, her pride insisting she fight even though she knew it was futile.

Mikel grabbed her chin and jerked her face toward his. "You will do this, Quinn. I'll give you forty-eight hours to make your peace with it, and then I'm going to start with your mother and work my way through each member of your family, gifting you with pieces of them as I go so you never forget whose fault it is they ever bled at all. And if that's not enough to convince you just how serious I am, or what will happen if I find out you've defied me, I will find that Guardian of yours and bleed him dry."

Quinn sucked in a shocked breath.

Mikel grinned. It was a slow, wicked thing that did nothing to bring any life to his cold green eyes.

"Yes, I know about him too. I pay very close attention to my most prized possessions. And make no mistake, Weaver. You are the most prized piece in my collection."

She shivered and gave him a terse nod as she reached for Lina. "Guess I'll be seeing you in forty-eight hours then."

He'd left without another word, no longer interested in delivering threats when he'd so clearly won. Quinn hadn't been able to get out of that room fast enough after she'd constructed the flimsy wall in Lina's mind, blocking her from the events of the day, but nothing else. She'd stolen her friend's memories once; she had no intention of ever doing it again.

Quinn had only just made it streetside when a hand grasped her wrist and pulled her into a darkened alcove. She cried out, but a second hand wrapped around the bottom half of her face, covering her mouth.

"Shh, it's just me. I'm here to get you and Cora somewhere safe."

She sagged against Finley's broad frame, reveling in the feel of him wrapped around her for one perfect second before driving her heel into the top of his foot.

"What the hell, Satori?" he hissed, jumping away from her with an accusing glare.

"Is this your idea of foreplay, Batman? Dragging unassuming women into dark alleyways? Because let me tell you, it's not sexy."

His eyes narrowed incredulously. "I already told you. I'm here to rescue you."

Quinn scoffed, but her mind was still reeling from Mikel's words. Seeing Finley so soon after knowing what Mikel had planned for him sent her heart galloping with fear. She needed to get him away from here. Now. He couldn't possibly know how much danger he was in, or he'd never have set foot in Mobius territory on his own.

"Well, that's adorable, but I do not now, nor have I ever, required a man to rescue me."

Something flashed in Finley's eyes, but it was too dark for her to read the emotion before it vanished.

"Nord sent me—" he tried again.

Quinn held up a hand and shook her head. "Then you probably already know he needs you right now more than I do. I'll be fine. I know what I'm doing."

"Do you? Because from the looks of things back there, none of us seem to be holding any cards right now."

"If you know that much, then you should also know that's only more of a reason for you to get the fuck out of here as soon as possible."

His expression tightened, and he stepped right up into her space, his chest bumping into hers and pressing her back against a brick wall. "I saw what you did to Lina. And I know what you took from me."

Quinn's heart stuttered in her chest.

How? He's bluffing.

She clung to the thought; it was the only way to keep her expression blank. She couldn't deal with this, with him, right now. "Fin—"

"I want it back," Finley growled, his face less than an inch away from hers. "All of it. Those memories are mine. *You* are mine." Her lips parted on a protest, her eyes flaring wide at the molten heat burning in his eyes and the determined clench of his jaw. "But this will suffice for now."

He cupped her face between his hands, his lips crashing down to claim her mouth in an act far too carnal and possessive to be labeled anything as innocent as a kiss.

Oh. Oh, God, I've missed this.

Her body hadn't seemed to get the memo that Finley represented everything forbidden and off-limits to her. She was too focused on how good it felt to be surrounded by him, his clean, masculine scent seducing her as deftly as his delectable lips.

Quinn whimpered against his mouth, her tongue thrusting against his, her hands lifting to push him away but curling into his shirt and pulling him closer instead.

A chime rang out, hauling Quinn out of the single most terrifyingly perfect moment she'd experienced, possibly ever, and straight back to the penthouse's entryway. Heart racing and lips tingling from the mere ghost of Finley's kiss, she pulled her phone out, eyes quickly scanning the screen. It was a text from her aunt, Sheridan.

We're ready.

Quinn blew out a breath, knowing the worst was yet to come. Steeling her shoulders and cutting herself off from everything except the matter at hand, she stepped away from the door—and the people safely tucked inside. A quick scroll through her recent contacts revealed Mikel's name, which she'd punched in as THE DICKtator.

She pressed the call button before she could second-guess herself.

It didn't even ring twice before he answered, "Do you have what I want?"

"I'm on my way."

Download your copy of Call of Danger now and find out what happens in the epic conclusion...

GLOSSARY & PRONUNCIATION GUIDE

AUTHOR'S NOTE: These are the notes I send to my audio narrators. I am no pronunciation expert, as you'll see, so when I go for phonetic spellings, I base it off what makes most sense in my mind (which you should all know by now is a scary, scary place. Ha!) In some case, pronunciation can vary depending on region, and while I generally default to the Old Norse and Norwegian versions of words, sometimes a matter of personal preference may sway me to something else. All of this is to say, while I do my research, I am far from an expert and this is all just how I hear things in my head while writing. You may keep or disregard these as you will.

Animagi (plural): Ani (as in animation) Maji (hard J)

Animagus (singular): Ani (as in animation) Mag (as in magazine) Us

Barchetta: (Italian) barrr-ketta

Drøm søtt: (Norwegian) – Drem Sut *Sweet dreams*

Gunnar: Goo (like goose) na (like nah) r (soft – a British v. American r) *Gunnar is a male first name of Nordic origin (Gunnarr in Old Norse). The name Gunnar means fighter, soldier, and attacker, but mostly is referred to by the Viking saying which means Brave and Bold warrior (gunnr "war" and arr "warrior").*

Kærasta: Ki (like in Kite) ra (like radish) stuh *Nord uses it as a term of endearment, like sweetheart, though a more direct translation would be girlfriend.*

La Voiture Noire (French) *The black car*

Minn: min *My*

Móðir: (Old Norse) Mow-Dear (o sound slightly extended) *Mother*

Mon coeur: (French) mon kurr *My heart*

Mon petit chaton: (French) Mon Peh (like pet sans T)-tee Sha-tah-n *My little cat/kitten*

Novasgard: Nov (as in nova) – as – guard

Pagani: pah – gah - knee

Þǫkk: (Old Norse) – Thock (rhymes with lock) *thank you*

Skål: sk-ool *the Danish-Norwegian-Swedish word for "cheers", or "good health", a salute or a toast, as to an admired person or group.*

Son: soon *Son*

Veneno: (Spanish) Ben – en – o

<u>Zonda</u>: (like honda)

<u>Novasgardians</u>:

- Arrick: Eric
- Björn: Bee - Yorn – (like horn)
- Brynhild: Brin-hild (with r slightly rolled)
- Søren: Sore - en
- Strega: Stray - ga

A NOTE FROM MEG

I mean...it wasn't the worst ending I've left you with. And, he had it coming, right? I know a lot of you wait for me to finish series by now because you can't hang with the cliffies, but I super appreciate those of you that suffer between books along with me. And for those that can't...I understand. I definitely have a well-deserved reputation.

For those of you that might hang out on TikTok, or perhaps watched the TV show Vikings, or even play Assassin's Creed, you might have recognized the lullaby Nord sings to Lina. It's an actual, genuine Viking poem, believed to be written by the war-poet (and alleged berserker) Egill Skallagrímsson. How cool is that? I already loved the song, but once I learned the story behind it, I couldn't resist borrowing a real piece of history. I use lots of traditional folklore to inspire my Novasgardians, though I do take liberties when creating my Norse inspired fantasy culture. But I hope you enjoy it! And, if you're looking to listen to the song, one of my favorite renditions is by Natidredd (you can check it our on Youtube or Spotify). It's so good!

I can't wait for you guys to see how it all comes together in Call. And while Call will mark the end of Nord and Lina's journey. It's not the end of this world. I hope you've been enjoying this rollercoaster as much as I have. These characters mean so much to me, and I love being able to share them with you.

Until next time, stay safe and happy reading!

XOXO,

♡ Meg Anne

If you enjoyed this book, please consider writing a short review and posting it on Amazon, Bookbub, Goodreads and/or anywhere else you share your love of books. Reviews are very helpful to other readers and are greatly appreciated by authors (especially this one!)

Want to know when I have a new release or get exclusive access to my newest works? Join my mailing list: MegAnneWrites.com/Newsletter All subscribers get a free Chosen series prequel upon sign-up!

ACKNOWLEDGMENTS

Thank you to all my Chosen for helping come up with kickass band names, but a special shout out to **Kristi Reetz** for suggesting Apocalyptic Unicorns.

Sarah: I feel like I tell you this everyday, but thanks for being my cheerleader and just an all-around awesome person. I couldn't imagine writing this book without you. It definitely wouldn't be as incredible as it turned out thanks to all our late night idea-bouncing and brainstorming. You're stuck with me forever :D

Kim: You have been an amazing friend and endless source of support and encouragement. I'm so thankful to have you in my corner rooting me and these characters on.

My Moose: You have been an absolute rock. I love you all of the muches. Thank you for bringing me food and coffee, and never questioning my obsession with Jolly Rancher gummies and understanding it's all part of my process. A girl couldn't ask for a better #1 fan.

Sprint Syndicate: Thank you for existing. You kept me on task when I needed it most.

Mo, Dom, Suzi: Thank you for making my words shine. Your contributions are invaluable.

Shane and Stella: Working with you has been one of the highlights of my career. You make this little indie author feel like she's struck gold. I am so blessed to have your talent bringing these characters to life. What you are able to do with your voices continues to blow me away.

Shaneiaks: Thanks for giving this fan girl a home and welcoming me and my characters with open arms! I love you madly and hope you appreciate the little easter eggs I sprinkle in just for you ;)

And as always, thank you to my readers. I write these stories for you. I hope you continue to enjoy them for years to come <3

ALSO BY MEG ANNE

THE CHOSEN UNIVERSE

THE CHOSEN

A FATED MATES HIGH FANTASY ROMANCE

MOTHER OF SHADOWS

REIGN OF ASH

CROWN OF EMBERS

QUEEN OF LIGHT

THE CHOSEN BOXSET #1

THE CHOSEN BOXSET #2

THE KEEPERS

A GUARDIAN/WARD HIGH FANTASY ROMANCE

THE DREAMER (A KEEPER'S PREQUEL)

THE KEEPERS LEGACY

THE KEEPERS RETRIBUTION

THE KEEPERS VOW

THE KEEPERS BOXSET

THE FORSAKEN

A REJECTED MATES/ENEMIES-TO-LOVERS ROMANTASY

PRISONER OF STEEL & SHADOW

QUEEN OF WHISPERS & MIST

COURT OF DEATH & DREAMS

Brotherhood of the Guardians/Novasgard Vikings

<u>Undercover Magic</u> *(Nord & Lina)*

A Sexy & Suspenseful Fated Mates PNR

Hint of Danger

Face of Danger

World of Danger

Promise of Danger

Call of Danger

Bound by Danger (Quinn & Finley)

<u>Standalones</u>

My Soul To Take: A Forbidden Love Meets Fated Mates PNR

ABOUT MEG ANNE

USA Today and international bestselling paranormal and fantasy romance author Meg Anne has always had stories running on a loop in her head. They started off as daydreams about how the evil queen (aka Mom) had her slaving away doing chores, and more recently shifted into creating backgrounds about the people stuck beside her during rush hour. The stories have always been there; they were just waiting for her to tell them.

Like any true SoCal native, Meg enjoys staying inside curled up with a good book and her fur babies . . . or maybe that's just her. You can convince Meg to buy just about anything if it's covered in glitter or rhinestones, or make her laugh by sharing your favorite bad joke. She also accepts bribes in the form of baked goods and Mexican food.

Meg is best known for her leading men #MenbyMeg, her inevitable cliffhangers, and making her readers laugh out loud, all of which started with the bestselling Chosen series.